The Midnight Rodeo

By Chad R Martin

ISBN: ISBN: 978-1-944583-46-0

Library of Congress Control Number:

Email: chadmartin39@gmail.com

Contents

Chapter 1: Blinking Light

Still Creek, Texas, wasn't much more than a memory with a blinking light.

The light hung crooked on a rusted pole where the cracked two-lane blacktop split through the middle of town. It blinked yellow every four seconds, or five, or not at all—depending on its mood. There were no stop signs, no street names. The road simply *was*. A long, faded stretch of nowhere where everything came to die, including the cattle, the people, and the stories.

June Weaver sat beneath that blinking light with a warm beer in one hand and a socket wrench in the other, her work shirt stained with sweat, oil, and the smell of everything she'd tried to outrun. The sign for Nettie's Store and Grill flickered behind her, half the letters burned out. It read "NE _ _ IE'S STO _ _ & GR _ _ L."

The night air held heat like a grudge. Somewhere far off, a cicada sang its dry, rattling song. June took a long swig from the bottle, wiped her mouth with the back of her arm, and glared up at the stuttering traffic light.

"Make up your mind," she muttered.

The light blinked once. Paused.

Then went still.

A low sound stirred on the horizon—not quite thunder, not quite wind. A kind of rolling vibration that settled in her spine. She stood slowly, wrench dangling from her fingers. Her gaze drifted toward the west where the land stretched into shadow and scrub brush.

The desert just went on forever.

June sighed heavily into the endless night.

Every day was the same; the occasional customer passing through from out of town, filling up on the lone gas pump, grabbing snacks, maybe the random friendly banter then they were gone, disappearing back into the distance, off to wherever this place wasn't.

She wondered for the thousandth time what she ever did to deserve this sentence to the ass end of hell.

Why hadn't she just packed up and left?

June launched the burnt out cigarette into the street, sighing once again.

The low rumble grew louder, and she felt it in her chest now, a staccato thumping that was either a series of muffler-backfiring explosions or a dozen angry horses stampeding toward town. She squinted against the moonless dark.

Motorcycles.

A gang of them, headlights blazing, engines roaring. The first bike shot past June with a whoop from its rider, a leather-clad blur, followed by three, four more in rapid succession. Then they all skidded to a halt beneath the blinking light. Men in denim and tattoos swung off their bikes and stretched their legs. One of them—the tallest, with a bandana wrapped around his head—looked at June like he'd found water in the desert.

"Hey there," he called out. "We're lookin' for gas." He had an easy grin that belonged on a billboard.

June pointed to the ancient pump beside Nettie's, its paint chipped and peeling. "Got just enough to get you out of town."

The man laughed. He pulled something from his pocket—a pack of gum—and tossed it her way. "Good enough for me."

They moved toward the pump like a pack of coyotes, loud and loose, shoving each other just for fun. A couple peeled off and headed for the store, boots clomping on wood planks. June ducked inside after them, fumbling in the dim for a switch. Fluorescent tubes buzzed reluctantly to life.

"Fellas," she said, eyeing their cuts and colors as they started grabbing chips and jerky from the dusty shelves.

She didn't need trouble tonight.

Didn't need it ever again.

The taller one sauntered up to the counter with an armful of snacks, as if he owned the place and everything in it.

"Slow night?" he asked, handing her a crumpled twenty.

"You could say that." She rang him up quickly, fingers twitching over buttons like she still had somewhere else to be.

He nodded toward the half-dark sign outside. "Nettie's your mom?"

"Something like that."

He let out a low whistle then peered out at the others fueling up their bikes. "This where you're from?"

Her mouth twitched like she wasn't sure if it was going to smile or spit him right out of the place.

"Not really," she said slowly.

He laughed again, shaking his head like there was some kind of joke between them that she'd missed. "Yeah," he said. "Me neither."

The bell over the door jingled, drawing their attention.

Deputy Mason King walked in, his six foot, two inch frame filling the doorway. Mason was in his early forties, a career lawman who transferred from Dallas a few months earlier. He didn't say a lot and no one knew very much about him but one thing was certain, the aura that surrounded the deputy spoke of someone who didn't care to be trifled with. He was friendly enough, but that underlying angry disposition seemed to bubble just below the surface.

Seeing the motorcycles was probably enough to kick it up a notch.

He scanned the room, taking in June and the biker with a glance that put both of them on notice, then stepped forward and rested one hand on his belt buckle. "Evenin', folks."

"Officer," the tall biker said with a nod, all the swagger gone from his voice. He took his bag of snacks and eased past Mason like he was backing away from a rattlesnake, joined his friends outside.

The deputy watched them through the glass for a moment before turning to June. "Trouble?"

She shrugged, but her shoulders stayed tense. "Just passin' through."

Mason watched her carefully, his eyes sharp beneath the brim of his hat. "You good here?"

"Always am." She tucked the twenty into the register, closing it with a thud. The bikers were already revving their engines and she could hear them hootin' and hollerin' like coyotes again.

"Keep it that way," Mason said, a hint of something like concern in his voice. He turned and strode back out into the night.

June let out a breath she didn't know she'd been holding.

She followed Mason's shadow onto the porch, watched the bikes tear off into darkness under the blinking light. Their noise faded down the highway until it was just her and Mason standing in silence.

He squinted at her through drifting dust. "You look tired," he said finally.

"I don't sleep much," she replied, reaching for another cigarette. She lit it and drew deep, feeling something loosen in her chest when he nodded and didn't press further.

"Lock up after yourself," he told her as he climbed into his car and pulled away slow, lights flashing once like a wink.

June sat back down on the stoop. The beer was warm as spit by now but she drank it anyway, watching as Mason disappeared over the horizon.

Another reminder that even he had somewhere else to go when this place got too quiet.

The cicada started up again; relentless, endless, like everything in Still Creek except for people. She flicked ash into its hum and wondered if it ever got lonely calling out to nothing like that.

She finished her beer and stared down at the socket wrench in her hand as if it held an answer or maybe just an excuse to keep busy until morning.

The air seemed to chill, the wind shifted and kicked up slightly, blowing dust across the highway.

June blinked.

The beer slipped from her hand and shattered.

The blinking light above her head turned solid yellow and stayed that way.

***

Eli Boone sat atop of his dad's ramshackle house, taking a hit off a blunt and watching the night sky. The eighteen year old senior dreamed of far away places that would finally take him out of that shitty little town. His girlfriend, whom he had met online through a study group was about to attend the University of Texas. That one little fact propelled Eli to study harder, as if he needed any more inspiration.

When he left Still Creek he vowed to never come back. He didn't hate the town, there was simply no future there for anyone. It was a town for the lost and hopeless and Eli had plans for his life. His dad traveled an hour to and back from work every day and drank every night to drown the memories of his deceased wife.

Eli didn't blame him for the drinking but wondered how anyone could settle for a life like that. He would visit his dad often, though, if nothing else to remind himself of what he escaped.

He took another hit and held it in. The rumble of motorcycles in the distance broke the silence and soon Eli was watching their headlights as they roared past the house and into town. They disappeared, leaving only faint echoes of laughter and raw engines behind.

The blunt was nearly gone so he jumped off the roof with a soft thud and walked toward the back of the house where a rusted basketball hoop hung above a cracked driveway. He picked up an old ball and started taking shots, hustling after each miss with a dogged persistence that would make his father proud.

"Eli," a voice called from inside. "Get your ass in here."

He sighed, made one last shot then shuffled through the screen door.

The inside of the house smelled like mildew and stale beer. It was cluttered with years of collected junk— broken furniture, yellowed newspapers, empty bottles. His father sat in front of a flickering TV with a can of Lone Star in his hand, looking older than his forty-five years.

"Yeah?" Eli said, standing awkwardly near the door.

His dad turned around, eyes glassy but focused. "Ya seen them bikers?"

"Just now."

"They're trouble," he muttered, although there was something like fascination in his voice.

Eli shrugged. "They'll be gone soon."

His dad grunted and turned back to the TV. Wheel of Fortune was on but he wasn't watching it; just staring through it like it held some kind of answer he'd never get to hear. "You eat yet?"

"Not hungry."

"You should eat."

"Yeah," Eli lied. "I will."

His father nodded slowly, taking another swig from his beer. "Don't stay up too late."

"I won't," Eli promised and slipped out before there could be anything else—any other request or reminder hanging in the air between them. He loved his father, and his father absolutely made it clear that Eli was his only priority. Their relationship wasn't like those tv tragedies. They both wanted something better for Eli and his dad would move hell and high water to see that his son had a better life than he did.

He grabbed his skateboard from beside the porch and glided down Main Street toward Nettie's, feeling more alive with each push against the pavement. This time of night felt like freedom; no cars, no noise except for wheels hitting asphalt and the hum of cicadas all around him.

The town stayed dark as he passed under streetlights that had burned out long before he was born.

When Eli rolled up to Nettie's he saw June sitting on the porch smoking her millionth cigarette of the night. Smoke curled around her head like she was dreaming or drowning; maybe both.

"Hey Junior," she called out as he skidded to a stop.

"What's up?" He sat next to her and looked at broken glass scattered across wood planks.

"A whole lotta nothin'," she replied with a smile that seemed too tired to reach her eyes.

Eli laughed softly then nudged some shards with his foot. "You smash this or what?"

She nodded at the light above them, still shining steady yellow against night sky.

"That thing finally die?"

"Just woke up." She flicked ash into its glow then glanced sideways at him. "How's your dad?"

"You know..." he half-smiled.

The wind kicked up again, bringing another cool blast of air.

Eli shivered, "what's up with this wind tonight? It's usually not this cold."

"The riders..." an old, raspy voice whispered at them.

June and Eli both turned to see Old Man Thompson rocking in a chair, a huge wad of tobacco in his jaw. The former cowboy spent most of his days and nights rocking in that chair, just watching and reminiscing of better days when the town was full of cowboys, cattle, and trail drives.

Pat Thompson was a big deal then, a cowboy when cowboys were rough, determined, and got things done. Once the cattle moved off to bigger, grass heavy pastures, the old towns life blood disappeared with it and ole Pat was left to the dust with the rest of the vacated ranches.

His stories were often repetitive, full of history, and always entertaining. But tonight there was something different about his tone, as if what was causing the weird wind was supernatural.

"Awful late for ya, ain't it?" June asked. The old man was usually in bed by eight.

"The riders are back." He spat into a paper cup and wiped his chin. "Just like '87."

Eli raised an eyebrow. "You mean nineteen-eighty-seven?"

Thompson gave him a long, crooked grin. "No boy, eighteen."

He let the statement hang in the air.

The wind picked up again, dust swirling around their feet like a ghostly partner to his words. Eli blinked, unsure of how to respond.

"Okay…" he said at last, standing up. "I'm gonna grab a drink before you start tellin' me what century I'm livin' in."

June laughed as he walked into the store, letting the screen door slam behind him.

She glanced back at Thompson, who continued to chew methodically and rock his chair at a steady pace. Her curiosity got the better of her.

"What happened last time?" she asked.

The old man leaned forward, eyes glinting like he finally had someone listening close enough to hear. "Storm rolled in," he said slow and deliberate. "Blew through here hard for three days straight, soon as them riders came through."

"Bad storm?"

"It was," Thompson nodded sagely. He settled back into his chair and spat again. "Ain't been one like it since."

June watched him rock in silence for a moment then put out her cigarette and went inside.

Eli was at the cooler, rooting around for something that wasn't expired. She grabbed a broom from behind the counter and started sweeping up broken glass while overhead lights buzzed and flickered with tired electricity.

"You hear what he said about the storm?" Eli called out as he slammed the cooler door shut.

"I heard," June replied, trying not to sound interested.

"You think there's anything to it?"

She paused with the broom mid-sweep then shrugged one shoulder thoughtfully. "Probably just old stories."

He grabbed a soda and joined her at the counter, handing over crumpled bills that looked like they'd been washed too many times with his jeans before she could even ring him up.

"Later," he said as he headed for the door.

"Later Junior." She watched him go then locked up for real this time; keys jingling in her hand like bells on an abandoned church.

Outside it was still eerily cool but calm now; no wind, just near-silence stretching across Main Street all the way out to desert and beyond.

Thompson had disappeared from his chair when she wasn't looking—back home or maybe hunkered down waiting to see if history would repeat itself once more.

June looked up at the light hanging over her head; solid yellow against dark sky like some kind of warning or promise or both.

She pulled her collar tight against the chill air that felt foreign after so many years of heat and stepped gingerly over shards of glass as she made her way toward home.

***

Out in the rocky desert, not three miles from town, dark clouds surged, rolling across the rugged terrain swallowing everything in its path. Emerging from the clouds three pales horses, clouds whirling off their hind flakes, steam flowing from flared nostrils. The steed's eyes burned like embers, their jaws set firmly with angry determination.

Pale riders, draped in dark clothes, black leather dusters, wide-brimmed cowboy hats, gun belts and embellishments highlighted the dark clothes in the color of deep dark blood, rode their steed with expressions of hate.

They bore down on the little town of Still Creek for the first time in a hundred and fifty years. Appearing out of the roiling clouds behind them was a long, dark stagecoach, black as death. The coachman sitting above drove the eight horse team, with dead eyes and a tortured grin.

The riders never broke stride as they approached the small town, ripping through the night and leaving an angry wind in their wake. They stopped just short of the blinking light, circled once, then disappeared into the darkness.

The storm pushed forward with them, lightning crackling the sky as thunder echoed across the plains, the yellow street light whipping about in the possessed winds.

The Dark Rodeo had come to Still Creek.

Chapter 2: Shut Eye

June lay in bed, staring up at the thin cracks in her ceiling. The wind rattled the window frame, and she listened to its hollow sound as it sought out places to settle and get comfortable. Sleep felt distant, just like everything else these days.

The storm was growing louder; the kind of noise you could hear in your bones. She closed her eyes against it, but the old man's words kept creeping back into her mind.

Ain't been one like it since.

She tossed and turned until the sheets wrapped around her legs like a straightjacket. Finally, she kicked them off and got up, pulling a sweatshirt over her head. Maybe some late night TV would beat back those creeping thoughts. She padded quietly across the living room to the small kitchen, opened the fridge, and cracked open another beer.

The place looked as tired as she felt. Nettie's furniture hadn't changed since the seventies— paisley couches and dusty macramé curtains. Her mother's presence lingered there like a ghost June couldn't quite make peace with.

She stared at the TV, not really watching but letting the images wash over her until her eyes grew heavy and the beer sat warm in her hand. The lights flickered once, then twice before plunging into darkness.

The storm must've taken out power lines this time instead of cattle.

She swore softly into the blackness but stayed on the couch, too worn out to do anything about it till morning.

***

Eli woke to find his room filled with strange light: greenish-yellow, almost sickly looking against his walls that were plastered with band posters and faded maps of places he'd never been.

He blinked groggily at it then went to the window and saw that it was still coming down hard outside; clouds thick enough so they seemed to press low against rooftops. The storm had hit full force while he slept.

He pulled on a hoodie over his T-shirt and padded down narrow hallway toward kitchen where his dad already sat at table with steaming mug of coffee.

"Power's out," Eli said by way of greeting.

His father nodded without looking up from newspaper he was reading by battery-powered lantern. "Came back on for 'bout an hour around dawn."

Eli grabbed a Pop-Tart from a pantry shelf and tore open the foil wrapper. "You sleep?"

"Some." His dad gave him a sidelong glance over the top edge of the paper. "You?"

"Not much."

They fell into easy silence then—each absorbed in own thoughts or maybe shared ones about weather or past or future things they couldn't control but felt anyway like the distant rumble when thunder was still far off.

Finally Eli spoke again: "Think they'll cancel school?"

His dad shook head slowly; resignedly—as if the world might end before Still Creek cancelled anything because nothing short of the apocalypse would keep the town from carrying on the same way it always did.

"Doubtful," he said after moment; then added more gently: "Go see Nettie if you don't want to sit in the dark all day. I'll be working over for a little while tonight. Roger called and told me we had extra orders. I'm glad we're making products in this country again but damn, we gotta find people who want to make the products."

Father and son had a little laugh before Eli finished breakfast standing up and let door bang on his way out. "Later Pops," he shouted as he skated off into the distance.

The storm whipped around him, the wind pushing against his hoodie and making it hard to keep his balance. He sped down Main Street, careful over sidewalks that were slick with dust and rain. The blinking light near Nettie's shone solid yellow again, casting its sickly glow through the haze like it was keeping vigil over empty streets.

Nettie's sat dark but June was outside on the porch, bundled in a blanket and drinking coffee from a chipped mug. She looked up at him as he rolled to a stop.

"Thought you'd be in school," she said with a raised eyebrow.

He shrugged. "They'll probably send us home early."

"Probably." Her voice held a note of disbelief as she poured him a cup from the thermos beside her. "You see that sky?"

Eli nodded, taking the mug gratefully. "Feels like the world's ending out here."

She laughed, short and humorless. "Wouldn't be Still Creek if nothing died."

They huddled on the porch together, watching the storm blow through like it owned the place.

"What do you think?" Eli asked after a moment; half-curious, half-challenging. "Old Man Thompson gonna be right about this one?"

June considered him thoughtfully, eyes narrowed against wind that seemed to cut sharper with every gust. "I think..." she began but let her words trail off as headlights appeared through distant sheets of rain.

The car barreled toward them faster than anything had any business going in weather like this. Tires skidded as it pulled up in front of Nettie's and Mason jumped out, hat clamped down against flying dust and rain.

"June!" he called over the howling wind.

She stood slowly, bracing against railing and squinting through the storm at his approaching figure.

Eli stayed put beside her; part of him wanted to know what was going on—what could get Mason riled up enough to drive into town when most people were hunkered down waiting for the sky to fall.

The other part knew better than to ask.

Mason stopped at the base of the steps and fixed June with a look that went beyond business; something personal simmered beneath the official urgency. "Need you to come with me."

She blinked at him; surprised, suspicious—or maybe just resigned that even in the middle of nowhere there was no hiding out forever.

"What for?"

"Ain't got time to explain," he said tersely. Then added more gently: "Please."

June hesitated only long enough for Eli to get an uneasy sense that whatever waited wasn't good news; then she set down her coffee and followed Mason to his car without another word.

He watched them go—taillights glowing faint in the swirling dust until they too disappeared into the deepening storm.

***

Out past city limits where land flattened into endless scrub brush and rock-strewn fields, three riders pushed forward through wind that swirled around them like an angry specter.

They rode abreast of each other; their black dusters snapping wildly behind them and wide-brimmed hats pulled low against fury of advancing tempest. Steam rose from their mounts' haunches with every pounding stride across rugged terrain.

The stagecoach rattled behind them—driver grinning his manic grin as the horses strained at their leather traces and whipped up dust and chaos in pursuit.

Somewhere between Still Creek and nowhere, the riders reined in their horses and came to a stop.

They waited, silent and watchful as the storm caught up with them; thunder exploding like cannons overhead as they stared back towards town with eyes that burned like coals.

The wind howled defiantly but they did not move— only shifted slightly in their saddles, patient as they had always been.

***

Mason's car skidded to a halt outside the small police station, its windows rattling like they were ready to crack under pressure of the wind-driven rain. He cut the engine and turned to June, urgency written across his face.

"Come on," he said, almost pleading.

She followed him inside where the lights flickered weakly against cinderblock walls. The place was empty except for one other deputy who looked barely old enough to shave. He hovered near a desk full of paperwork, looking nervous—or maybe just unsure why anyone would bother showing up for work under circumstances like this.

Mason led June down a narrow hallway lined with filing cabinets; records kept on people long gone and towns that had disappeared into dust before Still Creek ever took shape around its lone traffic light.

He stopped at an open door near the end of the hall then stepped aside to let her see what waited on the other side of the one-way mirror:

A man sat slumped in a metal chair; cuffs on his wrists where they rested limply against his thighs. He wore dark clothes—denim and leather streaked with dirt—and his hair fell loose over eyes that stayed closed as if he couldn't be bothered waking up from whatever nightmare landed him here.

June stared at him for several moments before speaking: "You think I know this guy?" Her voice was unreadable; somewhere between anger and disbelief.

Mason ran a hand through his hair, eyes searching hers intently. "Driver found him out by 287 this morning."

"And?"

"And he said just one thing, your name."

June kept her gaze locked on Mason's for a long second then looked past him at the unconscious man again. There was something familiar about those features; something like recognition tugged at edge of a memory she'd buried deep enough never to feel it again.

"Shit," she whispered, barely audible over growing sound of storm battering outside walls.

Her legs felt unsteady beneath her as she pressed her hands against the glass, eyes fully taking in the man slumped in the chair in the next room.

"June," Mason's voice called behind her, startling June into standing abruptly as if caught doing something she shouldn't have done or wanted seen.

She turned but it wasn't Mason speaking—not really: it was on a tape recorder sitting next to two freshly placed coffee cups on a nearby desk.

The deputy who looked too young for his badge poked head in nervously; like he wasn't sure whether witnessing any part this situation might get him fired—or worse—wrapped up in whatever storm seemed ready to tear everything apart inside station just as thoroughly as it did out there beyond the brick walls and dusty desert streets.

"Bout all we got so far," Mason said; apologetic now instead of urgent or pleading. He stood and walked around the desk, touching her shoulder lightly as if to offer reassurance.

June pulled away from his touch; not unkindly but like she couldn't bear any more people reaching toward places she kept locked tight inside herself. Finally she looked at Mason, a thousand emotions playing across her face, "he's my ex. Those bikers that came through last night? Rival gang to his." June studied the bruised and beaten man sitting before her, clueless that she was standing in the next room. "I haven't seen this asshole in years."

"Look, I'm sorry for pulling you into this. Your name was the only lead I had and he sure as well wasn't saying anything," the deputy told her sincerely.

She stared at the man for a few more seconds before turning back to Mason, her mind made up. "His name is Frank Garrison, probably wanted in a few dozen states. Drug running, theft, who knows what else," she spat out with disgust. "Be careful, Mason. He's a piece of shit."

Mason laughed briefly then escorted her back up front, "No worries, guys like that don't bother me."

As they met walked to the front door their exit was interrupted by Sheriff Wally Mott, a portly, bully of a man who was more prone eating marathons than stepping on a treadmill. The sheriff didn't particularly care for anyone, especially his new deputy but a favor was a favor, and this was one favor he couldn't back out on.

"You make any progress?" he grumbled, brushing past June.

"Working on it Sheriff," Mason replied.

"Work faster," the sheriff snapped and waddled down the hallway, his resentment following him like flies on a gut wagon. "Don't want such riff raff in my town," he drawled out slowly, eyes looking pointedly at June. "Gonna need you to stick around, Miss Weaver," he said with a dismissive glance in June's direction. "These guys sometimes don't know what they're sayin'." He looked away from both her and Mason, making it clear he had more important things to do.

June hesitated, her eyes narrowing at Mott with a mix of contempt and resignation. She was too tired for this kind of fight today. After a moment she nodded at Mason, her expression softening slightly. "Call me if anything changes."

He met her gaze steadily, something like gratitude in his eyes. "Will do."

She pushed out the door into the teeth of the storm, the wind tearing at her hair as she made her way across the parking lot and back to something like freedom.

Once outside June pulled the blanket tight around her and studied the sky. "This storm looks like it could hang around a while," she muttered to herself.

Mason followed her gaze, "You gonna be okay?"

"Always am," she said softly. "You know me."

His eyes lingered on her for a moment longer than they should have. "Guess I do." He hesitated then took off his hat and ran a hand through short hair that was damp from rain. "I'll bring you in when he wakes up."

June shook her head, "Don't bother."

Mason didn't try to argue; just nodded with that same look of concern he'd worn ever since he first laid eyes on her beneath blinking traffic light.

She turned and walked off into the wind that bit down harder as if punishing everyone in Still Creek for daring to think they'd survive another round.

***

The storm clung to Still Creek with dogged ferocity. By midday its presence felt almost alive; a heavy and insistent thing that refused to budge no matter how many people cursed it or stared silently out their windows and hoped it would leave them alone.

Eli took refuge at Nettie's with June after school grudgingly let out early; groups of kids waiting for rides stood huddled beneath overhangs, backpacks held above their heads in feeble attempts to shield themselves from weather that had slipped into bone-chilling cold.

Now he sat cross-legged on one of the counters inside the store while June dug through boxes and old inventory lists with an air of restless determination—like keeping busy might keep those creeping thoughts at bay.

"Power's probably out all over town," Eli ventured as he watched her sort through shelves of canned goods that looked older than both of them combined.

"Yup."

"Think we should just close up?"

She paused briefly then resumed digging through yellowed papers. Her voice was steady but distracted when she answered: "What else we gonna do?"

Eli didn't have a good answer for that so instead he jumped off counter with graceful ease and grabbed another soda from cooler; warm now but still drinkable if you didn't mind taste of metal under your tongue.

As he cracked it open the door banged wide with sudden gust of wind and Old Man Thompson shuffled in, looking more alive than Eli'd ever seen him—not just animated by stories past but invigorated by something happening right here; right now.

"They're back," he rasped triumphantly at both of them, spitting tobacco juice into paper cup. "Didn't I tell ya?"

Eli raised an eyebrow at June who shrugged; maybe skeptical but not entirely convinced that Thompson's words were any crazier than everything else going on around them these days.

"You did," she said as she offered a box full of batteries he could use for his radio or flashlight; whatever creature comforts held him together while wild weather pounded the outside walls of his sagging old home.

He took it gratefully, nodding at June and Eli both as if bestowing some kind blessing—or maybe curse— on them before turning back toward the door without another word.

The storm seemed ready to swallow him whole as soon as he stepped outside again; dark clouds spinning down low enough almost seem parting just for him like they knew someone who belonged there had come along at last after being gone far too long.

Eli watched through dingy window as the rain suddenly stopped. It was an abrupt end to the torrential downpour. The wind, however, kept howling. A slight clicking sound could be heard on the window and as Eli looked closer he could see the sand hitting the glass panes.

He didn't notice Nettie step up beside him until she spoke, her usually loud, gruff voice cracking like a whip came out in a dreadful whisper, "It can't be."

A shiver slow crawled through Eli's body as he strained to see what her old grey eyes were peering at through the swirling clouds of sand.

——

They said the dust came first.

Not the wind, not the thunder. Just the dust— crawling low like a sickness on its hands and knees. It slithered over the hard-packed earth outside Still Creek, rising in tendrils, climbing fenceposts, curling into the broken boards of barns and biting into the cracks of tired, sunbaked homes. The horizon boiled with it, though the sky was moonless and dry.

Old Man Thompson was the first to see it—crouched behind his barn with a rifle across his knees and a bottle of something mean in his hand. He'd seen storms roll across the plains before. Seen wildfires chew through the grasslands. But this dust didn't come from the earth. It came from *somewhere else.*

"Something's setting up out there," he whispered, squinting into the growing dark. "Ain't natural."

Beyond the cattle gate, across the fallow pasture where no crops had grown in years, the wind began to *whistle.* Not like air. Like a *calliope* out of tune, sputtering with rust. Lights blinked in the haze—dim yellow, like gas lanterns or dying bulbs swaying in an unseen breeze.

And then came the silhouettes.

Tents snapped into being where there had been nothing seconds before—faded canvas striped red and black, rising as if dragged from the soil. Poles drove themselves into the ground. Ropes tightened with a shriek. A Ferris wheel taller than any building in town creaked into the sky, its motion slow and aching, like something waking from a long, bitter sleep.

A banner unfurled at the gate:
"THE MIDNIGHT RODEO — ONE NIGHT ONLY"
It shimmered, just for a moment, and then went still.

Back in town, lights flickered. Radios lost their signal, replaced with static and whispers that didn't quite speak words but still *meant something*. Horses in their stalls began to kick. Dogs howled once, then cowered. And far above, the stars seemed to blink out, one by one.

Sheriff Mott stood on his porch, staring toward the fields. His coffee trembled in his cup. His breath caught.

"What in God's name...?"

Because now came the riders.

Six of them. Pale shapes on pale horses. Cloaks of shadow trailing behind them, their faces hidden beneath wide-brimmed hats that glowed faintly red from beneath. They moved without hoofbeats— gliding across the dirt like memories, or regrets. Wherever they passed, the ground darkened, the grass blackened, and the sound of bells followed like a funeral procession.

The sixth rider dragged something behind him—a long chain, rattling, looped in barbed wire and meat hooks. At the end of it, a crooked shape twitched.

A voice whispered across town, carried by no speaker. It slid through windows, under doors, into dreams:

"Still Creek... the show is ready."

The rodeo ground pulsed once, like a heartbeat. Lights flickered to life—sickly gold, carnival red. The ring stood at the center, surrounded by empty bleachers that hadn't been there yesterday. Rusted turnstiles waited with open mouths.

Then silence.

Still Creek held its breath.

Because the rodeo had arrived.
And it was *hungry*.

Chapter 3: The Dark Carnival

The rodeo sat in the distance, just outside of Still Creek, like some ominous shadow, flickering with gold and red lights but not much else. There was no hint of life. Mason King parked his patrol car on the edge of town and watched, through the winds and sand, waiting for an signs of life. Someone had to have built the rodeo, but how? When? It wasn't there and then it was. Just like that.

A car pulled up next to his.

"Where in the hell did that come from?" June shouted over the howling wind as she got out of her car.

"Beats the shit outta me," Mason admitted with a shrug.

"The old man was right," she said like it half surprised her. "It's just like he told us."

"Who?"

"Old man Thompson," she answered, recounting the old cowboy's tale.

Mason gave her a skeptical glance. "You think that's possible? Sounds like folk tales and superstition."

"Still Creek ain't exactly a town that does possible." Her eyes stayed fixed on the strange scene ahead.

"And I'm not one for the hocus pocus, heeby jeebies, but this, it's somethin' else."

They watched the dark horizon as it crackled with red and yellow lights against swirling clouds of dust.

"You wanna drive out there?" Mason asked, his voice even but with an edge of something almost like excitement.

Before she could answer, a third car pulled up alongside them. It was Sheriff Mott, looking more flustered than ever. His face was ashy and drawn.

"You two see that goddamn thing?" he bellowed through his window.

Mason nodded. "We ought to check it out."

The sheriff snorted. "It'll wait till morning, I reckon."

June leaned against her car, arms crossed defiantly. "What are you scared of, Mott? Clowns?"

His eyes narrowed but he didn't rise to the bait; instead he gave a dismissive wave and headed back towards town.

"Waitin' till morning my ass," June muttered when his taillights disappeared into the storm.

Mason grinned at her sidelong then started up his own car again. "We goin' then?"

"Let's do it." She jumped into her car and they both sped off down the highway—leaving lines of fresh tread marks in dry cracked ground as they cut through wind and weather toward whatever waited beyond those wild electric lights.

***

The ride out dragged on interminably, each yard seemed a mile, a grueling journey beneath ominous clouds that threatened to unleash not just rain or dust, but something far more sinister. June's eyes remained locked on the flickering carnival lights ahead—those lights tugged at her soul with a force that defied mere curiosity, an irresistible pull that seemed to gnaw at her very being. They could have walked the few hundred yards easily but with the instability of the weather and, more importantly, not knowing what they would find out there, it made more sense to be mobile.

When they finally reached the edge of the rodeo grounds, an eerie stillness enveloped them—a profound silence, as if the world itself held its breath, acknowledging their presence in a place the high, dry desert had long since swallowed from memory.

Mason parked beside one of the turnstiles and stepped out cautiously, testing the solidity of the ground beneath him before venturing further towards the ghostly, pale horses standing motionless near a warped wooden gate.

June joined him after a tense moment, her flashlight slicing through the darkness, carving an uneasy path over the dirt packed hard by parades long forgotten—parades for which thinking too deeply about their purpose or audience seemed an unfathomable exercise.

"This is the part where we should just turn around, get back in our vehicles, pack up and leave town," June quipped, half-joking, half-serious.

"You're not wrong," Mason chuckled then became solemn, "but this place..."

"...it does feel wrong," June finished for him.

"Yeah..."

The wind ceased abruptly, leaving only the lethargic hum of generators echoing from somewhere deep within the labyrinth of tents and trailers sprawling into the desolate horizon—all deserted save for the crooked carnival signs that loomed over walkways leading to nowhere anyone in their right mind would dare to venture, unless they were driven by desperation or the reckless abandon of those lost to the night—or perhaps to eternity itself.

Together, they made their way to the center ring, the heart of the unusual spectacle. The bleachers stood silent beneath the heavy atmosphere, filled with the kind of anticipation June recalled from childhood fairgrounds, when everything seemed new and needed to be discovered each time the lights shone brighter than the stars in the vast Texas sky. The sky stretched wide above her young eyes, eager to absorb everything at once, while the towns around them quietly faded, unnoticed by feet not yet fast enough to realize.

As they neared the ring where splintered boards reached upwards as if longing for stray cheers of unwilling spectators, Mason halted abruptly. June turned her gaze to see what had captured his attention.

He nodded toward three dark shapes.

They approached with the stealth and grace of a storm moving in from the west-- deliberate and unstoppable.

"Evenin' folks," the tall one said, his voice a gentlemanly southern drawl that dripped with velvet menace.

June took an instinctive step back as Rook tipped his hat, revealing jet-black hair and a mustached face elegantly out of time with Now; a face that had watched over boomtowns just like this when they thought they might live forever.

Mason's hand moved toward his sidearm then relaxed. "We're looking for the owner," he said evenly.

Rook dismounted in one fluid motion—an old-world apparition wrapped in creased leather and shadow. "Then it seems you've found him."

The other two riders stayed mounted, their silhouettes stark against ragged tents, still as sentinels guarding against another century of absence.

Rook strode forward with an uncanny calm that belonged to someone who knew every step by heart even after years buried beneath creeping dust. He studied June with curious eyes that shone faint red beneath wide-brimmed hat before shifting focus back to Mason then addressing them both in slow, polished tones: "I must say, we were expectin' more of a crowd."

"Ain't usual for rodeos to just show up," Mason replied; cautious but not backing down. "And especially without permits."

Rook gave him an approving nod and smile like someone who'd finally taught a dog to heel then glanced at June again—a look so penetrating that she felt words crawl up under her skin, waiting to be spoken whether she liked it or not.

"What's your name?" she blurted; sharper than intended but softened by the need to know more than just surface answers.

"Folks call me Rook." He held out a hand like an old-fashioned gunfighter challenging enemy or friend—or maybe both—to draw first. June hesitated then shook it briefly; half-expecting a cold ghostly chill but feeling only warmth instead—the dreadful kind you couldn't shake even when everything else went dead around you.

"This thing on all night? I don't see any workers," Mason asked tightly, nodding towards glowing banner at entrance that promised more than anyone could deliver in lifetime full of honest living and quiet deaths.

"Just finalizing set up, been a long ride. We are a finely run show, no time for doddlin' about. My people need their rest. We like to make sure we are set and ready to go, fast as possible. Never in one place very long."

"Never seen a Ferris wheel at a rodeo," June spoke matter-of-factly.

"We got a show fer everyone," Rook said while turning away from them as if to indicate end of the momentary audience; then looked back over his shoulder with eyes lit by lightning-cracking storms inside deep desert twilight. "Even fer those who think they ain't got no business bein' here."

Mason and June watched him walk away but the strange man paused and spoke one last time, "I'll see bout them permits first thing in the morning, deputy."

His voice trailed off into the crisp October air—a bitter reminder that seasons always outlasted memories—mounted his horse and he and the other two riders swept past them both without another word.

***

Back in town, Sheriff Mott sat uneasily at his kitchen table, flipping through reports and invoices that made no mention of dark rodeo shows. He poured himself another cup of coffee then leaned back in his chair; heavy eyes drifting towards the window where the storm still ran riot across brittle October sky.

His wife, Lucille, stood at the sink washing dishes with studied precision; shoulders hunched forward like she'd spent too many years leaning into a never-ending chore. She didn't look up when she spoke: "You gonna let that nonsense run wild?"

"Don't know what I'm lettin' till I see it myself," he muttered defensively, more to the room than to her.

She wiped her hands on a towel whose once-vibrant red had slowly faded to a gentle pink, and over countless years steeped in watery sunlight and the weight of small-town existence, it had become an almost translucent whisper of color. "Last time this town went crazy, you ended up as sheriff," she said, her voice steady and unyielding as she turned to face him; her soft gray eyes meeting his with a fierce, unflinching resolve that cut through the haze of memory.

He muttered a low, discontented grumble under his breath, then abruptly pushed himself from the timeworn table. With deliberate movements, he grabbed a threadbare jacket that hung like a faded relic over the back of a rickety chair, his rough fingers lingering for a familiar pocket, as if expecting to find a packet of smokes—a habit he had abandoned a decade ago. Whether he smoked or not no longer made a difference; in his mind, as Doc Bradford had repeatedly warned him, the real damage had been done long ago.

Lucille observed him with a cool, impassive detachment as he stepped toward the door. For a moment, he hesitated with one foot planted in the familiar domestic space—a sanctuary that now felt uncomfortably confining—and the other half stepping into a world where lingering ghosts and forgotten regrets from dusty decades might still be waiting to greet him. Over his shoulder, her voice carried a gentle, yet weighted warning: "Some folks build their lives waitin' on trouble."

Without even a flicker of alarm when the door slammed behind him, she returned to the rhythm of her chores, her hands resuming their work among the dishes as she set the radio to a country station. Even with its comparatively clear signal over much of Still Creek, the station struggled to escape the omnipresent static and disjointed fragments of songs laden with heavy regret—ballads of lost love, battered trucks, or the fraying edge of sanity on endless desert highways disappearing into nowhere.

In a neglected corner, where an old pickup pressed insistently against a collection of vinyl records that hadn't played since the last rodeo swept through town before their marriage, an aged, scribbled flyer peeked out like a half-forgotten specter. It boldly promised thrills for every member of the family—cattle, women, and kids—its golden letters once dazzling enough to make promises enticing and dreams plausible, even if, as the evening darkened, those very same promises turned to shadows of despair, summoning a hunger for retribution that overtook all who dared to dream.

———

From his rooftop perch, Eli surveyed the shifting storm clouds from a distance that now felt safer. The turbulent sky had descended low enough to enshroud the entire horizon, wrapping the town in a somber shroud reminiscent of a massive gravestone marking ancient sorrow. It was as if the heavens themselves were attempting, in vain, to hold restless spirits at bay—spirits whose stories had been long since consigned to the tattered pages of the town's history books, even as men like Pat Thompson pivoted to advertising reliable pickup gas mileage to distract a community trapped in an endless cycle of dust, wind, and slow decay.

Everyone believed they could outgrow the haunting memories, until those old recollections seized them by the soul, rattling their deceptive lives and exposing the raw truth behind every constructed fence of grief so immense that its weight spanned the horizon.

While that tumultuous scene unfolded before him, Eli reached for a pen and a battered notebook resting near his side.

With quick, deliberate strokes, he scrawled the word "Rodeo. One Night Only."

Around these words, he drew a thick black line—a stark, resolute border delineating a final separation between a community watched too closely and a fate destined to be sealed in an irrevocable moment of reckoning.

———

Nettie poured herself another shot of rot-gut. It had been many decades since she had partaken of her old vices but this long forgotten nightmare was reawakening on a community that had no idea what had just rode in.

She remembered the last time—how easy it was to lose yourself in promises of a different kind. Her hand shook slightly as she brought the glass to her lips and knocked back the whiskey. It burned all the way down, and her breath came out ragged, catching on memories buried as deep as the scars that lay beneath them.

Flashes of Ferris Wheels and pony rides, cotton candy and the smell of the dirt as horses pranced around the rodeo arena. She could almost hear the sounds of the crowds, the joy, the happiness, the clinking of metal as the chutes opened, horse and rider bucking into the night.

Then she remembered the screams.

Nettie downed another shot.

From her window, the dark outline of the rodeo cut into the stormy sky like a long-healed wound reopening against any sane desire to banish it to history. She watched its lights flicker faintly through swirling dust, glowing with a terrible allure that made her heart race with fear and something that felt an awful lot like excitement.

"They'll all come runnin,'" she whispered hoarsely to herself.

Nettie knew it was true; she knew more than she ought to let herself remember on a night like this. June's stubborn streak followed in her own wild little shoes, and she could already imagine her granddaughter standing in line for some front-row seat at disaster—and dragging along every other poor soul left lost enough not to know better.

The phone rang suddenly, jarring Nettie from the tightrope walk between past and present. It wailed its urgency into brittle air until finally she snatched it from its cradle.

"Yes?" Her voice cracked, more with impatience than age.

Static hissed on the other end—sputtering white noise that filled long seconds before resolving into words; words spoken softly but clear enough for Nettie to catch every one:

"See you there."

She froze in place as if struck dumb by lightning, then slammed down receiver with enough force to send tremors skittering across table like ghostly echoes of old horsemen finding their way back home again.

The whiskey bottle waited invitingly within reach but Nettie didn't pour herself another shot—not yet. Instead, she rose slowly from chair; a woman prepared for battle even when warriors ghosts only wore those they loved down inch by inch till nothing remained but cold desert bones.

A cackle broke the quiet—a laugh full of both madness and defiance as she steeled herself defiantly against what Lincoln called malice towards none and charity towards all, knowing instead those were two sides of exactly one dreadful silver dollar.

There would be no running away from this one.

***

Back at June's darkened apartment, Mason sat tensely on her worn-out couch, wiping rain from his face and trying not to look like he was waiting for anything at all.

June watched him pace through the shadowed room with eyes that lingered halfway between admiration and annoyance then opened the curtains just enough so the flickering rodeo lights could cast a faint glow across walls thick with bygone wallpaper patterns not even this new style of retro had decided yet to dig up again from thrift store landfills.

"You figured it out yet?" she asked finally; tossing TV remote aside since power wasn't coming back soon enough for distractin' anyone much more than they'd been already distracted around Still Creek lately.

Mason looked at her with a tired grin, running a hand through damp hair. "What's to figure? The damn thing appeared out of nowhere." He shook his head, incredulous. "You really think this is possible, just some old ghost stories comin' back around?"

June stared out the window towards the distant glow—an unsettling beacon in the thick night air. "In Still Creek, anythin's possible," she replied dryly and switched her gaze back to Mason, daring him to argue otherwise.

The heat between them stayed unspoken; growing hotter as lights from the Midnight Rodeo crept further into their lives like silent warnings or promises—which one depended on who you were asking—and they leaned into each other's company with intent eyes and careful space that left room for all kinds of trouble if this storm blew half as hard as everyone seemed pretty sure now it was gonna.

Finally, June grabbed her keys off chipped Formica countertop and tossed them at Mason who caught them with easy reflexes. She shot him an appraising look—half-joking but more than half serious: "You know me better than you think."

He hesitated only briefly then stood up and returned those steady eyes with ones that said maybe she was right about more things than ghosts extinguishing lights like dreams. "Suppose I do."

They slammed door behind themselves and laughed at the absurdity; outside the rodeo glowed its greedy invitation until the town started getting ready to let it eat them alive come morning—and how many mornings thereafter nobody yet wanted to guess.

***

Eli sat hunched over his notebook until the midnight shadows consumed every word he'd written, offering neither promise nor explanation in return. He furiously traced letters, circling some as if trying to trap wild animals in delicate paper cages. Eventually, he closed the notebook, deciding it wasn't worth chasing words that only ran in endless loops without ever finding solid ground where new dreams could grow.

His father snored softly in the back room they had shared since Eli started high school last year. They lived in a smaller place to save money, with the intention of moving on once Eli made his promised escape from the ghost towns neither of them wanted to linger in—even returning for visits seemed unlikely, but Eli went along with it, knowing plans could change quickly once you set yourself free.

He grabbed his skateboard by the front door and slipped outside through the screen, which banged in familiar silence into the porchless night. The hot breath of the night lingered after the cold storms, and he rode toward the horizon, unsure of what else to do when hope without answers drove him forward, wheels beneath his feet, running toward the wind before dawn broke and men dared to dream of being cowboys.

***

June and Mason made their way back toward town; the headlights sliced through the thick veil of settling dust—or perhaps it only seemed to be settling because everything after leaving the dimly lit rodeo felt achingly slow. The rush they had felt earlier was gone, leaving only the dry whisper of tires against asphalt, each mile a distant echo drawing them closer until they arrived at Nettie's place, where cars lined up side by side like silent sentinels.

The sign above Nettie's blinked erratically, illuminating one letter at a time in a haphazard dance. June nearly laughed aloud when she spotted her grandmother waiting patiently on the porch, a familiar bottle in hand—almost as if the old woman had sensed their arrival on this night filled with unresolved matters and vivid, unbroken visions.

"Go get some sleep, kid," June advised Eli as he coasted up on his skateboard, the wheels humming softly against the pavement. "You'll miss school tomorrow."

"I might be livin' the dream," he retorted, a playful grin tugging at his lips. There was no real bite to his words; just a bubbling excitement and the keen awareness that life was a game without a clear winner, though everyone still tried to keep score. Eli grabbed a coke and a snack then jetted back down the street towards home.

Mason cast an enigmatic glance at June as she drew near; he observed her pause midway, as if contemplating the possibility of wings sprouting from her shoulders, the kind that might let her soar beyond the reach of memories, allowing ghosts to outpace them until they circled back once more.

"You gonna be..." he began softly, his voice trailing off uncertainly, unsure how to finish the thought.

June smiled with a confidence that seemed almost too bold for someone who had lived in these parts as long as they had, where past and present sometimes blurred into an indistinct tapestry. It was a place where the gaps in memory loomed large, where truths were both remembered and rewritten, making it hard to leave despite the ancient game of departure that many had attempted but few succeeded in.

"Always am," June replied, her voice resonating in the dusty morning air. Her laughter rang out, mocking belief while clinging tightly to its opposite, like horses straining against the unyielding traces of fate, woven by hands that seemed to belong to another realm entirely.

The sun had just started dipping behind the hills when Eli walked around the back of the house, wiping axle grease from his hands with a rag he'd probably never wash. His dad was usually on the porch by now, half asleep with a beer in hand and a country record humming through the screen door.

But tonight was different.

The porch light was off. No radio. Just the hush of early evening and the faint rustle of the wind through dying trees.

"Dad?" Eli called.

He heard a garage door creak open.

Eli rounded the side of the house—and stopped.

His dad stood next to a dirt bike. Brand new. Matte black with chrome trim. It caught the last of the sunlight like a whisper of something impossible.

For a second, Eli just stared.

"You kiddin' me?" he said finally.

His dad didn't smile much these days, but right now there was something close to it on his weathered face. He gave the seat a pat. "Figured you were gettin' too big for that beat-up skateboard."

Eli blinked. "Where'd you—how—?"

"Been savin'," his dad cut in. "Worked extra shifts over at the plant. Roger owed me some overtime. Figured I'd rather spend it on somethin' that might actually mean something before it gets eaten up by busted plumbing or property tax."

Eli walked up and ran a hand over the bike's smooth handlebars. "Damn, it's beautiful."

They stood there in companionable silence, the only sound the creak of a wind chime and the faint chirp of crickets trying to find their rhythm.

After a moment, Eli looked over. "Why now?"

His dad took a long breath, then let it out slowly. "Because I know you ain't gonna be here much longer."

Eli frowned.

"You're leavin' soon, and that's good," he said, voice thick with pride and something harder to name. "But I want you to remember what it felt like to ride. To be free. Before the world starts tryin' to own you."

Eli didn't know what to say. He surprised his dad with a quick, fierce, hug then climbed on the motorcycle, gripping the handles, adjusting to the weight like it already belonged to him.

His dad gave the fuel tank a tap. "Go on. Let her breathe."

The bike kicked over with a deep, satisfying growl. Eli gunned the throttle just enough to feel it in his chest.

As he turned to take off down the dirt path behind the house, he heard his dad call after him:

"Don't ever forget how it feels right now, Eli."

He didn't.

Not that night.

Not the next.

And not when he'd later find himself at the gates of something ancient, with that same engine rumbling beneath him—and a wooden coin in his pocket, still warm from a clown's hand.

Chapter 4: Dust and Silver

The Still Creek Municipal Building stood like a defiant relic—a heavy, sun-baked block of cinder and resignation that oozed decay. Its air reeked of old paper, aggressive mildew, and coffee long scorched on a hot plate. The flag at the entrance, drained into ghostly pink and ashen gray, flapped in the wind like a battle banner from a forgotten war, while the lobby clock labored, its heartbeat a beat too sluggish, mirroring the town's perpetual struggle to keep pace.

Mayor Otis Pride sat behind a scarred desk, surrounded by the artifacts of his crumbling reign—a cracked leather blotter riddled with memories and an ashtray stuffed with the remnants of unlit cigar stubs. With a rotund, almost feral face and jowls that drooped like those of a battered hound, he exuded the restless anxiety of a man born not to win elections, but to endure the fallout of one-man show politics. His powder blue tie, once a beacon of optimism, now hung like a tattered ribbon, a feeble remnant against a white shirt stained ominously yellow under his arms.

Across from him, Sheriff Wally Mott radiated raw exhaustion, his eyes bloodshot as if he hadn't closed his eyes since the first light of dawn. His shirt, carelessly untucked on one side, and a belt fastened askew, testified to nights of relentless vigil. The staggering weight of his gut rested heavily as he drew slow, measured breaths, each one a sigh of a man teetering on the edge of relentless routine.

Then, as though summoned by an unholy premonition, the air itself cooled and thickened—the front door groaned open with a sinister whisper, its sound too smooth for the ancient hinges—and in strode Rook.

Rook exuded a bygone elegance in his impeccably tailored black coat, his high-polished boots reflecting the dim light like shards of broken glass, and a broad-brimmed hat that cast his sharply defined features into a dramatic interplay of light and shadows. His face, pallid and almost otherworldly, crisscrossed with lines not of senescence but of brutal, hard-earned experience. He embodied the perilous blend of a gambler, a prophet, and a gunslinger all at once.

"Morning, gentlemen," Rook drawled, his voice silky yet crackling with dangerous old-world charm, as if each syllable carried secrets older than the town itself. Removing his hat with a flourish that bordered on theatrical, he laid a neatly folded piece of parchment onto Mayor Pride's desk. "I thought I'd drop by to settle our formalities."

Mott's eyes narrowed, coiled like a viper, as he scrutinized the paper. "What in the hell is that?"

"Permit," Rook replied effortlessly, as smooth as molten lead. "For the rodeo."

Pride's trembling fingers unwrapped the parchment, revealing deep red ink that whispered of iron and hidden dread. The elegant, looping cursive shimmered menacingly in the light.

"This ain't no state-issued document," Mott growled, squinting at alien symbols stamped near the signature line, suspicion burning in his eyes.

"No, Sheriff," Rook countered with a smile that flashed dangerously, baring a hint of gleaming teeth, "but I assure you, it'll do for this town."

Almost in perfect timing, Rook plunged his hand into his coat pocket and produced a small leather pouch. With a dull, resounding click, he let it drop onto the desk.

Pride, with an almost ritualistic carefulness, opened the pouch and allowed its contents to cascade across the surface: ancient coins of gold and silver etched with mysterious emblems—a ram, a wheel ablaze, a gallows tree—that did not merely glimmer but burned with a searing, embattled heat as though echoing the clamor of long-lost, violent histories. It was more than fifty times what an actual permit usually costs.

Pride's breath hitched in his throat. "Well, I...I suppose everything appears to be in order."

Mott leaned forward, his gaze ferocious as he examined one of the coins, his voice low and dangerous. "Where'd you get these?"

"Same place I got the Ferris wheel," Rook replied with unsettling calm. "Old treasures have a way of sticking to you when cherished."

Mott's gaze darted between Rook and the mayor, the tension slicing through the stale air. "This town's got rules, you know."

"And every single one will be obeyed, me and mine will do nothing more than what the town of Still Creek requests," Rook confirmed, bowing his head with a gravity that promised consequences. "Our visit is transient. We need nothing more than one night."

Pride cleared his throat with a shaky chuckle that barely masked the anxiety beneath. "Well, why not? We don't exactly get much stimulation around here. Perhaps a spark of chaos is exactly what this town needs. Good old fashion western rodeo. This used to be an old cattle town, you know."

"Oh yes, I am very aware," Rook said smoothly, a dark twinkle in his eye.

Mott remained silent, his fingers drumming against the table like a prelude to an impending storm.

Rook pivoted toward the door, pausing with one hand on the cold metal of the knob. "I appreciate your hospitality, gentlemen. I look forward to seeing you—right from the center of the action."

Without another word, he vanished into the tense gloom outside.

Leaning back, Pride's eyes remained transfixed on the enigmatic coins. "Hot damn... I ain't seen authentic silver like this since my granddad passed. That old man was either out-of-his-mind eccentric or—"

"He wasn't from around here," Mott muttered bitterly.

"Damn right," replied the mayor, cradling the coins as though they were relics of divine power.

Mott's gaze hardened as he watched the empty doorway, his jaw set in a grim line. Far off, the wind shifted, carrying with it a sinister perfume of burnt sugar and scorching gunpowder—a harbinger of the chaos that promised to return.

——

The jail in Still Creek was nothing more than a barren corridor lined with cold, unforgiving bars. A bizarre aroma of strong, fresh coffee mixed with country biscuits invaded the senses. In the holding cell stood a lone metal cot, bolted firmly to the unforgiving floor, and a toilet that groaned in contempt every time it was remembered. Harsh morning light sliced through the slatted blinds of the station's only front window, casting harsh, striped shadows across the floor that stretched like prison bars far beyond the cell's confines.

Frank Garrison slumped on the cot, his elbows resting on his knees while his greasy, sweat-crusted hair fell over bruised cheeks and battered temples like a ruined crown. He clung to the same black denim jacket and jeans from the previous night, now reduced to ragged remnants—scuffed and coated in grime. Not a word had escaped him since Mason dragged him in, except for one charged utterance.

June's name.

Outside the cell, Mason King loomed with arms crossed, his weary eyes locked on Frank. The badge on his chest caught a fleeting glint of light from the window, and in that brief flash he resembled not a mere deputy but a relic of a bygone era—coiled, silent, and chiseled from unyielding granite.

"He's clean," declared the young deputy Tyson— barely twenty and already drowning in regret over his chosen path—as he handed over a thin, almost insignificant file. "No record, no warrants. Not even a citation in Texas."

Mason's scowl deepened as he flipped through the report. "You sure you got the right guy?" Tyson ventured timidly.

Mason remained silent, his gaze fixed on Frank. Finally, Frank met his eyes with a cocky half-smile— the same defiant smirk that surfaced when fate was about to turn against him.

"You boys missed me that bad?" Frank drawled, his voice etched with the roughness of disuse and the sting of cigarette smoke.

"No one missed you," Mason replied curtly.

With a languid stretch of his arms that made his injured body wince, Frank stood up. "Then I guess I'll be going."

Mason stepped aside and grudgingly unlocked the cell. The heavy metal door protested with a screech that echoed too long. Frank swaggered out like a man reclaiming his place at a high-stakes poker table, casually flipping his disheveled hair aside and dusting off his soiled jacket with an air of indifference.

"Still Creek," Frank drawled, his tone laced with a resigned familiarity. "Not much ever changes."

"You do," Mason warned, his voice low and ominous. "You show your face near June again, and I won't be nearly as polite."

Frank paused, turning slowly to fix Mason with a long, challenging look. "Got someone new looking out for her, huh? Thought she was grown enough by now."

Mason's jaw tightened, his silence heavy with unspoken threat. Frank chuckled darkly and strode out the door but Mason wasn't done. "Some friends of yours rode through the other night, Frank. Maybe it's coincidence, maybe not. Maybe you're running to them or from them, either way I could give a shit less. But if you bring trouble to this town, a tiny little jail cell will be the least of your worries. We clear?"

Frank's posture stiffened at the mention of the biker's who had ridden through. Damn, he thought, they know I'm close, boxing me in. But he couldn't let this nosey deputy know that though. As much as Frank wanted to push his buttons he sensed this Mason fella meant business, and Frank survived by listening to his instincts. He forced himself to relax. "Crystal," he answered, stepping out of the building.

The dilapidated hotel across from Nettie's was a tired relic—a cramped space of ten rooms each draped in tired shades of beige from another era. The hand-painted sign above the office, faded since the sixties, served as a silent witness to countless sorrowful departures.

Frank leaned heavily against the antiquated bell at the front desk until an old man with coke-bottle glasses and a crackling hearing aid emerged from the back.

"Need a room," Frank grunted, his voice edged with urgency. "For a night or two."

"Sixty-five a night. Cash only," the clerk replied without missing a beat.

From his jacket, Frank extracted a neatly folded wad of bills—a couple of crisp twenties and a wrinkled hundred.

"Keep the change," he rasped. "Give me one upstairs. Facing the road."

Room 7.

The key dangled from a metal hook; no bureaucratic nonsense, no ID checks, just a curt nod and an exhale from the clerk who'd seen too many lost souls drift through Still Creek to care about names anymore.

Frank ascended the worn steps slowly, his shoulder protesting with every movement. He lingered before a door stained by time, then unlocked it and stepped into a room thick with the scent of cheap soap and older, buried secrets. Dropping his bag onto the bed, he made his way to the window.

Across the street, Nettie's Store flickered in the dusty daylight, its neon signs blinking beneath layers of neglect.

And then he saw her.

Not Nettie—but June.

There she was, standing on the storefront step with a steaming cup of coffee in her hand, conversing with a teenager. Her posture was guarded yet deceptively serene, like someone who had forgotten how to truly live but was desperate to reclaim a semblance of freedom.

Frank's eyes burned with long-held fury and longing as he took in her sight, his expression masked in shadows of unreadable intent. With deliberate slowness, he raised two fingers to his brow in a mocking salute.

June remained absorbed in her own world, refusing to look up.

But Mason had already caught the gesture.

Sitting in his cruiser a few corners away, Mason's gaze was locked on the second-story window as his hand edged toward the radio.

A hint of a smile curled Frank's lips even as he pulled the curtain shut, sealing the intensity of the moment away like a final act in a dangerous game.

———

The sun hadn't dared to break through the oppressive shroud of clouds and choking dust all morning—a pitiful smear trying to ignite a fury above Still Creek, as if unleashing reckoning upon the land. The air was a suffocating miasma, heavy with the stinging tang of ozone, burning rust, and the ghost of crushed sagebrush. The road to Old Man Thompson's was less a proper pavement than a punishment of crumbling potholes, and the farther you ventured from town, the more it felt like you were barreling headlong into the gaping maw of something ancient and hungry.

Mason's cruiser roared over the dirt path, its tires unleashing a furious storm of dust and grit. June sat rigid in the passenger seat, her fingers drumming on the door with restless intensity, her jaw set like hardened steel.

"You really think he'll talk?" Mason edged out.

"He'll talk—to me," June snapped, her tone carrying both determination and dread. "He might not like what he says, but talk he will."

Thompson's shack loomed at the edge of a barren field like a forsaken relic from another era—a squat, one-story ruin with peeling white paint and a sagging roof barely held together by patched corrugated metal. Horseshoe charms clattered from the porch in muted protest, their dissonant clicks a grim symphony in the stagnant air.

Even before they knocked, the screen door groaned open.

Old Man Thompson sat entrenched in his battered chair on the porch, a living monument to time itself, swaying deliberately in the stillness. His long gray beard, streaked with bloodshot yellow tobacco stains, and his wide-brimmed hat shadowing eyes that had witnessed too much, gave him the look of a man carved from despair. One hand gripped a dented jug while a rifle lay casually across his knees like a silent sentinel. A spit cup, already brimming before noon, sat defiantly beside his boot.

"Well, if it ain't the crawlin' wreck of the town," he rasped. "The wrench and the ghost."

June stepped onto the porch as though treading sacred ground, nodding sharply. "Mornin', Pat."

Mason followed, hat in hand and eyes wary. "Hope you don't mind the intrusion."

Thompson snorted, a dry laugh cutting through the tension. "Boy, you think anyone drags themselves this far by accident? You ain't intrudin'—you're bein' summoned."

They sank into worn chairs across from him—June with an unsettling calm borne of hard truth, Mason stiff with the anxiety of heading into the heart of a haunted secret.

"We saw it," June declared after a pause. "The rodeo."

At her words, Thompson's slow rocking came to a halt, his lips twisting into a grim smile of displeasure.

"Rook," Mason continued, voice low. "He's callin' the shots. Even paid the mayor in goddamn gold."

A slow, deliberate exhale rumbled from Thompson, morphing into a curse heavy with bygone anger. "That son of a bitch is back."

"You knew him?" Mason pressed.

Thompson's eyes darkened as he spat into the cup with a harsh hiss. "I know what he is. He ain't no ordinary man. He ain't the devil himself—but he's on first-name terms. Might even be kin."

June leaned forward, her curiosity edged with foreboding. "You told me once that the riders came before, that after the storm… after the chaos, what exactly happened, Pat?"

Thompson's answer came slow and deliberate, as if each word weighed a ton. He took a long swig from the jug, wiped his mouth with the back of his calloused hand, and stared across the brittle, desolate grass as if the truth was trudging in from the barren horizon.

"They came in '87," he said, each syllable heavy with regret. "Not nineteen. Eighteen. I was just a kid, but my grandpappy listened to his mamaw's tales. They said it began just like this—weather twisting, nature holding its breath, animals silenced, and people drowning in unsettling dreams. Then came the searing lights, the grotesque tents, the pungent

71

stench of burnt sugar and spilled blood. Folks laughed at first. They thought it was a twisted carnival, a fleeting burst of joy in the dusty heartland."

He leaned in, his voice dropping to a conspiratorial growl.

"But it wasn't joy—it was bait."

Mason's brow knit together. "Bait for what?"

Thompson locked eyes with him, and in that charged moment, the old man's fear was as raw as an open wound.

"For what's lurkin' beneath," he whispered. "This rodeo is just a flimsy disguise—a mask. The real horror festers below, feasting on your name, your sins, your very blood. Once invited in, it's here to stay until it's sated."

"Why Still Creek," June asked, unaware at how shallow her breathing had become listening to the old man talk.

"It ain't just Still Creek, it's all over. It seeks out small towns, hopeless places so far off the map that no one will be missed. They say it's been going on since the first settlers started making the west their home."

A weighty silence crashed over them, oppressive and foreboding, like the final click of a door sealing their fate.

June's throat tightened. "So what do we do?"

Thompson snorted like a dying beast. "Do what you do when a tornado's coming—duck, pray, and cross your fingers that it doesn't rip away your roof or your soul."

He hoisted his rifle, setting it upright against his knee with deliberate defiance. "I told you before, Junebug—when that wind shifts, you stay locked in. Shut your doors. Steer clear of that cursed arena. Don't eat the food, don't play the games, don't even watch."

Suddenly, Mason's radio erupted with harsh static— a maddening reminder of isolation—only to fall silent moments later, amplifying the eerie quiet.

June rose slowly, resignation and determination warring in her eyes. "Thanks, Pat."

"Don't thank me," Thompson barked, resuming his relentless rocking. "I'm not here to save souls. I'm just old enough to see the damn storm coming and wise enough not to stand out in its path."

As they trudged back to the cruiser, Thompson's voice called after them, loaded with grim finality.

"Rook don't knock twice," he warned. "You see that ferris wheel spinning? That means the deal's already been sealed."

Without a backward glance, they drove off into the dark uncertainty.

—

The storm had subsided by early afternoon, yet the atmosphere remained thick with an electric menace—as if lightning had scorched every surface, leaving behind a dangerous, simmering charge in wood, wire, skin, even thought.

Eli Boone roared through the oppressive silence on his new dirt bike, slicing erratic arcs down the barren spine of Main Street, his hoodie pulled taut against a chill that hinted at unseen terrors. The engine murmured under him, a dark, dependable rumble that pounded in sync with his racing heart. Around him, Still Creek resembled a forsaken ghost town hastily sketched with smudged pencil lines—faded, incomplete, and blurred at its edges.

Yet the rodeo was anything but abandoned.

It pulsed at the outskirts like a sinister, living beast. Tattered tents shivered in a wind that wasn't really blowing, and lights blinked in a deliberate, menacing pattern—red like fresh blood and gold like cursed embers, reminiscent of carnival fireflies on a haunted night. The Ferris wheel turned with an eerie, unhurried motion. Impossibly slow. Without any sound or engine, it moved like a spectral relic caught in a timeless loop.

Eli came to a stop at the edge of the grounds, his front tire bumping against a strip of dry, trampled earth. A corroded sign arched over the entrance, swaying gently as though it too were alive.

MIDNIGHT RODEO – ONE NIGHT ONLY

He cut the engine and sat there for a heart-stopping moment, as the silence wrapped around him like a sodden shroud—the kind of silence that buzzes in your ears until it hurts. He drew a deep, cautious breath, like one prepares before plunging into dark, icy waters without knowing what lurks beneath. Then he swung his leg over and stepped forward.

The gate offered no creak; instead, it exhaled softly, as if breathing after a long, suffocating slumber.

Eli walked slowly past faded tents whose still, unmoving flaps watched him with unseen eyes. No music dared break the oppressive quiet, yet a visceral, low throb pulsed beneath the earth—an undercurrent of dread that hinted at something awful stirring below. He passed a carousel that had appeared overnight, its horses frozen mid-gallop, mouths twisted open in silent, eternal screams. One of them stared with human eyes, glimmering with unspeakable fear.

Eli forced his eyes away.

A disturbing flicker caught his peripheral vision.

Ahead, leaning against a warped wooden booth painted with peeling stars and stripes, stood a clown.

But this was no whimsical jester from a children's party or a circus act.

This clown wore a perfectly tailored suit of midnight black, accented with thin, blood-red pinstripes. His face was smeared in bone-white makeup, and his red lips were caught in an unyielding, macabre grin that refused to waver as Eli stared. His eyes were abyssal pits rimmed with shimmering gold, gleaming like cursed coins, and a crooked bowler hat sat askew on his head. In his gloved hand, he held a cane topped with a silver knob fashioned into the grim outline of a noose.

He uttered no words. Instead, he slowly extended one gloved hand.

Gripped in that outstretched hand was a coin.

It was wooden. Round. One side bearing a star, the other a spoked wheel.

Eli stepped closer, his throat tight with dread. With a hesitant, almost ritualistic motion, he reached out and took the coin.

The clown's fingers were ice-cold—not merely the chill of death, but a deep, hollow cold, as if they had never known warmth.

Eli turned the coin over in his hand; it was unnervingly smooth and had warmed to an almost sinister heat. Looking up, he found the clown had vanished without a sound, leaving behind only undisturbed dust where he'd stood.

Eli's pulse drummed fiercely in his neck. He shoved the coin into his hoodie pocket and made his way back toward his bike. Behind him, the Ferris wheel persisted in its relentless rotation, a ghostly sentinel silhouetted against a bruised, ominous sky.

He couldn't recall riding home.

He couldn't remember shutting off the engine or even stepping back inside.

But later that night, when he emptied his pocket, the coin was still there—warm and waiting.

And on its reverse side, beneath the etched image of a wheel, an ominous message had materialized, burned into the wood in small, slanted letters:

"SEE YOU SOON, RIDER."

The store lay suffocatingly quiet—a silence that both unnerved and strangely soothed Nettie Carson. As she stood behind the counter, she observed the red numbers on the unplugged register with a mix of suspicion and longing, as if they might suddenly reverse their count and undo the past. Dust motes floated listlessly in the stale air under failing fluorescents, while a jar of pickled eggs on the shelf fixed her with a gaze full of disquieting, yellowing eyes.

Not a single customer had come in all morning—neither the Boone kid nor even June. That barrenness left her conflicted: part relief at the brief solitude, yet deep disquiet at the eerie absence of life. It wasn't merely the silence; it was the way the town's spirit seemed to be shifting, tilting subtly as if the very air or gravity preferred new, mysterious destinations. With a heavy heart and trembling resolve, she sighed, rotated the "OPEN" sign to "CLOSED," and locked the door—a motion so automatic she almost doubted it was her choice at all.

In the cramped back room, the lights flickered again, as though echoing the uncertainties that roiled inside her. The bare bulb above the old rocking chair buzzed with the relentless anxiety of a trapped wasp, a sound she wished to ignore. Instead, she moved to the shelf by her sewing machine, pushing aside a stack of long-forgotten receipts and a dusty radio that had long since fallen silent. Beneath these relics of a former life, she discovered an old cigar box, its exterior wrapped in fraying twine—an object that stirred a torrent of conflicted memories.

Her hands trembled as she opened the box. Inside she found ashes, faded ribbons, three small brass bells, and a horseshoe-shaped locket, its face now tarnished to a dull green-brown. The locket was a relic from over thirty years ago, a remnant of a time when things still felt real and warm. With both trepidation and a desperate nostalgia, she snapped the locket open. Instead of a cherished photograph, she found a pressed piece of blood-red fabric and a single word burned into the metal: REMEMBER.

Nettie exhaled harshly, sinking into the creaking rocking chair—a chair that, much like her heart, seemed reluctant to bear its burdens any longer. A familiar, forbidden pull tugged at the base of her spine, a hollow hunger behind her ribs that she had thought long buried. It was as if the rodeo—once a wild dream and a symbol of things lost—had returned to reclaim parts of her identity she had hoped were gone.

With conflicted determination, she poured herself a shot of rotgut whiskey from the bottle stashed under the sink. The burn ignited unshed tears, a bitter acknowledgment of pain and desire intermingled. Her gaze drifted toward the window where, amidst a storm-draped horizon, the lights danced—golden and red, like elusive promises that whispered hope even as they warned her of danger.

From her apron pocket, she retrieved a flyer slipped in under the back door earlier that morning— knowledge kept secret from June and everyone else. Printed on heavy parchment with edges singed and curling, the ink shimmered as if still drying in the heat of a long-ago fire. "Midnight Rodeo – VIP Invitation; Special Appearance by Netta Carson; Admission Paid in Full," it declared boldly. Beneath the invitation, an emblem—a spoked wheel set within a radiant sunburst—evoked childhood dreams and ancient altars in the woods, stirring emotions she had long tried to ignore.

In a moment of inner turmoil, she crumpled the flyer, only to smooth its creases again with trembling fingers, as if wrestling fiercely with her urge to both forget and return. In the bathroom mirror, her reflection blinked a moment too slowly before her lips moved almost on their own: "I told him I'd never come back." Then, in a surreal echo of her inner conflict, her reflection smiled softly and mouthed, "But you will—tonight." Nettie stared, her body wracked by an uncertain passion until her knees nearly gave way.

She moved back to the room and donned her old black coat—the one she had buried in the crawlspace so long ago, its scent of sawdust and smoke a lingering reminder of past choices. As she fastened the buttons, the shaking in her hands subsided into a fragile calm. Clutching the tarnished locket close, she slipped it under her blouse, as though safeguarding it might mediate the war between longing and fear that churned within her.

Outside, the wind had intensified, moaning through the eaves like a warning or an invitation—a duality that perfectly captured the turmoil in her soul. Stepping onto the porch, her hair whipped uncontrollably across her face, mirroring the storm inside. With each hesitant yet determined step into the tempest, Nettie felt the relentless pull of conflicted destiny, knowing that through the chaos awaited answers she both craved and dreaded. And despite the tumult within, she resolutely did not look back.

——

Nettie Carson strode through the Midnight Rodeo's towering arch without pause or interrogation. No ticket was given, no name was demanded. They simply accepted her into this otherworldly carnival.

The grounds lay unnervingly silent—an expanse of decay and distorted beauty. Tents, gaunt and stretched over cracked earth like withered skin on a corpse, fluttered in the dusty wind, their red and gold stripes bleeding into one another. A twisted Ferris wheel loomed above the horizon, its deliberate rotation void of any creaks, as if it were a sentient watcher in the gloom.

No revelers haunted this place yet—no laughter, no playful shrieks of children. Only the grim workers—Rook's minions—moved amid the shadows, as if fused with the decaying structure. They exchanged not a single word; clad in mismatched, tattered rodeo uniforms, their spurs produced an eerie, rhythmic jingle reminiscent of chains scraping along a deserted ballroom. Some clutched buckets brimming with a substance far darker than water; others meticulously scrawled cryptic messages in reverse on battered signs.

In the midst of this macabre labor stood one peculiar figure: a barefoot man, his eyes hidden behind a blindfold, methodically pounding horseshoes into the dirt in a perfect, unsettling spiral.

Nettie's gaze was steeled; she paid them no mind—they were mere specters of worse things she'd encountered.

At the far end of this dread-filled fairground, nestled between two ominous pavilions, rested a trailer that defied expectations of performers or livestock. This mobile parlor exuded an eerie charm: windows frosted over and glowing with a dim amber light, while gold trim danced along its blackened surface like sinister veins throbbing beneath paper-thin skin.

Rook awaited at the foot of a narrow set of steps, as unchanged and timeless as ever.

He remained unscathed by time—a figure clad in a long black coat adorned with silver embroidery along the collar and cuffs. Leaning casually against the trailer's rail, one boot resting on a step and his hat cradled in his arm, his eyes caught the lantern's flicker, transforming it into an incandescent blaze that belied ancient secrets.

"Netta," he uttered softly, with an unsettling sincerity.

She halted five paces from him, her stare icy. "I didn't think you'd come in person."

"I come for those who truly matter," he murmured.

"You've got a lot of nerve," she retorted.

"I always did," he replied, his smile neither cruel nor warm, but like the forbidden taste of something long suppressed.

A heavy silence stretched between them, punctuated only by the sound of sawdust being swept and the intermittent, almost ritualistic tap of a hammer driving iron into bone.

"You're early," she finally accused.

"And yet you came all the same," he countered.

Nettie stepped closer, her voice low and wary. "I knew you'd drag it back with you."

"It isn't something I carry," he said as he turned toward the trailer door. "It follows where debts must be paid."

With a silent gesture, Rook swung open the door. "Come in. No witnesses, no strings. Just you and me."

Nettie ascended the steps deliberately, her hand gripping the railing as if to test the searing heat of an unholy brand. The door closed behind them with a ghostly whisper.

Inside, the air was oppressively warm, as if the room itself remembered a false sense of comfort but could never fully recreate it. The walls were draped with ancient photographs—sepia-toned portraits of riders and clowns, bleachers filled with once-cheerful faces now marred by decay. Some of these fractured images bore uncanny resemblances to people she once knew. One, disturbingly, looked like her.

A small table, covered in scarlet velvet, sat at the center. Two chairs faced each other across it, and a bottle of rye alongside two already-poured glasses awaited like silent witnesses.

"You kept everything exactly as I left it," Nettie observed, her voice barely above a whisper.

"I never break my promises," Rook replied evenly.

"Strange, I can't recall you keeping your last one," she hissed.

Rook sank into the chair, motioning for her to sit across from him. "Tell me, you didn't die, did you?"

Nettie remained standing, defiant.

He swirled the amber liquid in his glass. "Do you remember what you entrusted me with?"

"I remember every sacrifice I made for you," she shot back.

"Not every fragment," he intoned, tapping the table once with a slender fingertip. "But I kept the essence of it. All of it—bound in ribbons, still warm."

"You promised I could leave," she accused. "Start over—and that it would never return."

"I never claimed it wouldn't chase you," he replied coolly. "I never said it wouldn't visit."

Nettie's hands trembled slightly, yet she refused to sit.

Leaning forward, Rook folded his fingers with ritual precision. "There is a place for you here, Netta. It has always been so, and it always will be."

Her eyes met his, filled with the wary scrutiny one reserves for a flame that has burned them before.

"I'm done with your twisted rodeo," she declared.

"You were never one of the performers," Rook murmured, rising to his full, ominous height. "You were the one who truly understood the macabre rhythm—the weight of fear and the thrill of terror. They adored you for it."

"I gave you everything," she spat, voice trembling with both rage and despair. "And still, it was never enough."

Stepping closer, Rook's voice dropped to a hushed, mournful cadence as if reciting a blood-soaked prayer.

"Not everything," he whispered. "You kept your name."

Nettie turned, intent on leaving.

"I refuse to ride your nightmare again," she declared, firmly. "Not for you, nor for anyone."

"I'm not asking you to ride tonight," Rook replied, his tone laced with sorrow. "Not yet."

She stopped at the door, poised between worlds.

He raised his glass behind her in a final, chilling toast. "To memories."

Without turning, she left. Outside, the wind had died, leaving an eerie stillness. The silent clowns had dispersed, and the blindfolded worker continued hammering horseshoes within his mystic spiral. At her feet lay a new flyer, pinned to the dirt by a glinting silver tack.

She did not reach for it.

Nor did she need to.

She already knew its grim promise:

"One Night Only. VIP Returns."

Chapter 5 – The Parade

The morning light in Still Creek arrived like an admission half-heartedly made—soft, gray, and hesitant. It bled slowly across the horizon, failing to break through clouds that loitered like unsaid apologies over the hills. The town was cloaked in a lingering gloom, as if each street corner bore the weight of too many unspoken regrets. The dampness of the streets wasn't born of rain but rather the prolonged sweat of a community caught in a breathless state, each heartbeat a reminder of unresolved tension.

In that fragile space between the weary sorrows of yesterday and the uncertain promises of tomorrow, the town stirred with quiet disquiet.

June Weaver stood before Nettie's, clutching a steaming mug of black coffee as if it might dissolve the knot tightening in her chest.

Beyond the glare of a reluctant dawn, the Ferris wheel continued its slow, soundless rotation—a mechanical metronome in a landscape that had lost its natural rhythm. Its dead, eyesome lights pulsed in a beat that felt out of place, as if even inanimate objects were caught in a conflicted trance.

Narrowing her eyes, June watched each turn of the gears—a constant reminder that something was off, as though the wheel itself was breathing in time with a troubled heartbeat.

"You sleep at all?" Mason's voice cut in from behind—a low, scratchy murmur clinging to each word like remnants of a long night filled with too many cigarettes and too few answers.

June didn't look back. "Barely." She took a measured sip, trying to find solace in the bitter warmth. "You?"

"Didn't bother trying." Mason stepped up beside her, eyes locked on that unsettling wheel. "It wasn't moving when we left last night. Was it?"

"No." She finally met his gaze, an uneasy flicker in her eyes. "Something's changed. Again." The word hung between them like a verdict they both dreaded to fully comprehend.

Mason's hand rose to caress his stubbled jaw as he stared into the horizon, seeking, perhaps in vain, some sign of resolution. "I went out to Thompson's this morning."

June's brow lifted in a mixture of curiosity and apprehension. "Yeah?"

"He's gone. The place was empty. And the rocking chair... it was still moving when I got there." He paused, his words heavier now. "Gun's gone too."

A charged silence fell over them, dense and unresolved, like a confession trapped in the space between exhaled breath and an unanswered prayer. Somewhere down the street, a dog barked once before dissolving into a whimper—a brief note of disturbance in an otherwise too-quiet town, as if the silence had become a canvas for all their unsettled thoughts.

"I think something's coming," June murmured, her voice barely above the whisper of conflicting memories and hard truths. This time, she didn't look at Mason but instead fixed her gaze on the storefront window across the way. In its reflection, she saw herself—a tired, fragmented image that clashed with the ghost of who she used to be. "Something bigger than before."

Mason shared the sentiment without a word, their mutual understanding as bitter and unresolved as the dawn itself. They lingered in that uncertain moment, shoulders tense beside one another, both caught between resignation and defiance. Then, as if to remind them that time waited for no one, the wind shifted.

It wasn't a strong breeze—just enough to disturb the trees, to murmur unsettling secrets in their ears, carrying with it the faint scent of burnt sugar and old sawdust; carnival smells that shouldn't exist here, smells out of place and stirring even more inner turmoil.

June's eyes flickered with sharpened doubt. Across the street, pinned to a power pole with a solitary silver tack, was another flyer. Drawn to it, she crossed slowly, the security of her coffee forgotten as she approached with hesitant steps.

The weathered paper felt like a relic that shouldn't be there, its once-vibrant edges curling inward, as though the weight of unspoken warnings had aged it overnight. The script sprawled across in tall, looping letters, rendered in a red so deep it nearly seemed black.

MIDNIGHT RODEO – ONE NIGHT ONLY

GATES OPEN TOMORROW AT SUNDOWN

ALL WELCOME. NO REFUNDS. NO RETURNS.

June tugged the flyer from its place, feeling a subtle jolt—like electricity dancing beneath her skin. Tucking it into her pocket, she turned back towards Mason with a conflicted resolve.

"I think we just got our invitation," she said, her voice brittle with both hope and uncertainty.

Mason responded with a grim nod, his eyes returning to the slow, uneasy spin of the Ferris wheel. "Let's hope it's the only one."

As they moved to rejoin the shelter of the storefront, neither noticed the solitary figure in Room 7 of the hotel across the street. Half-hidden in shadow, a man watched with half-lidded eyes, a cigarette burning slowly between his fingers. Frank Garrison's faint smile was a paradox—an acceptance of the inevitable mixed with the quiet tension of secrets kept. He leaned back into the gloom, drawing the curtain closed as if to seal away further unrest.

Outside, the Ferris wheel continued its interminable turn, each slow rotation a metronome marking an uncertain future. And somewhere in the fields beyond town, a drum beat rose—low and steady—as if something deep and conflicted were finally stirring awake.

———

It began just after noon. Not with a gentle melody or carefree laughter—but with the grating, tortured groan of wheels. Not the slick, familiar sound of rubber skidding over asphalt, but creaking, splintered wood that strained forward as if it despised each forced movement. It sounded not like machinery, but like ancient, creaking coffins dragged over a cracked, unyielding ground.

An eerie fog roiled across the street, almost alive.

Eli Boone heard it first. He sat outside Nettie's, half-ensnared by the suffocating heat of a lazy afternoon, a wrench clutched tightly in one hand and a sticky MoonPie in the other. His dirt bike, its chain freshly anointed with oil, lay dormant next to him, eagerly poised to devour any back road that crossed its path. Yet, as the sound reached his ears, it severed his chewing in an instant.

Creak. Groan. Clink.

Eli leaped to his feet, squinting against the harsh glare of the sun. Then he saw them.

The clowns.

They emerged from behind the courthouse like a waking nightmare, as though the very earth had vomited them forth. Not the cheery, balloon-twisting clowns of birthday parties or circus tents—these were relics of a twisted, archaic terror. Their faces were smeared with cracked makeup that flaked away like dry, desiccated skin. Smudges of pallid white and rusty red contorted into macabre grins, grotesque mustaches, and smeared tear tracks. Their wide-brimmed rodeo hats slouched at lopsided angles, and eyes—those dead, haunting eyes—gazed out from hollow sockets, either void and coal-dark or gleaming an unearthly, dying gold. Some donned dusters crudely stitched with animal bones; others sported seared, inverted stars and crescent brands, burned into their cheeks like the eternal scorch of an iron.

The first clown towered above them all—nearly seven feet of monstrosity cloaked in a tattered poncho fashioned from rattlesnake skins. His minimalistic face paint formed a grinning skull beneath lifeless eyes. Clutched in his skeletal hand was a jagged staff—a broken fence post scavenged from decay, its tip still entangled with rusted barbed wire.

One after another they advanced. A pair of twin clowns reared up on mechanical horses that moved with an eerie, unnatural lurch. A juggler hurled cowbells marked with grotesque bite marks, their clangs echoing like the clamor of some unholy congregation. One clown, dragging a shrieking suitcase that thrummed with every jolt, made his presence known with each tortured bounce. Another, his chest a canvas punctured by painted bullet holes, limped on backward-bending stilts, reminiscent of a starving elk's desperate limbs.

They surged onward in relentless succession. A fire-breather burst forth, his plume belching out a toxic green flame that hissed like venom, reeking of sulfur and decay. A blindfolded clown fiddled an instrument whose wail mimicked the last, tortured cries of a dying beast. One danced madly with marionettes wrought of razor barbed wire, their jerking motions punctuating his every step with sinister precision.

The townsfolk began to pour out of their homes. Doors creaked wide open. Blinds shuddered upward. An unfathomable dread clawed at the hearts of everyone in Still Creek.

"What the hell is that…" someone whispered in broken terror.

"They're clowns," another stammered, voice shaking with disbelief. "But not the kind from any circus I know."

Mothers clutched their children with desperate arms. The old-timers stared in horrified disbelief, as though the very specters of their buried past had risen again.

June Weaver, unyielding, stood beside Mason King outside the diner, her arms folded and eyes sharply fixed.

"This ain't no parade," she snarled, voice edged with grim conviction. "This is a damn warning."

Mason's jaw tightened into a rigid line as he nodded once, wordlessly acknowledging her truth.

Then came the float—a grotesque chariot pulled by a team of pantomime horses. Their skeletal forms were smeared with deathly paint, their eyes rolling in sunken sockets as if mocking the living. Behind them dragged a warped, splintered wooden platform, doused in the dried stains of paint and blood. Atop this abomination rested a mock throne, hewn from the broken steer horns of fallen giants, adorned with buzzard feathers and scavenged bar stools.

Perched atop the throne sat a rodeo queen—a spectral figure draped in decay. Her sash boldly declared "Still Reigning," though the letters were as cracked as her tilted tiara. Her makeup had long since run like melted wax, revealing a visage that belonged to something not wholly alive. Her skin shone with an unearthly, artificial perfection, and her eyes traced the crowd with a slow, disconcerting rhythm as the float rumbled by.

June felt an unnerving familiarity stir within her, an inexplicable connection that gripped her with terrified confusion. Mason noticed her haunted look and followed her unwavering gaze.

"What is it?" he demanded, voice low and tense.

June replied slowly, her eyes unyielding as they clung to the queen, "I don't know... I feel like I ought to recognize her, like I truly do. Is that crazy?" she finally asked, desperation lacing her words as she turned to Mason for reassurance. But his eyes were fixed elsewhere—at the sad figure of Nettie, standing at the porch's edge, her head slumped, a single tear trailing down her weathered cheek.

"That's impossible."

Even the deputy, gripped by doubt, sensed that certainty was slipping away.

There was no triumphant music. No heralding announcement. No revelry. Only those horrifying, painted faces and the echoing symphony of ancient wheels and crackling, dry wind.

The procession slowed at the town square, the clowns dispersing like shadows into narrow alleys, into the broken seams of the air. One stepped into the post office, swallowed by darkness, never to be seen again. Another vanished behind the church, dragging his living, screaming suitcase until all sound was consumed.

Only the float remained.

And the queen.

She sat there, immobile and foreboding... until, in a moment that shattered the silence, her stillness gave way to unholy motion. Her mouth unlatched ever so slightly. And from its gaping maw drifted a whisper—not borne on a voice, but a deeper, more ancient rumble.

"Soon."

Then her head slumped, like a puppet whose strings had been violently yanked away.

No applause erupted. No smiles broke the paralyzing dread. They all stood motionless, entombed in the searing midday heat, as a horror unlike any other clawed its way into their hearts with rusted hooves and melting greasepaint.

The parade was over.

But the show?

It hadn't even started.

———

The sun bled a bruise across the western horizon, its dying light staining the sky with raw, violent passion as long, fractured shadows sliced through Still Creek. A parched wind howled down the streets, whipping dust devils into frenzied life and scattering brittle, faded newspapers like remnants of shattered memories. The town, still reeling from the nightmarish clown parade, trembled in stifled silence—drawn curtains, bolted doors, watchful eyes peering from every crack. But the silence was about to shatter.

They struck just after sunset.

Engines roared to life—deep, ravenous beasts tearing through the darkened asphalt like wild, frenzied wolves. Their sound cascaded over the town in a relentless surge, building into a guttural growl that rattled the windows and left dogs cowering in impotent fear behind their fences.

Frank Garrison was already crouched by the hotel window when the rumble hit. He hadn't dared move from his spot. Sweat slicked his shirt as he fixed his gaze on the street, anticipating its violent awakening. And now, the nightmare had arrived.

He yanked aside the curtain.

Six bikes, their chrome gleaming like snarling predators in the dim half-light, roared hard onto Main Street, tires shrieking as they split past the blinking streetlight. These were the same bikes from that gas station encounter—the riders, clad in oil-black leather, bearing on their backs a jagged red insignia: a skeletal wolf crowned with vicious thorns.

Frank growled a curse under his breath.

"Goddamn it," he spat. "They found me."

The lead rider—Griff—cut his engine sharply, lifting his helmet to reveal a head shaved almost clean apart from a scarred mohawk running like a battle-worn ridge down the center. He inhaled deeply, the air tainted with the scent of fear and adrenaline. His grin erupted into a savage snarl as he nodded to the hounds at his side. "He's here."

The bikers fanned out like predatory hounds encircling a trapped, quivering rabbit.

Frank didn't hesitate.

He yanked open his room door and bolted down the back stairs, his boots slamming against cold metal steps as his heart hammered and his ribs tensed in each desperate stride. He plunged through the alley, darting past the back of Nettie's, every step fueled by raw, unyielding terror.

And there it loomed—a neon blemish carved into the darkness, beckoning him like a bleeding wound etched into the heart of the land.

The rodeo.

Its lights flickered in a violent heartbeat—burning red and molten gold, twisting into the night like acrid smoke from a seething inferno. The Ferris wheel turned with a slow, predatory deliberation. Tents gaped open as if inhaling the despair of the night. There was no laughter, no music—only a potent, inescapable tension.

Frank felt it deep in his bones. He didn't dare question it. He ran. Out the back of the hotel he bolted, quietly snaking through the shadows until he hit the town's edge then he took off running, hoping his legs wouldn't give out or his lungs didn't explode.

Griff sniffed the air again.

"South," he snarled. "He's headin' for the lights."

"You gotta be fuckin' kiddin' me," muttered Preacher, a wiry man with a snake tattoo slithering up his neck. He spat venom onto the dirt. "That freakshow? No place for hide and seek."

Griff revved his engine low and menacing. "It's exactly the kind of rotten place he'd think we wouldn't chase him down. But we sure as hell aren't playing fair, are we?"

"The cop?"

"Nowhere in sight."

They barked short, ugly laughs—a sound like clattering chains.

Then they roared off.

Frank crossed the perimeter just as the air shifted, thickening with an oppressive force.

It slammed into him like a monstrous wall: warm, suffocating, heavy with the grime of dust, the iron tang of blood, the burnt sweetness of scorched sugar, and an underlying stench of ancient decay—as if bones, long abandoned under the relentless sun, were exhaling their secrets. His legs moved on pure instinct, so automatic that he only realized he'd abandoned the cracked concrete for soft, treacherous earth when the familiar sounds of town faded behind him like a closing door.

The midway lay eerie and deserted. No workers, no clowns—just aging tents creaking under the unseen weight of a sinister wind, the Ferris wheel ticking in relentless, beat-like rhythm, and the distant, disquieting churn of something unfathomable stirring beneath the ground.

Frank stumbled forward, past a row of abandoned trailers and a toppled popcorn stand, until he beheld the big top.

And there, silhouetted by flickering neon, stood someone waiting—a man in a pinstriped vest, his face as pale and unnervingly calm as a phantom's, hands locked in a poised gesture as if expecting a long-overdue visitor.

Rook.

Frank froze.

The man didn't shift; he only tilted his head in a slow, deliberate arc.

"You seek sanctuary," Rook intoned—no question, just the stark, undeniable truth.

Frank's throat tightened. "I need somewhere to hide. Just... just for the night."

Rook nodded once with measured gravity—as gentle as a priest absolving a penitent sinner on borrowed time. "We don't judge your past. We only demand that you play your part."

Behind Rook, the flap of the tent rustled open not by any hand, but by a breath of something beyond human.

Inside, darkness exhaled.

Frank stepped into the void.

As he melted into the tent's embrace, the lights pulsed once—first red, then gold—before falling silent again.

Moments later, the bikers reached the edge of the rodeo grounds. They halted.

None dared cross the threshold.

Griff stared at the pulsing lights, the quivering tents, the relentless Ferris wheel with eyes narrowing in uneasy suspicion. A cold dread coiled in his gut.

Preacher fumbled for a cigarette, lighting it with trembling hands. "We really gonna go in there?"

Griff said nothing. He slowly turned his bike.

And one by one, they followed suit.

Like wolves who'd caught a whiff of something ancient, malevolent, and waiting in the dark.

And inside the tent, far away from the last vestiges of ordinary life, Frank stood alone beneath a canvas so black it devoured the stars.

Deep within that oppressive void, a calliope began to wail.

It was off-key.

It was soft.

And it was unsettlingly, irresistibly welcoming.

———

The hour weighed down like a slumbering behemoth—unyielding, suffocating, its silence pounding in your ears like the distant rumble of an impending storm, even when nothing stirred. Still Creek lay in deceptive slumber, its dark windows flickering with muted light through parted blinds while the static of an old television droned like a warped lullaby for those too afraid to face the night.

But Eli Boone was not asleep.

He lay in bed, fully dressed and his heart wound tight from the day's relentless terror—the deranged parade of clowns, the cursed coin, the unyielding, sinister grin. That very coin now sat heavy in his pocket, its warmth unnaturally fierce against his thigh, pulsing like a heartbeat from some malevolent source.

The house groaned around him, every creak a whisper of foreboding; his dad's low snore bellowed from the next room like a bear awakening from its feral slumber.

Without hesitating, Eli swung his legs over the bed's edge and snatched up his hoodie. He didn't pause to ponder—the act of moving drowned out the storm of thoughts that paralyzed him. For stillness was an invitation to relentless, torturous reflection.

He crept through the kitchen, boots clutched tightly as he slipped out the back door into the suffocating, breathless haze of the yard. The moon had been swallowed by dense, choking clouds, leaving only the whispering wind to sketch dark, twisted shapes in the night. He hoisted his hoodie higher, nudged the garage door open just enough to squeeze through, and rolled out his dirt bike with hands trembling from a volatile cocktail of dread and anticipation.

The engine coughed into life with a rough murmur, then settled into a low, sinister purr—as if it too yearned to slip back into a realm of unspeakable horrors.

Slicing through the back alleys of Still Creek, Eli merged with the coarse dirt and gravel, a spectral figure on a mission dictated by dark inevitability.

The rodeo grounds had mutated yet again.

They always did.

It wasn't merely the grotesque, bloated tents— sullen, rotting husks stretched unnaturally—or the Ferris wheel, now in reverse, its every creak groaning under the weight of some unseen burden.

It was the oppressive, sickening aura that clung to the place.

Eli killed the engine at the field's edge, allowing his heavy steps to carry him onward, his bike abandoned behind a half-collapsed hay wagon—an eerie relic of decay.

He melted into the shadows, sliding low behind sagging fence posts and tattered, dying popcorn banners until he reached the back of one of the massive tents—a subordinate structure, not the towering big top but far too large for any ordinary sideshow.

Something was happening inside.

A feeble, blood-red light seeped beneath the canvas—flickering like a sinister flame filtering through a veil of crimson, as if steeped in spilled blood. Eli edged closer, crouching low until he discovered a narrow seam in the aged fabric, just wide enough for him to pry it open.

What he saw stole the very breath from his lungs.

There were no chairs, no expectant crowd—only a dirt floor and a ring of ashen debris etched in a perfect circle. In the center, Frank Garrison stood barefoot, stripped down to ragged jeans and an undershirt, his expression a raw blend of fury and confounded dismay. And he was not alone.

Around the ring, three grotesquely painted rodeo clowns loomed, their tattered suits marred by smeared, distorted makeup that hinted at alien, contorted forms lying beneath. One had eyes that glowed with an eerie, spectral gold; another clutched a bell-shaped lantern that threw erratic, dancing shadows against the dilapidated walls.

And then there was Rook.

He lingered just beyond the circle, dressed in his trademark long black coat that absorbed the darkness, now accented with a blood-red sash dangling like a duelist's trophy. He fixed his gaze on Frank like a man watching a pot whimper into a violent boil.

A guttural growl tore from Frank—a sound Eli barely caught over the pounding of his own heart.

Rook answered with a slow, ritualistic gesture, and the clowns stirred into action. One advanced, extending something on a faded velvet cloth—a mask.

It was ancient and sinister. Cracked leather, scarred by time, adorned with faded carnival swirls. Its eyeholes were edged in tarnished brass, and the lower lip boasted a jagged row of teeth stitched in black thread, reminiscent of a predatory altar.

Frank reached for the mask with trembling, hesitant hands, as if the very act were an unholy surrender.

"No," Eli whispered, his voice quivering as his fingers dug into the tattered canvas, desperate to hold back the inevitable.

Frank fixed his gaze on the mask for a long, brittle moment; then, as if compelled by dark fate, he slipped it over his face.

There was no blinding flash or bursting storm. Only the distinct, suffocating snap of air—like the final seal on a tomb—and Frank collapsed to his knees within that macabre ring. In unison, the clowns clapped once—a single, eerie sound—and Rook executed a measured, contemptuous bow, the motion as deliberate as a conductor commanding a deadly symphony.

Eli staggered backward, his body buckling as he crashed onto his trembling hands. Like a cornered beast, he scurried away through the encroaching grass, his movement frantic and raw. His heart pounded an erratic, violent rhythm; his limbs quivered under the weight of unspeakable horror. The mask, the deranged clowns, the haunted expression on Frank's face before he vanished into an abyss of leather and madness—it was all unequivocally, horribly wrong.

He didn't dare stop running until the sickly flicker of streetlights broke through the darkness.

Finally, when he collapsed back into his bed that night, boots still on and heart still hammering against his ribs, the cursed coin slipped out of his pocket and rolled under the bed.

It was no longer merely warm.

It seethed with an unholy heat.

And on its underside, etched beneath the image of the wheel, had appeared a single, damning word:

"WITNESS."

———

The bell above the door let out its reluctant, ominous chime as June stormed in, her boots slamming the dust of the fading evening into submission. Mason followed close behind, flicking off gritty layers from his jacket and an unease that clung to him like a curse.

Inside Nettie's store, the dim light of the overhead fluorescents flickered with an anxious hum that tonight felt more like a dire warning than the usual comfort. The air reeked of burnt coffee and the chemical tang of pine-scented cleaner—a scent as familiar as it was foreboding—but this time there was an undercurrent, a razor-sharp edge, a pressure that didn't belong.

Nettie sat behind the counter, her hands mechanically folding a stack of old receipts with the precision of someone who'd seen too much. Her eyes remained fixed ahead, avoiding any hint of connection.

June slammed her arms over her chest and leaned aggressively against the counter. "What the hell was that, Nettie?"

Without so much as a glance upward, Nettie continued her methodical folding. "You'll have to be more specific."

"That parade," Mason interjected, stepping forward as if daring the silence to break. "Those freaks, those damn clowns... You froze when they passed by. We were all rattled, but you—Nettie, you looked possessed, like you'd seen ghosts from a nightmare."

Still, Nettie's eyes didn't flinch until she finally sighed and glanced up, her face etched with a deep, haunting exhaustion not just of age but of a soul thoroughly drained—as if she were a candle burned down to a stubborn wick.

"You two think this is some twisted sideshow—a bizarre carnival rolling in under a tempest of neon and deceit," she began, her voice low and jagged with resignation. "But that rodeo... it ain't natural. It ain't of this world."

June's arms dropped, her unease blossoming into alarm. "What do you mean, 'ain't of this world'? Like, not from Texas?"

"No," Nettie whispered, her voice a delicate yet cutting rasp. "Not from here."

Mason's eyes widened. "Wait, are you saying it's… alien?"

Nettie's steely gaze said it all—a silent command to stop being foolish even as it hinted at unutterable truths. "I'm saying it's not of this earth," she replied flatly. "Not in the way you imagine. Not every otherworldly visitor wears green skin and blasts lasers. Some come riding in with spurs and crooked smiles. They don't need spaceships—they only require a door."

June took a step back, her heart hammering as dread seeped into her bones. "You've seen it before, haven't you?"

Nettie offered no immediate answer, only a heavy silence.

"You have," June pressed fiercely. "That's why you were so deathly quiet when it appeared. That's why you vanished out there the other night."

With trembling hands, Nettie lit a cigarette, drawing in a drag that seemed to carry centuries of secrets, her gaze fixed on some distant, shadowed memory. "You don't need to know everything I've witnessed," she murmured. "And I'm bound by rules—rules I'm damn well not willing to break. Not again."

"Not again?" Mason echoed, the implication hanging like a storm cloud in the stale air.

Nettie shot him a withering look and ignored his protest. "You want answers," she said, rising and leaning heavily on the counter as her voice dropped to a conspiratorial whisper laden with raw conviction. "But you're asking all the wrong questions. That rodeo didn't start here. This town isn't the first to be gripped by its unholy lights—it's merely the next doomed soul in its path."

June's voice came out rough as gravel. "How many towns?"

Nettie's reply was barely audible, a choking whisper: "Too many."

"That's what old man Patterson said," Lucy murmured to Mason, her voice small against the swelling tension.

But Nettie laughed hollowly, a sound that dismissed old tales and feeble minds. "That old coot doesn't know shit," she scoffed. "He's heard whispers and legends, and yeah, he was one of the cursed towns. But that's all he knows. He was smart enough to run."

"Then why hasn't anyone else heard of it?" Mason demanded, his voice edged with a desperate need for logic.

Nettie exhaled a plume of acrid smoke through flared nostrils. "Because those who witness it keep their damn mouths sealed. And those who survive barely remember it right. That's the damned deal."

"What deal?" June insisted, her voice trembling with a mix of fear and fury.

For a long, suffocating moment, Nettie said nothing—the tension coiling between them like a living thing. Finally, she reached into the pocket of her cardigan and retrieved a battered flyer, its edges singed and creased, its lettering pulsating with an eerie light under the store's flickering ambiance. Midnight Rodeo – One Night Only—the promise of a curse etched into every fiber of the paper.

She passed it to June, her eyes dark and unyielding. "This isn't printed—that's *etched*. And it showed up inside my house without anyone knockin'."

June stared at the flyer and then at her aunt, confusion and terror wrestling in her eyes. "Nettie..." she began, but Nettie was already melting away into the back room.

Just as the door creaked and sealed her fate, Nettie's voice sliced through the silence. "Lock your doors. Stay far from the lights. And whatever you do... don't stray near the arena when the dust starts to rise. I would tell you both to run but we all know there's nothing that could convince you of that."

And with that, she vanished into the darkness.

June, who had always believed her aunt was as immovable and unyielding as granite, now felt an icy dread unfurling in her chest—a chilling bloom that no truth could ever dispel.

———

The night over the desert stretched out like a vast, empty void beyond the dying lights of Still Creek. The two-lane highway snaked into a black horizon that seemed eager to devour every stray beam of headlights. Six bikes roared along the asphalt in loose formation, engines howling like a savage pack of metallic wolves. At the head of the pack, Griff – a hulking brute marked by prison tattoos – led the charge astride his custom hog emblazoned with iron crossbones. Hot on his tail, Preacher rode with a long, tattered coat billowing like a battle-worn flag, his machete's hilt glinting as though promising retribution. The rest – Crow, Tank, Buzz, and Dimes – followed in steely silence, fueled by a singular purpose: get reinforcements, return, and reduce that abomination to smoldering ruin.

"Frank's hidin' behind something in there!" Preacher bellowed, his voice crackling fiercely over the comms. "We regroup, get everyone, and torch that wretched plague!"

Griff spat venom onto the scorched pavement. "We should've dragged him out when we had the chance."

Then, without warning, the crisp desert air morphed into a sinister mist. One moment the night was dry and clear; the next, a low, creeping fog slithered up from the earth, crawling over boots and pooling on the road like rapidly congealing spilled blood. Buzz's voice cracked through the tension, "Uh... this ain't normal, right?"

No one answered.

The mist thickened with alarming speed, metamorphosing into a blinding wall of white that sent their headlights scattering. Instinctively, Griff eased his throttle; the rest followed until the roar of their engines dwindled to a trembling murmur. They came to a complete stop.

"Eyes open," Griff ordered, his tone a mix of urgency and dread. "Something's off."

And indeed it was. The atmosphere pulsed, heavy and suffocating, like a drenched wool blanket drenched in oil and sorrow. The bikes idled in a dead, oppressive silence—no crickets chirping, no wind rustling through, no far-off rumble of trucks. Even the moon seemed to recoil, hidden behind the encroaching clouds.

From the murk, the soft, rhythmic clopping of hooves emerged—clop... clop... clop... steady and insistent, heralding a grim omen. Out of the milky fog, three towering figures on horseback appeared, otherworldly and menacing. The riders did not charge; they drifted forward like ghosts on spectral steeds—massive horses with steaming bodies and too many shifting shadows clinging to their skins, moving as if the laws of gravity had been forsaken.

Their riders were draped in long, obsidian coats and wide-brimmed hats that concealed their faces, save for the baleful glow of red eyes burning from beneath. One wielded a rusted, menacing chain that scraped the pavement. Another gripped a jagged, crescent-hooked staff with a predatory calm. The third—the tallest—wore a coat trimmed in bone-white fringe that fluttered without a whisper of wind.

Griff's voice dropped to a growl. "You boys seein' this?"

"Hell no," Crow muttered, his tone trembling with disbelief. "This has gotta be one twisted dream."

The Riders remained mute, their presence exuding an ominous calm as they observed. Then, with a sudden, terrifying snap, one of them cracked his chain like a whip. It lashed the pavement just inches from Griff's front tire, unleashing a shockwave that splintered the asphalt like shattering glass.

"MOVE!" Griff roared.

The engines screamed to life as the pack barreled toward Still Creek with desperate speed, tires screaming in protest and hearts pounding wildly, the fog clawing relentlessly at their heels. But the road, once a familiar escape, was no longer theirs. The mysterious mist twisted unnaturally around them, funneling them back toward one another like a tightening noose. And the Pale Riders pursued without a sound—swift, silent, and utterly merciless.

Chaos exploded. Crow was the first to fall, his bike spiraling out as an impossible stretch of road vanished beneath his wheels. He fought to steady himself, but nothing was there; his scream dissolved into the fog. "Crow's down!" Dimes shouted, lashing out as he swerved desperately.

Then the rider with the hooked staff materialized beside Buzz. There was no struggle—only the cold, decisive tap of the staff against Buzz's chest, and in an instant, Buzz was gone, swallowed by the night along with his bike, like a candle abruptly snuffed mid-prayer.

Preacher's face, slick with sweat, turned in alarm. "We're not outrunnin' 'em!"

"Then we stand our ground!" Griff roared as he skidded to a halt, leaping down in one fluid, determined motion. Tank and Dimes immediately joined him, whirling to face the advancing Riders, while Preacher gripped his machete in trembling defiance.

The fog had now encircled them completely. The Riders advanced with measured, infernal calm. Tank hefted his shotgun and hollered, "Come on then, you demon fucks—let's see if you bleed!" With a thunderous blast echoing like a cannon's boom, Tank fired. The buckshot slammed into its target—only to pass straight through, as if his ammunition were nothing more than ghostly shrapnel.

The lead Rider did not even flinch; he simply raised a hand. In that brutal instant, Tank's head jerked violently to the side, as if yanked by unseen, spectral fingers. His body crumpled, lifeless, to the ground.

Dimes bolted, but fate was equally swift with him. A vicious swing of the chain caught his ankle, yanking him screaming into the snowy expanse of the fog.

Only Griff and Preacher were left—back-to-back, encircled by an evil beyond measure.

"I'll be damned," Preacher whispered hoarsely, tightening his grip on his blade. "You think we're in Hell?"

Griff's jaw clenched darkly. "Nah. Hell's got rules."

Then the third Rider dismounted with imperceptible sound; his boots kissed the asphalt as he approached relentlessly. Slowly, deliberately, he removed his hat to reveal a face crafted from stitched shadows, as if the very darkness of the night had been sewn into flesh.

Griff began to reach for his pistol, the .9mm tucked in his waistband. The Rider offered a smile that was both inviting and macabre, flipping aside his dark coat to reveal ruby red revolvers. Griff seemed to understand what was being offered without a word being spoken. The Rider tilted his head, extending a single, beckoning finger. The biker leader's hand snapped toward his pistol. He had barely cleared his waistband when the Rider snapped the revolver from its holster, lightning quick, and sent a lead bullet, radiating with red spectral residue, right between Griff's eyes. The force lifted the biker up and slammed him back into the asphalt.

Preacher's grip on his machete faltered, and he let it drop. He stepped forward, drawn inexorably toward the figure. And then, as if unveiling a terrible secret, the Rider opened his coat to reveal not flesh, not bone—but a mirror that reflected Preacher's own agonized expression, every sin and every scar of his past converging in one horrifying moment.

The biker crumbled to his knees as the Rider stepped past him, leaving only a quivering Preacher in his wake.

"Why?" Preacher croaked, voice riddled with terror and disbelief.

The Riders said nothing. Wordlessly, they remounted their spectral steeds and faded into the consuming fog.

When the mist finally receded, the highway lay utterly abandoned. No bodies, no bikes remained— only suffocating silence and the faint, haunting aroma of burnt sugar drifting on the night wind.

Chapter 6 – The Dead Hour

It began just before dawn—when the quiet town of Still Creek lay exposed in its most delicate state, bathed in a ghostly pallor that hovered between the remnants of night and the very first, trembling hints of light. There was no forewarning, only the violent scream of metal slicing through the deep silence.

The source of the chaos was the railyard on the south side of town—a place left to the ravages of time since the early '90s, now a broken panorama of rusting tracks, train cars defaced in fresh graffiti, and wild, overgrown weeds thick enough to devour a boot. No living soul should have been there. In fact, no one had set foot there in years.

Yet, in the dim pre-dawn light, something impossible happened: all twelve of the long-dead railcars began to move. They did not roar to life with the familiar grumble of diesel engines, nor did they hitch themselves to an inviting locomotive. No human hand flicked any switch or cranked a lever. Instead, the cars simply began to roll on their own.

At first, their movement was tentative—a slow, eerie crawl marked by the high-pitched squeals and grinding scrapes as their wheels fought against the timeworn rails that should have securely held them in place. Gradually, the pace quickened, as they looped around the ancient switchback track, their progress punctuated by harsh screeches that echoed the sound of something ungodly gripping the wheel.

Mason King, on his overnight patrol, was the first to witness this surreal spectacle. Stationed by the south bridge, he was finishing up his routine when the ground beneath his cruiser began to tremble. Initially, he chalked it up to one of the minor quakes that had become increasingly frequent since the annual rodeo had come into town. But then the lights revealed a more disturbing truth.

Hanging from the last two railcars were lanterns— old-fashioned, gas-fed hurricane lanterns with wide, imposing mouths. They swung gently as if in a slow dance, painted in a deep soot-black and dripping with crimson wax that caught the dawn's fragile light. Within the flickering glass of each lantern, tiny, unsettling details became apparent: small coiled snakes, knotted ropes twisting like ancient curses, and miniature skeletal dolls that floated as though suspended in some unseen, fluid realm.

The train hurtled past the bridge, a spectral force with no conductor, no visible mechanism binding it to its tracks anymore. Mason stood frozen, watching with wide, unseeing eyes, as the air around the moving cars shimmered like the furious heat of a furnace, a stark contrast to the biting, freezing wind that whipped across the valley.

As the final railcar disappeared into the early morning gloom, the town itself reacted. The lights in Still Creek dimmed and flickered erratically before surging back to life with a violent intensity. At that very moment, every mirror in town—whether nestled in a compact purse, mounted as a rearview reminder in a car, or proudly displayed in the antique vanity in Nettie's back room—cracked all at once. The fractures spread like lightning, whispering with a sibilant hiss as if the glass were actively resisting some invasive, crawling force.

And then there were the clocks. Every single clock in Still Creek froze, its hands stubbornly fixed at exactly 5:19 a.m.—no exceptions, no moments before or after. They simply stopped, leaving behind an eerie silence in their wake.

At Nettie Carson's house, she had already been awake when the mirror in her kitchen began to spider-web itself, breaking apart on its own accord. She did not jump in fear. Instead, with a calm that belied the surreal chaos unfolding, she murmured, "It's begun."

Just down the block, June jolted upright in the middle of the night. The sound of her bathroom mirror shattering snapped her completely out of a half-formed nightmare—a nightmare where a massive, spinning wheel made of bones turned in reverse, accompanied by a discordant melody played backward.

The strange phenomena did not end there. Telephone lines began to stutter and glitch, radios emitted bizarre, unexplainable static surges, pets howled with an unearthly urgency, and from the gnarled trees near the old church, a brood of crows—far too many for the quiet season—took flight en masse, circling the town like a ragged, black halo.

By the time Mason reached the edge of the rodeo grounds once more, he found that the old Ferris wheel, a relic of happier times, had come to a complete, eerie stop. And, as if nature itself were sending a final, cryptic message, a new sign had appeared at the entrance. It was not hung or nailed like the others; it simply seemed to have grown there, as if emerging organically from the earth.

Chiseled from a slab of dark red wood that appeared to be soaked in an ancient, unspoken substance, the etched sign read in bold, almost prophetic script:

"TONIGHT: THE MAIN EVENT

ADMIT ONE. NO RETURNS."

——

The Still Creek Retirement Home loomed on the ridge like a ruined toy lost to time—a crumbling shell with flaking siding, sickly pale green stucco warped by relentless decay, and a flickering neon sign that hadn't buzzed to life in years. Inside, dim corridors exhaled a muted, oppressive glow—just enough light for nurses to furtively check vitals without rousing the sleepers, but far too feeble to banish the lurid shadows that slithered under beds and lurked in every dank corner.

In Room 108, three beds huddled in a grim horseshoe around a dusty television and a shared, counterfeit faux-oak nightstand, as if bound by an unspoken curse. For nearly seven harrowing years, three women had been chained to this dismal space.

Dorothy Meeks, 83, cloaked her true hair color in mystery. Miss Evelyn Hart, 91, was razor-sharp in her demeanor, her words slicing through the silence. Lucinda Ray, 86, plagued by failing sight yet haunted by a relentless compassion, whispered fervent prayers even for the wicked souls in the building.

That night, the room reeked of an unbearable stillness, as if time itself hesitated, holding its breath in dread.

Within that suspenseful void, they found themselves trapped in the same nightmare.

They stood, side by side, beneath a sagging circus tent with tattered stripes of dying gold and sickly crimson. The air reeked of putrefied hay and burning sulfur, and each step on the spongy floor—a floor that whispered of unseen decay—resounded like a wet squelch beneath their distraught slippers.

In the shared dream, their awareness converged. "Dorothy, Lucinda? Are you here too? When did we stumble into this accursed circus?" one whispered, voice trembling.

Dorothy's eyes flickered in startled surprise. "Not exactly, Evelyn—we're just here. Oh wait...I realize I'm dreaming, and my dearest friends are with me. I usually love these dreams, truly."

"This isn't your dream, Dorothy—it's mine," countered another, incredulous with a bitter edge. "My mind insists I'm trapped in someone else's nightmare."

Then, like a trapdoor snapping shut, a spotlight burst to life.

"Allow me to clarify, dear ladies," crooned a maddened, cackling voice that slithered from every shadow, "this nightmare is yours—each and every one."

And from the darkness, he emerged.

The clown.

Not the jolly harlequin of childhood fancies—this was a twisted abomination. His face resembled cracked, peeling wallpaper; his eyes were voids, glassy and dark like blood-soaked marbles. His painted smile stretched unnaturally wide, slack and devoid of joy, more a predator's sneer revealing a row of ragged, filed-down teeth.

He wore a vest crafted from human teeth, strung together with brittle, faded thread, and his gloves were pristine bone-white satin, an eerie contrast to his animalistic gait on hooves. Tiny silver bells dangled from each earlobe, their delicate chimes cruelly ringing out even in the stagnant air.

"I've been waiting," he hissed, his voice a tortured rasp like a bow scraping across oiled violin strings. "Tonight's show demands three tickets—but only two of you will awake."

They clutched each other in terror, hands quivering as if anticipating doom.

"No," whispered Evelyn, defiance mingled with dread.

"You can't kill us in a dream," insisted Lucinda, voice trembling with disbelief. "That's not how it works."

But Dorothy turned to her friends, her face drained to a ghastly pallor.

"You fail to grasp," she murmured, voice saturated with despair, "that I have seen him before. The night Henry died, his smile was just like this—and his words, the same chilling promise."

The clown stooped forward, his spine creaking like brittle twigs snapping under winter's bite, until his eyes—ominous and unyielding—hovered inches from Dorothy's.

"Do you know what happens," he rasped in a voice of raw menace, "if you awaken too quickly?"

No sound came in answer.

Slowly, he straightened. "Then do not."

The light above them blinked out, swallowing them in total darkness.

And then, the screaming erupted.

Evelyn jerked upright in her bed, drenched in cold sweat, her hands seizing a rosary so fervently that the beads carved painful crescents into her palms. She gasped as if dragged from the deepest abyss.

Moments later, Lucinda awoke, her first breath strangled by a choking sob. "I...I saw him, Evelyn—I swear I saw him!" she stammered.

But Dorothy remained unmoving.

She lay there, not in peaceful rest, but rigid—her mouth frozen in a silent scream, her eyes unblinking in a terrible stare.

Not at the benign ceiling.

But fixed on a shadowed corner of the room.

Lucinda followed her gaze.

The corner was empty.

Yet in the near silence, the eerie ring of a tiny bell echoed—a solitary chime slicing through the darkness.

Chime.

Then nothing.

Twenty minutes later, the night nurse found them. Evelyn and Lucinda wept amidst despair, while Dorothy's lips were a ghostly blue and her hands chilled by an otherworldly stillness.

On her wrist, the hospital bracelet lay turned inside out, its vinyl marred by an inexplicable etching—a tiny, spoked wheel.

And that was the night Room 108 welcomed its first empty bed in nearly a decade—a sinister void that foretold horrors yet to unfold.

———

While the old ladies woke to the devastating loss of their dearest friend and most of Still Creek lay in uneasy slumber, something abominable erupted near the Kincaid farm. It started with a sound—a deep, bone-shaking rumble, as relentless as a freight train or the growl of distant thunder. Yet there were no ominous clouds, no encroaching storm—only a pristine, unyielding sky and a moon that pooled its eerie light over frost-slick fields, turning fence posts and dry irrigation pipes into sinister, gleaming sentinels.

Then, the animals began their unholy scream.

Chickens erupted into a frenzy of shrill squawks, thrashing in their coop until splatters of blood marked the wood like splattered paint. Horses bucked in their stalls with a wild, almost inhuman fury, their hooves and flailing limbs battering stable doors until one shattered its own leg, unleashing a cry of unearthly agony. The old milk cow cried out once—a long, dreadful bellow that hinted at unbearable torment—before falling into a ghastly silence; later, she was found dead, eyes staring wide in terror, her tongue grotesquely swollen and hanging limply from her mouth.

Dale Kincaid—a battle-hardened ex-Army man who had once fired at shadows in three distant war zones and never once faltered—bolted outside in nothing but his boxers and a rifle, his bare feet slapping against the frozen ground. He discovered his barn doors swinging open, not rent apart by a raging wind, but left deliberately ajar, as if an unseen presence had entered and exited with a chilling courtesy.

In that moment, the wind ceased its mournful howl, and the temperature plunged by ten degrees in an instantaneous, bone-chilling drop.

Dale lifted his rifle and stepped into the heart of darkness.

He never spoke of the ghastly vision that awaited him.

Just after sunrise, his wife found him curled up in a corner of the hayloft, clutching a severed bull skull— a relic that hadn't roamed the property for years. His mouth gaped open in a silent scream, his eyes fixed on horrors unseen, while his hands bore burned, circular blisters that twisted into patterns resembling wheels, brands, and ensnaring ropes. In a voice scarred by terror, he repeated one fateful line:

"They're not men. They ain't ever been men."

With Sheriff Mott nowhere in sight, Mason took command, demanding silence from his deputies. A doctor was sent to tend to Dale, and his distraught wife, April, was asked to keep the night's events shrouded in secrecy until Mason could get to the bottom of it. Yet by midday, every soul in town whispered that something had gone horribly, irrevocably wrong at that farm.

The rumors ignited like wildfire.

"Dale saw a faceless clown."

"No, it was three riders—ablaze like fire yet moving like ghosts."

"They weren't after Dale. They were hunting someone else—he merely stared too long."

By the time June heard the tale—first as a frightened rumor, then confirmed by Tyson who had helped carry Dale to the house—the Ferris wheel of fate had already begun its slow, deliberate turn once again, as if it sensed the dreadful climax was near.

And in the shadowed back room of her store, Nettie Carson stood hunched in darkness, her trembling fingers tracing the cold iron key that dangled from her neck, as she whispered a name long locked away by fear and time:

"Ashbride."

———

Eli Boone sat at the kitchen table, trying desperately to seem normal. The cereal bowl lay abandoned, and his spoon dangled uselessly in his trembling hand. Overhead, the harsh buzz of the fluorescent light seared the air, merging with the relentless clack of his father's boots on cold linoleum. In the living room, the TV droned on about a local feed outage, its monotony a grim counterpoint to the oppressive, suffocating weight that burdened the very atmosphere—too heavy for spring, too thick for breath.

"Eat something, son," his dad growled without so much as a glance upward. "You're twitchin' like a raccoon in headlights."

Eli mustered a smile that tasted bitter and weak, nodding in response. "Yeah. Just… weird dreams." But even as he said it, he knew: it wasn't a dream.

It wasn't.

It was the tent. The mask. The clowns. Frank's scream—echoing before the world's sound was violently sucked away. Eli gripped the spoon as if it were a lifeline, a fragile tether against the unraveling of reality. Yet, even as his fingers clutched the cool metal, the shadows within him grew, stretching like sinister fingers at mid-morning—silent invaders not in his yard, but in his mind.

In a desperate bid to expunge the nightmare, he splashed cold water on his face in the bathroom, expecting the shock to burn the memory away. It didn't work. When he met his gaze in the mirror, he didn't see himself. He saw Frank—wearing that monstrous mask. But it wasn't merely on his face; it had become his face. Crude stitches marred the hardened leather that had fused with flesh, and from hollow eyeholes oozed slow, tar-thick black tears. His head jerked in a dissonant, marionette-like tilt, as though controlled by a malevolent puppeteer.

Then came the whispering. Low and warped, the murmurs slithered like venomous parasites, as if their sinister words were meant for another time and another soul. They seeped through the glass, their incomprehensible syllables leaving a hungry residue. With each whispered word, the mirror fogged, and jagged, looping glyphs etch themselves into the condensation, writhing like tiny, maddened insects beneath the surface.

Eli stumbled backward, heart pounding in terror. One blink later, the mirror cleared, revealing only him— pale, shaking, swallowed by isolation.

That night, shattered sleep gave way to the sound of his own name, softly echoing in his ear. It wasn't shouted—it was a hiss: "Eli…" A rasp filled with smoke and biting teeth emanated from his jeans pocket, where the cursed coin still lurked like a venomous spider curled in the dark folds.

He snatched it out, and a scream tore from him as he felt a burning—not the searing heat of metal, but a misbegotten fire, as if the coin had scorched its mark from within someone's very soul, pressed against pure hatred. In a blind panic, he flung it across the room. It struck the closet with a dull, final thud, coming to rest in an eerie silence.

For what felt like an eternity, he watched the coin lie still on the cold floor before exhaustion dragged him back into a troubled sleep.

The next morning, the coin was back in his pocket, exactly where it had always been. School was an impossibility—he simply couldn't face it. Instead, he curled up on his bed with his battered notebook open; the pages that once captured sketches, lyrics, and flashes of strange ideas now served as his frail anchor to sanity. Absentmindedly, he flipped through them until his eyes landed on a photograph.

Tucked between pages that hadn't seen the light of day in weeks, the black-and-white picture was curled at the edges like a relic from another era. It showed a rodeo crowd, grandstands filled with hollow, blurred faces, and dust swirling ferociously in the arena. A clown, frozen mid-stride, was trapped in time. And then, amid the formless sea of spectators... there was him.

Eli Boone. Still wearing the same hoodie, his hair unaltered, his expression vacant yet laden with an unspoken terror. Staring directly at the camera, it was as if he was confronting his own reflection—an image that chilled him to his core.

His hand trembled violently as he flipped the photo over. On the back, a faded, smeared message scrawled in desperate handwriting declared:

"One of you must ride. One of you must fall."

A heavy thump echoed in the hall. Was it his father's heavy footsteps? Or the ominous pad of the dog's paws? No. Eli knew, with a dread that burned through every fiber of his being, that it was something else entirely—something relentless and close, creeping nearer, demanding that he remember.

———

The blazing noon sun loomed in the sky like a desiccated skull, its glare offering no comfort—only a cold, relentless scrutiny. Still Creek was uncommonly hushed, not in a soothing way but as if the land itself were holding its breath, bracing for some unspeakable horror to fully emerge into the world.

June Weaver pulled her truck to a stop just before the dusty lot at the edge of the rodeo grounds. The Ferris wheel had halted once again, its skeletal structure slanted ominously in the dead, windless air. Tents drooped under the oppressive heat and ragged banners hung like rotten, shedding skin, their edges twitching with a life of their own in a silence that mocked the very idea of movement.

She disembarked with deliberate caution, her boots crunching over crushed straw and scattered dirt—the harsh sound clashing violently with the suffocating quiet.

There was no sound of music, no burst of laughter, no gleam of lights, no flicker of movement.

Except for her.

Up on the bleachers.

A figure sat frozen and poised—as if a photograph had been left to bleach in the relentless sun. At first, June wondered if her eyes deceived her, maybe mistaking the shape for a mannequin abandoned from last night's twisted parade. But as she edged closer, a cold dread slithered through her gut.

The woman was perched in the highest row of creaking wooden benches, legs crossed with an unsettling elegance, her dress trailing behind like tarnished lace dipped in smoke. Clad in a cracked, yellowed sash and crowned with a tarnished tiara missing its jewels, her messy curls framed a face so pale and still it defied recognition.

It was her.

The rodeo queen from the parade.

Each step towards the bleachers sent sharp spikes of terror through June's heart, drawing her inexplicably toward this eerie specter. There was an unyielding compulsion, a desperate need to see what was unfolding.

The woman remained motionless, her gaze fixed straight ahead as if witnessing an invisible spectacle in the dust-choked arena—an act performed for a forgotten dead or perhaps for some unseen, malign audience.

June climbed onto the bleachers slowly, every wooden plank groaning in protest under her weight as though cursed by discomfort.

Reaching the top row, she froze, breath shallow, caught in a surreal trance.

Then, with an unsettling gentleness, the woman turned. Not with a violent jerk but with a languid, eerie grace akin to turning the pages of an ancient tome that should have remained sealed.

But her face was wrong.

Not hideously disfigured, not outright monstrous—just profoundly off, as if time itself had smeared the memory of her features with distorted, clinging oils. Her lips were unnaturally vivid, her cheeks unnervingly flawless, and her eyes, too wide, glowed with a spectral intensity.

When she opened her mouth, the sound that emerged defied humanity—a voice as if gasping in a vacuum, devoid of any warmth or life.

"You're late," she whispered, her cracked lips barely parting. "Late to your fate."

June's mouth dried up, and a piercing chill shot down her spine, freezing her blood as she blinked in disbelief.

In that instant, the woman vanished.

There were no echoing footsteps, no lingering sounds, no trace that she had ever occupied that space at all—save for what was left behind.

On the bench by where she sat lay a locket.

Small, ancient, its clasp broken. The chain was snapped, and it was smeared with a dark, sticky substance—fresh blood that smeared onto her fingers as she gingerly picked it up.

June recognized the locket immediately. It was the same one that had nestled around her mother's neck the day the car careened off the road into the ravine.

She had not seen it since.

Nearly tripping over a wooden bench behind her, June staggered back, trembling as the locket gripped her hand. Her heart thundered in her chest like an impending storm.

She stared out at the desolate arena and whispered hoarsely, "What the hell is happening?"

From the far edge of the bleachers, deep within the dust-shrouded shadows, an unseen presence stirred. Rook emerged from the darkness, his eyes glinting with a ravenous hunger. "I have such plans for you, my dear," he hissed through gritted teeth, an ancient, malevolent smile creeping across his face. "Will she be mine?" he crooned into the void.

But the void offered no reply.

Instead, Rook's relentless gaze tracked her retreat as June drove away, his low, sinister murmur trailing behind, "hmmmm…"

———

The decrepit municipal building loomed under the scorching daylight, its facade cracking like parched, blistered skin. The flag above sagged listlessly, tangled in its own cord like a defeated serpent, unmoving. In this forsaken part of Still Creek, time seemed to stagger, as if the town's very heartbeat was snapping in agony. The air pulsed with more than scorching heat and choking dust—it carried the taste of a monstrous secret swallowed whole.

June burst through the front doors, her boots crashing on the marble floor like the salvo of a deadly assault. Mason King struggled to keep pace, trying to corral both sanity and speed. "June, wait—"

"No," she snarled, spinning on her heel with seething conviction. "No more holding back. Not you too."

She halted dead-center in the entryway, jabbing a finger into his chest with scorching purpose. "Why didn't you tell me about the Kincaid farm?"

Mason stiffened, his lips parting as if to protest—only to exhale a heavy, burdened sigh. "This morning has been an absolute shit show," he spat. "Thompson vanished without a trace. Patterson's trailer went up in flames, leaving nothing but charred echoes behind. And I got a voicemail from Pastor Cole's wife saying the chapel's walls are bleeding. An old woman from the rest home died after all her friends confessed to a shared, horrifying dream...of a deranged clown at a twisted rodeo." His hand massaged his face as his jaw twitched with the force of his weariness. "So no, June, I haven't had a second to breathe, let alone brief you on the case of a husband found clutching a severed bull skull. But yes, I know the Kincaids—and yes, I know that what happened out there has driven a good man mad."

June's mouth twisted briefly, but she clipped it shut with resolve. Instead, she drew in one long, shuddering breath and produced a blood-stained locket from her coat pocket.

"I went back to the rodeo grounds," she murmured softly. "I saw her again—the rodeo queen from the parade. She was alone in the desolate bleachers, sitting like a mourner at a funeral. She spoke to me, Mason. She told me I was too late, that I was fated to my own ruin. And when I blinked...she was gone." Holding the locket aloft, her voice hardened, "But this was left behind."

Mason's brows furrowed, darkening with dread. "What is that?"

"It belonged to my mother."

The air between them froze, laden with unspoken terror.

He stared at the locket as if it might begin to whisper its secrets, then nodded sharply, decisively. "Enough of this. Let's go. We're done playing nice—time to confront Pride."

———

The building's interior was shrouded in darkness despite it being high noon—as if someone had twisted reality's dimmer switch to near extinction. The corridor leading to the mayor's office was eerily silent. No groaning wood, no blaring phone, not even the low, sinister drone of that accursed coffee machine that normally reeked of decay and Folgers.

June burst through the office door without a hint of hesitation.

Mayor Otis Pride sat rigid behind his desk like a lifeless wax statue. Unmoving. Every inch of him was unnaturally perfect, as if sculpted by an unholy artist, and not a single drop of sweat marred his impassive facade despite the suffocating heat. A ghostly smile flickered at his lips—too polished, too deliberate—as though he were trying to mimic a human expression.

"Deputy. Miss Weaver." His voice resonated with an eerie echo, formally polite yet detached, as if spoken from the depths of a different realm.

June wouldn't waste a moment on pleasantries.

"We're shutting it down," she declared fiercely. "The rodeo. It's over."

Mason stepped up to her side, arms tautly crossed. "It's not merely a terrible idea any longer—it's a nightmare. It's dangerous, unnatural, and it's sending the town into a state of terror."

The mayor tilted his head ever so slightly. His eyes glistened, pools of glossy moisture, while their whites shimmered with an uncanny golden hue, reminiscent of oil slicking over water.

"You're too late," he answered steadily. "We gave our word. That solemn promise is what binds us."

Mason's confusion hardened into anger. "Your word?"

"To our guest," Pride replied with an almost dismissive gesture towards the scattered coins on his desk.

June's eyes locked onto the coins. They weren't coins anymore. Their surfaces were dissolving, melting slowly like wax caught over a flame—but instead of dribbling off the edges, they were dissolving into the wood. Each coin seared a perfect circular burn as it disappeared, leaving behind cryptic symbols scrawled in a red so deep it appeared black under the harsh light. A ram. A wheel. And a barren, leafless tree.

"You signed something, didn't you?" Mason snapped, voice thick with rage. "What curse have you doomed us to?"

Pride's smile broadened with sinister calm. "Hospitality. A night's welcome. Fair coin for a fair show. Nothing more."

"Where's Sheriff Mott?" June demanded suddenly, a gnawing pit of dread twisting in her stomach.

The mayor's serene smile never wavered. "He's... unavailable."

"Unavailable how? Is he sick? Missing? Dead?" Mason barked, stepping menacingly forward.

Pride's lips quirked in a barely concealed amusement. "Resting. Let's call it that."

June exchanged a fearful glance with Mason, her face drained of color, her jaw set hard.

Then Pride extended a hand, pressing his palm onto the final coin as it completed its slow, hellish subsidence. A shrill hiss erupted—a sound as wet and searing as flesh pressed against scorching metal. Still, he did not flinch.

"This isn't merely about town ordinance anymore," he intoned with clinical detachment. "If you two want to be heroes, go ignite bonfires and flaunt your badge, Deputy King. But the rodeo remains."

A suffocating silence cascaded over the room like a tide of despair.

June stepped forward, her eyes locked fiercely with his. "You were always a coward, Otis. But this? This is selling your soul because you couldn't stand being irrelevant anymore."

For the first time, Pride blinked—slowly as if the very act was a struggle. When he raised his eyes again, the golden gleam had intensified, burning brighter with a malevolent promise. He smiled wider, a smile that chilled the blood.

"Sometimes irrelevance is a mercy," he murmured, every word dripping with fatalistic irony.

Mason gripped June's elbow and yanked her back.

"Come on," he hissed tautly. "He's not here anymore."

They turned to leave, but not before June stole one final, desperate glance at the desk where the coins—completely vanished now—had left nothing but burn marks that pulsed like festering wounds.

And behind the mayor, on the wall, the portrait of Still Creek's founders had transformed in the unholy light. Where faded sepia faces had once resided...

now, a sinister fifth figure emerged at the edge of the painting.

A man in black. His hat pulled low, shadowing his eyes.

And he was grinning.

———

The bell hanging over Nettie's store door jangled with a weary, metallic clatter that barely stirred the cat dozing lazily in the window. It was early afternoon, yet the oppressive lethargy in the air made it feel as if midnight had seeped into their bones. Inside, light slanted through the dusty windows, catching motes of particulate matter in a lazy dance as the overhead fluorescent bulbs droned on like a swarm of fatigued bees.

June eased the door open with a gentle push of her shoulder, letting it swing shut behind her without protest. Her appearance was disheveled, as though sleep had become a stranger over the past week— and Mason looked even more worn, as if the weight of the world had pressed him down.

Behind the worn wooden counter, Nettie stood in her familiar apron, methodically sifting through a pile of receipts that had long lost any significance. As the bell's chime finally caught her attention, she looked up and fixed her narrow, discerning eyes on the two intruders. "You both look like hell scraped itself across gravel," she remarked in a tone that mixed humor with exasperation.

"We've earned it," June muttered under her breath as she made her way toward the glass deli case. Mason, meanwhile, carefully lowered himself onto one of the timeworn stools at the lunch counter, stretching his legs with a long, gravelly sigh that seemed to echo his exhaustion. "If I don't grab at least an hour of shuteye soon, I'm gonna accidentally shoot someone in the holding cell just to catch a nap," he said, his voice thick with fatigue and dark humor.

Without a word, June reached into the case and produced a sandwich—turkey and mustard, his usual choice when decisions were too taxing to make—and handed it to him. She then took a seat beside him, and together, they fell into a comfortable silence filled only by the sounds of gnawing and the soft hum of electronics.

After chewing thoughtfully for a couple of bites, Mason broke the quiet. "You should do the same, you know. Go lie down for a bit. That rodeo opens tonight...and if even half of what we've seen is a taste of what's coming..." His voice trailed off as he shook his head slowly. "It's gonna be a long one."

June nodded absently, but her gaze wandered to the large front windows where the towering Ferris wheel loomed in the hazy distance like a colossal parasite, its presence impossible to ignore. "I don't think I'll sleep, even if I wanted to," she murmured.

Their quiet companionship, bound by years of habitual ritual, held them together like glue under strain—until every screen in the room simultaneously went dark.

An old television, carelessly mounted above the drink cooler and cobwebbed by time since its unreliable kickstart in 2004, buzzed once before it suddenly burst into life with a flare of unnatural light. Mason froze mid-bite, his eyes locked onto the glowing screen. The ancient radio behind the counter began to hiss fervently, and even the silent cellphone tucked into Nettie's apron vibrated awake.

An identical image materialized on them all.

Rook.

But this was not the Rook of town whispers, the smooth, enigmatic figure clad in a dust-draped coat. No—this was Rook in full, extravagant regalia: a gleaming velvet coat lavishly embroidered with silver threads that writhed like serpentine creatures; a silver mask polished to a reflective sheen that swallowed any hint of human emotion, leaving only a black void where eyes should be; and atop his head, a wide-brimmed hat that cast a perfect crescent shadow across his chiseled jaw.

He stood solitary on a pitch-dark stage, lit only by a singular spotlight that sliced through the surrounding darkness as if challenging the boundaries of time itself. Behind him, massive swirling curtains of the big top pulsed rhythmically, expanding and contracting like lungs filled with a toxic mix of smog and ash.

Then he spoke.

"Still Creek…" His voice emerged as a silken rasp, like velvet steeped in venom. "Tonight is the night."

At his words, June slowly rose to her feet, while Nettie's breath caught in her throat, rendering her momentarily silent. Mason's hand reached instinctively for the volume knob on the counter, but it spun uselessly in his fingers.

"The Midnight Rodeo opens its gates… for blood, for truth, for judgment." Rook's proclamation was not confined to the television alone; it resonated through the walls, seeped into the floor, and hung thickly in the very air around them.

As if in a grand, ominous invitation, Rook's gloved hands extended outward—a beckoning to an invisible congregation, promising a sermon of destructive fire. "Ride, if you dare. Watch, if you must. But remember… every show demands a price. And just like any good rodeo, there's a grand prize for the winner." He paused for a heartbeat, tilting his head ever so slightly so that the malevolent gleam in his mask shone with wicked mirth. "And tonight... the curtain rises for all of you."

In a dramatic flourish, the screen did not fade into darkness—instead, it erupted into a tumult of static. Not the usual crackle of failed signals, but a cacophony of shrieking, teeth-grinding sound that seemed to promise that something dreadful was slithering its way through the wires.

Throughout Still Creek, radios began to hiss in unison. Cell phones flickered erratically. Laptop screens sprang to life in dim living rooms and shadowed bedrooms, each one repeating the same eerie broadcast. And in the spectral seconds after the signal died away, a silence fell—a silence so profound and heavy it bordered on the unsettling.

Mason abruptly stood. "We need to prepare," he declared.

June cast one last lingering glance at the television before turning her attention to Nettie. "Did you know this was coming?" she asked in a voice tight with anxiety.

Nettie offered no reply, her eyes distant and solemn. There was no need for words.

Because, in a far-off corner of town, the Ferris wheel had ground to a halt.

And then, in a manner that defied both time and logic, it began to turn in the opposite direction— slowly, impossibly reversing the course of its eternal spin.

Chapter 7 — Walls of Dust

The hour before dusk crept in like a long-held, labored exhale. The sky bled strained purples and feverish ambers, sagging low over Still Creek as if the heavens themselves dreaded to witness what was about to unfold. The land was barren, its cracked surface whispering secrets to the parched air, which lay heavy with that sickly metallic tang that heralds both violent storms and darker omens.

Three miles east of town, old Walter Grigsby lingered on the back porch of his ramshackle ranch, a coil of rope draped in one gnarled hand and a half-smoked cigarette trembling in the other. His cows were off again—not ill, not wild, but unnervingly still, like eerie statues frozen mid-moment.

They had all gathered at the far side of the pasture, huddled stiffly along the rusted fence as though awaiting the rise of something ghastly over the hills. None of them chewed cud. None of them blinked. The only sounds were the creak of a warped windmill behind the barn and the low, uneasy whistle that escaped Walter's lips.

He was about to retreat inside—blaming the sultry heat or his advancing years—when he caught sight of the first anomaly. A lone rider on a pale horse, stationed high upon a ridge. Then another appeared.

And soon, two more joined them in eerie succession. Their movement was not that of ordinary men on patrol or cowboys roaming a trail—they moved as shadows, fluid and relentless, as if driven by a malevolent force. Their coats whipped in the rising gust, long dusters the color of funeral shrouds, and though they charged with unholy speed, their silhouettes exuded an timeless dread.

Walter squinted hard; his cigarette slipped from his lips and sizzled upon the deathly still grass. They were not heading toward town in any normal sense—they were dispersing, spreading out like the claws of some ancient terror.

As he watched, a fifth rider broke ranks and thundered toward the far edge of the field where the fence bowed low near the creekbed. In one hand he gripped something long and silvery—resembling a spike or a stake. With one fluid, unnerving motion, he leaned over his saddle and drove it deep into the earth.

The moment the metal struck the soil, the air itself seemed to shift—not in chill or heat, but in a burdened heaviness that pressed against Walter's ribs like a buried, terrible memory. His cattle, as if bewitched, turned their heads in unison, their unblinking eyes fixed toward the horizon, unmoving and silent. Not a single sound escaped them.

Then came the dust—but it was no ordinary dust kicked up by hooves or wind. This dust spiraled upwards unnaturally, whirling like a demonic funnel before lingering, suspended just above the ground as if defying gravity. In mere minutes, a vast, arching trail of it scrawled itself along the ranch's perimeter, connecting with other trails forming to the west and north alike.

Walter's heart pounded as the horrifying realization dawned upon him—they were inscribing a circle. A circle drawn around Still Creek.

He staggered backward, his gnarled hand fumbling desperately for the screen door. But then a piercing howl of wind tore across the fields—one singular, bloodcurdling sound, laced with something unnervingly sharp. It was not quite a voice, nor were they distinct words, yet it echoed like the low, ominous murmur of a grim crowd ready to unleash a maddening cheer.

A chill like a deathly grip crawled up his spine. Muttering a desperate prayer he hadn't uttered since his days in 'Nam, Walter fled indoors, unfinished supplications trailing in his wake. He bolted the doors and drew the blinds tightly shut.

Outside his window, the circle closed, and the riders melted into the encroaching twilight. And somewhere on the distant horizon, the first carnival lights sputtered to life—first red, then gold—before an overwhelming, suffocating silence descended.

———

Mason's truck roared up the gravel drive and slammed to a halt beneath the towering, crooked shadow of a pin oak. Behind them, the distorted world—the manic parade of clowns, a mayor liquefying into nothingness, bleachers whispering dark secrets—felt like a parallel nightmare as they stepped into the oppressive silence of the forest.

His house lurked at the edge of the woods like a forgotten relic, so modest and low that it could vanish into the gloom of the landscape. The tin roof was marred with rust, each streak a scar of relentless decay, and the sagging porch tilted like an old man burdened by too many years of sorrow. A screen door clung on by habit rather than strength, and from deep within drifted the faint but defiant scents of cedar and motor oil—a pungent blend of a hard, weathered life held together by sweat, nails, and a seething silence.

June halted on the creaking porch. "You never said you lived out here."

"I don't say a lot of things," Mason replied, shoving the door open with his broad, calloused shoulder. "Come on in. It ain't much, but it's home."

Inside, the chill was sharper than she'd expected—a low, dim refuge that somehow radiated a rugged welcome. The cramped space consisted of a single living room, a gritty kitchen, and a lone bedroom barely hidden behind a narrow hall—each fragment pulsing with an inexplicable heat. The pungent trace of woodsmoke clung to the pine-paneled walls like a ghost of fires past. Above a timeworn brick fireplace, a faded Texas flag drooped, its corners curled as if scorched by a relentless inferno. Worn boots rested silently against the wall beneath a row of coat hooks, remnants of journeys etched into history.

The couch, a patchwork of battered denim and worn leather, spoke of a secondhand existence fiercely cherished. A coffee mug boldly declaring "PROPERTY OF JASPER COUNTY SHERIFF'S ACADEMY" sat alongside a pile of timeworn Field & Stream magazines. But it was the mantle that snagged June's attention—a photograph of Mason in a pristine academy uniform, standing tall beside a grinning bloodhound whose muzzle bore streaks of worn gray. Beside this memory lay a small metal urn, its label scrawled in a rough hand: Rosie.

June's smile was a fragile thing, heavy with nostalgia. "She looked like a damn good girl."

Mason's silence was laden with grief. "Best I ever had. Wouldn't venture anywhere without her. Now, I hardly go anywhere at all."

She trailed him into the kitchen, watching as he methodically sliced cold brisket from the fridge, resurrecting it in a searing cast-iron skillet like a ritual against oblivion. They ate at a minute, two-chair table under a crooked ceiling fan, their silence as thick and longing as smoke that wouldn't clear.

Outside, the sun sank behind the dark tree line, bleeding bruises of violent purples and blood reds across the sky. Long, distorted shadows crawled over timeworn walls, dancing in erratic harmony with the fan's hesitant blades. Somewhere deep in the ominous woods, a whippoorwill let forth a lone cry before it vanished into the dark.

"This feels like the final breath," Mason whispered, his tone weighted with an unspoken prelude to ruin. "Just before everything collapses."

June's gaze lifted, revealing hair in disarray and a face etched with exhaustive battles, yet a fierce, unyielding brilliance lingered in those tired eyes. "I know," she murmured. "I keep thinking... if we don't hold onto something now, we might lose it forever."

Their eyes locked across the table, a meeting of raw, desperate souls—a silent acknowledgment of every unspoken word and lingering promise. Slowly, Mason rose and circled to her side, kneeling beside her chair. His rough hand reached out in a silent plea. "You don't have to stay."

She leaned forward, her fingertips gliding over his stubble-scarred cheek. "I do."

Their kiss ignited with a hesitant intensity that quickly burned into fierce urgency—a mingling of desperate need and the weight of buried secrets that tasted of fear and longing. They stumbled together toward the bedroom, stripping away their layers like discarded armor in a last, frenzied stand against the encroaching desolation.

In the secluded heat of that room, they undressed each other with trembling certainty, under the half-light of passion and the looming shadow of past horrors. Mason's calloused hands groped uncertainly, and June shuddered under his touch—not from a chill in the air, but from the overwhelming gravity of all they had witnessed and all that remained unnamed.

They made love with a slow, fierce urgency—as if every desperate kiss was a rebellion against a crumbling world, each breath a battle waged against the suffocating void. When he whispered her name into the dim hollowness of her neck, it was not a question but an anchor against annihilation. And when she wrapped herself around him, it was more than possession—it was an act of survival.

Outside, dusk deepened into a dense, unyielding darkness. The world beyond their fragile window twisted into chaos. From the distant hills, a malevolent wind stirred—not gentle, but ferocious and unholy. It began to whip up dust and memories, as spectral riders, ignited like ghosts on fire, advanced relentlessly, forming an inescapable wall around Still Creek. A barrier, not of stone or wood, but wrought from raw memory, paralyzing fear, and the unforgiving price of forgetting.

Within Mason's timeworn haven, the old floorboards groaned under the weight of their shared defiance, trembling with each entangled movement of their bodies. For one fragile, incendiary hour, the encroaching darkness was held at bay.

——

As the final blush of daylight bled into the parched soil and the sky gradually surrendered its vibrant hues to a ghostly ash, the perimeter roads around Still Creek began to tremble with an unearthly vibration. Not from the rumble of engines or the clamor of approaching storms, but from the relentless pounding of hooves.

A cloud of dust—red as oxidized rust and as thick as a veil of ancient sin—rose in heavy, deliberate plumes where not even a whisper of wind stirred. Beneath that churning veil, the earth itself groaned under a weight older than any law, predating the founding of townships, property lines, or even names. The riders had arrived.

At first, they emerged one solitary figure at a time, then came in pairs, and soon swelled into groups of tens—each cloaked in mystery as they astride towering beasts that bore no true resemblance to horses. These creatures were gaunt and angular, with limbs elongated to an almost unnatural span and eyes that betrayed a humanity deep beneath their fierce, wild demeanor. The riders were adorned in wide-brimmed hats and faded hoods, their identities hidden behind masks masterfully fashioned from stitched leather or carved bone—some masks offered empty, eyeless sockets, while others boasted painted snarls or grotesquely twisted carnival grins. They rode with spine-straight backs and heads held high, like spectral monarchs emerging from the mists of time to claim a debt long overdue.

They came from every corner—emerging from the rugged, pine-scorched hills to the north, flowing in from the barren, barbed wire-crisscrossed landscapes near the dried-up creek to the south, surging eastward from the blacktop highway dissolving into endless cotton fields, and materializing from the west where the ancient highway snaked like a restless serpent into memories of the past. They did not stop to chat or exchange words, nor did they break their relentless, unwavering pace. They simply circled the town—a great, ominous wheel of dust and silence, spun with an unmistakable, malevolent intent.

Residents in the surrounding farmlands and the town's outskirts watched in fearful silence from behind drawn curtains. Their mouths were as parched as the thirsty earth, trembling hands clutching desperately to crucifixes, rifles, or bottles—each item a testament to the particular god they had sworn allegiance to. As the riders passed by flickering windows like living shadows, their unyielding strides giving no acknowledgment to the sighted onlookers, it was as if the people had already been deemed inconsequential—already written off and irreversibly counted.

From a second-story balcony of the Still Creek Gazette, a man named Everett Pike—a seasoned photographer in town on assignment from a regional magazine—leaned over the rail, his Nikon trained with curious intent. He had come seeking relics of old Americana, lured by whispered rumors of the mysterious "Midnight Rodeo" that had begun to stir in hushed conversations. Until now, he had dismissed the stories as mere tall tales of small-town fantasias.

"Jesus," he murmured under his breath, lifting his camera as if in a silent salute. "They look like a damned posse of ghosts."

He snapped photo after photo—click, click, click—the shutter sounds reverberating through the charged air like the beating of an otherworldly drum. Yet the riders, still maintaining their distant, solemn formation, paid him no heed.

Emboldened by his curiosity, Everett made a fateful decision and edged closer toward the encircling ring of riders, thinking he might procure a better angle if he drove up County Road 5, toward a patch of road where the crimson dust had not yet completely coalesced. Packing his gear with a hurried determination, he ignored the desperate fervor in the voice of an elderly woman across the street, who cried out in a hoarse warning: "They're not for seein'—they're for keepin' in."

Ignoring her plea, Everett already sped off in his car, the tires shrieking against the loose, gravelly path. Yet fate would not grant him a safe journey. Before reaching the full mile he intended, from a ridge perched above the road, three riders silently broke from their formation. They descended as if they were predatory vultures, folding into a calculated dive. In a heart-stopping moment, Everett slammed on his brakes, sending his car skidding sideways in a riotous scream of burning rubber.

In the ensuing chaos, he fumbled to reverse and turn the way he came. His camera tumbled violently from the passenger seat—a casualty in this unfolding nightmare. Then, as if summoned by the darkness itself, a red-tinged fog fell suddenly, alive and purposeful, swallowing not only the vehicle and the road but engulfing Everett within its relentless grasp. In that moment, he vanished without a trace, never to be seen again.

Three days later, the only remnant of his doomed adventure was found—a battered Nikon recovered from a dry, secluded ravine at the base of the ridge. Its lens lay shattered, the film completely devoured. And etched into the back of the camera's casing, as if burned in by an unseen force with neither tool nor flame, were three elegant words inscribed in carefully pointed cursive: NO PASSES GIVEN.

Back in town, as if sealing a dark covenant, the rider ring finished its ominous encirclement. The red dust lingered in the air like spectral smoke rising from a ritual fire, and now the roads themselves seemed distorted—mysterious dead ends twisting through a labyrinth that had materialized overnight. Those brave or foolish enough to attempt an escape reported disorienting misdirections: landmarks that bizarrely repeated themselves, gas tanks draining with unnerving speed, and one woman even swore that after an hour's drive she had ended up face-to-face with her own house.

By the time nightfall draped its inky cloak over the land, the transformation was undeniable: Still Creek was no longer merely a town. It had become a stage—a meticulously crafted snare—and the audience, trembling in anticipation, had already taken their seats.

—

The house lay swallowed in darkness. Every blind was drawn, every switch remained cold and unused, and every corner lurked in a gloom reminiscent of a nightmare on its deathbed. Sheriff Wally Mott hadn't known real sleep in over 48 agonizing hours—if that was even enough time—while reality itself smeared and distorted like oily residue on a rain-spattered glass. Somewhere amid the parade of those infernal clowns and the sinister, hypnotic gleam of the mayor's eyes, something inside Mott had begun to unravel.

He paced relentlessly.

Barefoot on the icy, unforgiving linoleum, his trembling hand clutched a revolver as if it were a talisman. His sweat-soaked undershirt clung to a chest heaved with bitter exhaustion. Each ragged breath sounded like a man drowning in his own despair. With every cautious step across the creaking kitchen floor, a maddening echo ricocheted off the wallpaper frozen in 1984 and off cabinets that held nothing but expired soup and unspoken regret.

"They've brought it back," he murmured, his voice raw and splintered. "It can't be—no, it shouldn't be here again… not again…"

The revolver twitched in his unsteady grasp, poised like a silent predator, ever-ready. His bloodshot eyes flitted from shadow to shadow, from one dark crevice to another, fixating on every flicker of movement outside the grim windows. Yet, outside lay only the neglected porch light—dead for weeks—and an unsettling red haze that billowed low over the town like a fevered nightmare.

In a sudden movement, he pivoted towards the hallway closet and yanked it open with fierce determination. Within, amid a jumble of rain jackets, cracked boots, and a moth-eaten uniform from a more defiant past, lay three shoeboxes stacked like sealed tombs. With shaking fingers, he retrieved the top box, nearly letting it drop under the weight of his terror.

He peeled off the lid.

Inside lay a collection of newspaper clippings—old, brittle, and yellowed, folded like secrets from a bygone era, their edges curled like dead leaves. They all hailed from Callister, Nevada—a town that had been scrubbed from the map, erased as though it never existed at all. The headlines cried out in stark, black letters:

CARNIVAL FIRE CLAIMS 73—BODIES NEVER RECOVERED

STRANGE COINS DISCOVERED AMID ASHES—
INVESTIGATION CLOSED

SHERIFF'S DEPUTY WALTON MOTT CLEARED OF
NEGLIGENCE—SURVIVORS DEMAND ANSWERS

He lingered on the last headline, studying his younger self: a man barely thirty, hat primly stiff, shoulders squared with naive fortitude—a man who believed he'd seen everything.

He hadn't.

Without warning, the closet door slammed shut behind him despite the absence of any breeze.

Mott's body jolted with dread.

"Not again," he breathed, barely audible. "You bastards said it was over."

Stumbling back to the kitchen table, he found the coins exactly where he'd left them. Three of them. Gold tokens of heavy allure. When Rook had slid them across the table—smooth and all too pleasant—Mott had tried to convince himself they were simply a bribe, an old-fashioned inducement that he'd sworn to avoid, even though he'd witnessed too many men succumb to temptation.

But now...

Now the coins were no longer inert. They were seething. Not melting like metal in a flame. They perspired, oozed, and bled dark, mercury-black ichor that sizzled as it seeped into the grain of the wood, tracing burning spirals that looked like forbidden sigils etched by unseen demons.

One coin stirred.

It spun slowly—not influenced by wind, not by a tremor, but by an inexplicable, sinister force.

Mott leaned in, holding his breath. His lips parted imperceptibly when he heard it—a voice.

His own name.

It was spoken without malice, but with an eerie and ancient certainty.

"Wally…"

The whisper slithered out, as soft and sinister as velvet dragged over broken teeth.

He recoiled, the chair crashing behind him as he raised the revolver in a desperate arc.

"GET OUT!" he bellowed, though there was no one visible—only those accursed coins, pulsing ominously, their golden luster replaced by a slick, dark sheen, as if smeared with fresh, necrotic oil.

Another movement lurked just beyond his vision. "Wally," the voice cooed, lightly echoing.

"I said GET OUT!" he roared again, whirling around and unleashing a shot.

For a single, heart-stopping second the world froze.

As the smoke dissipated, Mott beheld his wife, her eyes wide with a shock and uncertainty. She clutched her abdomen as blood streamed uncontrollably. "Why..." she gasped, her voice fading as she collapsed, falling face first like a giant oak.

In that moment, Wally realized what he had done. His mind began to dissolve in a torrent of despair, tears mingling with anguished sobs until he was no longer himself.

Desperate, he pressed the cold barrel of the revolver against his temple—to feel its weight, and to remember the man he once was before the darkness descended.

He pulled the trigger—only to be met with a dead click.

Manic, unhinged laughter erupted around him, filling the void with chaotic madness.

He crumpled to the floor, hands clutched to his knees, swaying in a delirious rhythm, murmuring the same maddening refrain over and over between gritted teeth and saliva-streaked lips:

"They said it was over. They said it was over. They said it was over..."

Outside, the wind rose to a fierce howl, slipping through the eaves and raking the windows with fingers that felt like sand and smoke. And from the murky outskirts of town, where pale riders galloped in an eternal, ghostly procession, a lone whistle pierced the night.

It resembled laughter—a sound far too feral to be human.

———

The engine roared like a ferocious beast beneath him, a wounded monster clawing its way over the asphalt. Eli Boone didn't give a damn if the neighbors heard—it was better than obeying the damned coin. Better than the insidious murmur that slithered his name from the pocket of his hoodie, as if harboring a living, malevolent secret.

He hadn't meant to run. Not at all. But then the mirror had betrayed him—Frank's masked face, its grin a rictus emerging from the shadowed corner of his bedroom, spouting backward words that shredded his soul. In that moment, every shred of composure disintegrated, and instinct took over. He bolted without a helmet, without gloves—only raw throttle, screeching tires, and a deep, visceral panic pounding in his chest.

The night air whipped past, lashing his cheeks and evaporating the sweat clinging to his neck. He tore down the empty county highway, the dim, flickering lights of Still Creek in his mirrors like desperate ghosts trying to disappear behind him. And somewhere within him, he hoped desperately that he could outrun the nightmare trailing behind.

Then came the mirrors. First, there was nothing—just void and darkness, as is the nature of country nights. But then—a shift. Movement stirred in the blackness. He squinted, his heart hammering. A figure appeared. It wasn't running on human legs. It moved on all fours, its back arching like a wolf's, but the limbs were grotesquely off—long, gangly, and rubbery, like puppet strings snapped free. White greasepaint smeared across a face that twisted into a permanent, blood-red grin. A crooked hat sat atop its head, while cowboy boots clacked madly against the pavement, chasing him like some demonic rodeo hound.

Eli's throat constricted in a strangled gasp as he twisted the throttle harder. The engine screamed in protest as he shot around the bend, tires digging into gravel and sending sparks flying like errant shards of glass.

Another glimpse in the mirror revealed horrors beyond—to his left, two more figures appeared. One rode a skeletal hobby horse, its dangling legs like grotesque appendages from a nightmare, the creature balancing precariously yet unnervingly in step. The other skated across the imagery—a hulking mass on shattered roller skates, wearing a tattered sheriff's hat and a necklace of rusted spurs, its face marked with a sunken star and empty eye sockets that burned with unholy intent.

"WHAT THE HELL—" Eli roared, fighting for control as he cut hard right onto Miller's Bluff Road. Tires shrieked and the back end fishtailed wildly, the bike rebelling beneath him as though it knew better than to be part of this macabre circus. The rough, narrow road swallowed him whole, flanked by oppressive trees arched overhead like a grim tunnel, their gnarled limbs twitching in the wind like skeletal fingers ready to ensnare him.

Still, Eli pushed on, faster and faster. He dared not glance in the mirrors again—couldn't abide the horrors they held—and focused solely on the fractured road ahead, attempting to dodge gaping potholes, skim past treacherous ditches, all the while praying to a God he hadn't spoken to since his mother's funeral.

Then, after a mile, two—something emerged. Lights, red and gold slicing through the gloom. No. No, no, no. He blinked wildly, shook his head, and slammed his throat on the throttle once more.

The Ferris wheel loomed ahead, slow and ominous, turning languidly. Its massive, blinking light eye fixed on him with a hypnotic pulse. He skidded to a stop just before the midway entrance, gravel flying in every direction, the back tire scorching the dirt with its fierce burn. His breath hitched as his heart pounded in terror.

Gazing back down the road he'd fled, he found nothing—no clowns, no grotesque figures. The woods lay in suffocating silence. Yet ahead, the abandoned rodeo sprawled wide and menacing. Tents flapped listlessly, and the faint strains of calliope music drifted out like a deranged lullaby from inside a sealed coffin.

Eli's hands trembled uncontrollably on the handlebars. The road had led him in a looping circle, as if the very universe were contorting, bending reality to force him back here—to the epicenter of his living nightmare.

With a shuddering finality, he cut the engine. A devouring silence swallowed everything. Then, from somewhere within the labyrinth of tattered tents, he heard it: a single voice, cold and insidious, whispering from the shadows, "Witness."

In that moment, Eli dropped the bike and fled headlong into the night.

———

The house groaned with an uneasy stillness, each tick of the ancient wall clock sounding like a hesitant footstep drawing ever nearer. Outside, the wind had abandoned its song, leaving a strangely charged silence that seemed to promise an imminent storm— or perhaps something far darker. Dusk had barely begun to drape its long, conflicted fingers across Still Creek, its light painting the windows in a bruised and fading gold that whispered of beauty and decay.

In the back of her house, beyond the cluttered living room and the glow of an unplugged television that felt more like a distant memory than a comfort, Nettie Carson stood barefoot in the pantry. The cold linoleum under her feet was a stark reminder of her vulnerability. Without her apron and with bare hands, her familiar stoic face—etched by time, resilience, and an unyielding hope—was now imprinted with a raw openness that betrayed inner turmoil.

She moved slowly, each step heavy with both reverence and a deep-seated reluctance.

This wasn't simply rummaging.

This was a conflicted return—an exhumation of memories she wasn't sure she wanted to face.

Kneeling, she hooked her fingers under the decaying edge of an old floorboard, her muscles straining against a force that was both external and deeply internal. As she pried it open with a grunt, the board revealed a trapdoor, its rust-eaten hinges and nearly fused iron ring echoing the resistance within her own heart. Spitting in her palms, she gripped the ring, her knuckles white with the effort, until the hatch sighed free—exhaling decades of secrets and regrets in one reluctant release.

The odor that rushed upward wasn't merely mold or decay—it carried the dual scent of dry soil and charred pine, intermingled with the memory of horsehair and an unsettling hint of sweet, burnt sugar. It was the smell of a past too heavy to ignore.

Below, cocooned in cracked leather and bound in cold-forged chains, lay an old trunk. The top was adorned with symbols, carved so deeply into the hide that they shimmered with a conflicted radiance—a mixture of promise and warning, sigils intended to hold back one fate or invite another.

Nettie's hands trembled as she fumbled with the locks. With each released turn, her heart bristled with both dread and a strange longing. She murmured not words but tones—tones that recalled the taut pull of a rope and the hollow echo of footsteps on worn boards—as if summoning the ghosts of days past. The final lock surrendered with a hesitant clunk, echoing her own internal battle.

Lifting the lid, Nettie confronted the life she had fought so long to bury. Inside lay remnants of a bygone self—a black veil that folded like shadow in dim light, a sash held together by tarnished pins from another era, bones neatly wrapped in velvet cloth, a

174

horsehair braid tied with a red ribbon that hinted at both pride and sorrow, and a cracked mirror that had long failed to reflect her true face.

At the very bottom, as if awaiting a resurrection fraught with both hope and despair, lay her old rodeo queen regalia. Its dusty satin, faded to a bleeding bloodwine purple, spoke of lost glory, while the silver fringe and the crown beside it—melted and ravaged by time or fire—seemed to mirror her inner dissonance.

With lips trembling and her jaw set in a battle between defiance and vulnerability, Nettie shed all pretense, discarding her inhibitions along with her undergarments as the biting air caressed her exposed skin. Her weathered, purpose-driven hands worked with trembling determination as she redressed herself thread by weary thread. With every tug of fabric, her breath caught in a chord of both anticipation and regret. When the final clasp secured at her throat, her eyes shone—not simply with longing for a past life but with a conflicted fear of what might come.

Placing the cracked crown atop her head, she paused, a living contradiction between the persona of a fearless queen and that of a woman haunted by the echoes of her former triumphs and failures. Then she knelt before an old wooden vanity now stripped of any reflective glass. In place of the mirror was an abyss of soot-black emptiness—a stark void that mirrored her internal chaos.

Lighting three candles—one white, one red, and one black—their flames danced with a violent flicker as if battling an unseen inner tempest. Her voice broke before finding its steady cadence, and she began to murmur in a tongue not of this world. These were the words of the old riders, ancient incantations whispered behind veils of dust and under starless skies, each syllable a struggle between what was sworn and what needed to be remembered.

The shadows in every corner deepened with her every word, and the black veil on the adjacent table shuddered as if stirred by conflicting unseen forces. Her voice wavered on the final utterance—a trembling testament to the inner war waging within her—but then, with a sorrowful gentleness, she snuffed out the red candle. Its smoke curled upward, twisting into uncertain shapes that might resemble a noose or perhaps a broken crown—a symbol of both ruin and redemption.

"If this is the price," she whispered through tears, a voice thick with both anguish and reluctant resolve, "then let me pay it."

Silence fell over the room like a heavy, disapproving shroud, and even the flames seemed to falter in their glow. Nettie bowed her head, letting the crown slip slightly as silent weeping betrayed the fierce struggle warring within her spirit.

Outside, as dusk surrendered to encroaching darkness, the conflicted heartbeat of the Midnight Rodeo stirred—a promise of reckoning and remorse intertwined in one uncertain emergence.

Chapter 8 - The Midnight Rodeo

The world outside was suspended in a limbo between day and night—a spectral, blue haze that dulled every color and silenced every sound, as if the heavens themselves were holding their breath in anticipation. June stood barefoot on Mason King's front porch, her body swathed awkwardly in his deputy's oversized shirt. The fabric swallowed her small frame, while the faded stitched badge grazed her collarbone like a ghost of authority. The air was a fierce cocktail of cedar, parched grass, and the distant, acrid whisper of woodsmoke, though no fire burned in sight.

She cradled a chipped coffee mug in trembling hands, its contents long since gone cold, yet she remained indifferent, her eyes locked on the horizon where the Midnight Rodeo burst into life. It pulsed behind the treeline like a living, burning heartbeat—red and gold.

Red and gold.

Red and gold.

Each blink was unnaturally rhythmic, each glow impossibly hot and precise. It wasn't mere artificial illumination; it was a primordial blaze, awakening something ancient and sentient.

The screen door groaned in protest as it swung open behind her before snapping shut, and Mason emerged silently onto the porch. Bare-chested and exuding raw masculinity, his jeans hung low on his hips, and he carried the unmistakable scent of soap, worn leather, and the bitter tang of spent adrenaline. His arms encircled her waist with a deliberate tenderness, as if he feared that the moment—a fragile, burning instant—might shatter if he held her too firmly.

He softly placed his lips on her neck with a gentle, fever inducing kiss, and she yielded, as if surrendering to the warmth of a tempest before the downpour. Her breath hitched.

"I wish we could stay like this forever," she murmured, her voice raw and falling like fragile confessions in the charged air.

He kissed her neck once more, slowly, each moment stretching into eternity. "Me too," he whispered.

"Why did you come here, to Still Creek, I mean?" Her words cut through the charged silence. She sensed him stiffen at the question, only to then relax in a long, shuddering exhalation, his voice tinged with remorse.

"You saw my picture of Rosie," he began, his tone measured and heavy with memory.

"Yes," she replied, softly, as if every syllable carried a weight of its own.

"She and I were partners on a case. Back in Dallas, I was a detective, and Rosie was my partner. Though I wasn't a K-9 officer, I loved having her by my side. She could sniff out drugs, people—anything."

"Sounds like you two were inseparable," she said, her hand caressing the warmth of his arm, each stroke an unspoken empathy.

"We were... until one day, a routine shoplifting changed everything. We tracked a suspect into a field when, without warning, he fired upon us. Rosie charged forward like a force of nature—fearless..." His voice faltered, choking on the memory.

June felt the imminent surge of sorrow and terror ripple through her. She turned in his strong embrace to confront his haunted eyes, brimming with unshed tears and shattered memories. Gently, her hands cupped his weathered cheeks as he continued.

"...she took two hits while shielding me. I returned fire, downing the perp. I held her as she drew her final breath, locking eyes with me. I remember her eyes. The way she looked at me filled with a love and hope, believing I could ease her pain. I was so angry..." His words crumbled as tears fell unbidden, wild and unrestrained, drowning him in past anguish.

"It's okay," June whispered, her thumbs gently wiping away his cascading tears. "Mason..."

He met her gaze, his eyes heavy with guilt. "He was just a kid, June. Just a kid. It was senseless, stupid... I..."

She clutched him fiercely, overwhelmed by his raw confession—a vulnerability so intense it resonated deeply within her. "You couldn't have known," she insisted, her eyes burning into his, yearning to erase his pain altogether.

"I fled from everything, from everyone, June. I ran here..." he confessed, his voice raw with hidden torment.

"To me," she finished, fixating on his well-worn, unyielding eyes that had witnessed too much. She pressed her lips to his like a desperate plea to halt time, her hands gripping his shoulders in a fervor born of both hope and anguish. The kiss was not tender—it was an explosion before the inevitable deluge.

But the world refused to yield.

It trembled violently.

From the shadowed woods beyond the gravel drive, a jagged rustle shattered the disquiet.

Then came pounding footsteps.

Emerging from the darkness with an almost demonic urgency, a figure burst from the treeline—wild, erratic, stumbling as if fleeing from a personal hell.

Eli Boone erupted onto the scene like a bullet from a ruined prayer, sweat mingling with terror on his face, his breath coming in desperate, ragged gasps. His hoodie clung to him, drenched, while his shoes were caked in dust, blood, and all manner of dreadful debris from backroads best left forgotten.

"They're watching!" he screamed, his voice jagged with fear. "It looped me back again! I swear it looped me—!"

He collapsed onto the porch before they could react, his knees slamming into the wood with brutal finality. In his trembling grasp lay the cursed coin.

The one they'd all seen.

The one no one dared claim.

Now it hissed—a sibilant, menacing sound that sliced through the silence.

And it hissed his name.

In a burst of instinct, Eli hurled it away. The coin clattered against the floorboards, skittering into a shadowed corner, pulsating like a dying ember. As June knelt beside him, clutching his face and crying out his name in a desperate litany of concern, Mason backed away, his gaze fixed steadfastly on the distant, pulsating lights of the Midnight Rodeo.

Red and gold.

Red and gold.

Red and gold.

The lights blinked in unison with the eerie glow of the coin.

And somewhere, deep in the oppressive stillness of the encroaching night, a solitary bell tolled—low, heavy, final.

———

The screen door slammed shut behind them like a gunshot, severing the twilight and trapping the three of them inside Mason's no-nonsense ranch house. The living room reeked of pine cleaner mixed with the earthy musk of old cedar beams, its walls a gallery of faded Texas landscapes and antique rodeo belt buckles that hung like mythic relics. In the corner, a cast iron wood stove loomed like a silent guardian, its belly cold yet still echoing with the ghost of charred mesquite. The house itself embodied the man who built it—unyielding, secretive, and ruthless in its design.

Eli was slumped on the plaid couch, a broken figure hunched over with a pallid face and hands trembling against the worn denim of his jeans, as if he were summoning invisible forces. His gaze was fixed on the floor, eyes searching for a gaping chasm to finish what the cursed road had set in motion. June knelt before him, her steady hands gripping his arms, desperately trying to anchor his spiraling mind.

"You're safe now," she whispered, though her own voice betrayed a tremor of fear. "Whatever it was…it's not here."

Eli's bloodshot eyes shot up at her. "They weren't real. But they were. They were wearing people, June. Clowns in rodeo gear—one crawled on all fours like a monstrous spider, and another… it had a damn horse. Not a real one. It was a ragged stick horse, but it moved like it was possessed." His voice cracked under the weight of his terror. "And it screamed like a dying child."

He swallowed hard, closing his eyes as if to shut out the horrors. "I pounded every backroad. Took the hill through Bear Gulch, even tore through old Sawmill Lane. Every damn time…I ended up back at that grotesque rodeo entrance. The wheel—it saw me. I swear it did."

Mason stood at the kitchen counter, his eyes cold as he clutched the radio receiver to his lips. "Unit one to dispatch," he barked. "Come in. Do you read? We've got a situation—repeat, we've got a code black out here. Anybody copy?"

The radio sputtered, crackled, and then fell silent. He tried again. Nothing but static. Finally, Mason slammed the radio onto the table with a heavy, frustrated clatter. "Phones are down too," he growled. "This entire damn town is cut off."

"We can't just sit here," June declared, rising to her feet with a fierce determination. "We need to go see the mayor—find Mott, warn everyone, anything." She turned sharply toward Mason. "We're not going to wait here like characters in some horror flick, waiting to be picked off one by one."

Already, Mason strode toward the hallway closet, flinging open the door to reveal a long hunting rifle, two holstered pistols, and a worn tactical vest stained from battles past. His badge caught the feeble light, a silent reminder of the law he once believed in. "Then we go prepared," he stated flatly. "I've still got a few allies in town who'll listen. We bring them in. We fight back."

"I'm coming," June insisted, her tone unbreakable.

Mason's eyes narrowed as he turned toward her. "June—"

"I'm not staying behind," she interrupted, resolute. "Don't even ask. I saw her again, Mason. The rodeo queen. She spoke to me. She left something—a piece of my soul. My mom's locket. You really think I'm gonna just sit here and pray this nightmare fades?"

She snatched her jacket from the chair, zipping it up halfway as if arming herself mentally. "Not on your life."

Mason's lips twitched into a half-smile, half-laugh. "I was just gonna ask which pistol you preferred."

Her cheeks flushed as a smile cracked through the tension. "The Sig Sauer P322," she replied, both embarrassed and amused, "sorry."

Before Mason could retort, the porch creaked ominously. The knock never came—instead, the door slowly swung open on its own. And there, framed by the harsh glare of the porch light, stood Nettie Carson. Her long black coat shimmered like liquid obsidian, and silver conchos ran like threads of cold metal down her sleeves. A dark sash cinched her waist, and a faded purple ribbon dangled from an old pageant medal around her neck, dulled by the passage of time. Her face, powdered and stark, was a mask of pale horror, with lips drawn tight and eyes as empty and resonant as a church bell tolling at midnight.

June froze. "Aunt Nettie…"

Eli's expression crumpled as if he were about to collapse into unconsciousness.

Without so much as a word, Nettie stepped inside, her presence alone causing the door to close silently behind her.

"It's begun," she intoned, her voice low, calm, and laced with inescapable foreboding. "You'll need more than bullets to stop what's coming."

In that charged moment, no one breathed—not even the house itself, as if it were holding its breath before the storm unleashed.

———

Still Creek was changing.

It started with a soft, choking silence—a breath stolen from the very rooftops. The sun, already fading, sank deeper behind sinister, roiling red clouds, and the waning light bruised the cracked sidewalks with ominous, shadowed scars.

At exactly 6:06 p.m., every clock in town shuddered to a halt.

From the bakery's flour-covered wall clock to the digital green ticker at the gas station, time stuttered mid-tick. The ancient grandfather clock in the school lobby emitted one tortured, strangled chime before falling into a dreadful silence. Children on porches stared at their tablets as the time blinked 6:06... and then, as if snuffed out, the digits evaporated.

Then came the TVs.

One by one, they sputtered to life—even those that had long since been unplugged. Even the dead ones flickered back. This static didn't hum; it snarled like a beast awakening. The picture tubes hissed, writhed, and then, unfailingly, his face materialized:

Rook.

Adorned in his grotesque ringmaster's attire—a blood-dark velvet coat, a silver mask luminous like a cold, moonlit blade, and a wide-brimmed hat that cloaked his sinister, predatory smile—he stared out from every screen, silent at first.

Then came a whisper, crawling out from beneath the static, beneath a haunted breath.

"Still Creek... tonight is the night."

The TVs did not merely speak—they exhaled the words into stifling living rooms, shadowed back bedrooms, and deserted diners like a cursed confession.

"The Midnight Rodeo opens its gates... for blood, for truth, for judgment."

The words were not loud; they penetrated your bones. They slithered into the cracks of your mind, murmuring in the crevices where your oldest regrets lay hidden.

"Ride, if you dare. Watch, if you must. But remember—"

Rook leaned in from every screen, so near it felt as though his face brushed against your skin.

"Every show demands a price."

And then, suddenly, all screens died into black oblivion.

Some shattered into glittering shards.

Throughout town, beasts wailed in terror.

A barn cat clawed desperately through the walls of a farmhouse pantry. Dogs howled in maddened fear, scuttling beneath beds. Horses bucked violently in their stalls until they collapsed, overcome by exhaustion. At Nettie's, the canary dropped lifeless from its perch, its body cold and final. And from the tree outside the library, every crow vanished, leaving behind only scattered black feathers...and shattered eggs.

Then came the flyers.

At first, they seemed like a ghostly rain, a spectral shower descending slowly.

Soon it was dreadfully obvious that this was something far more sinister.

Ash and paper tumbled in chaotic spirals, fluttering from nowhere—no wind, no visible source—only the sky vomiting its hidden terrors. The flyers drifted downward, edges curling and blackened as though born of sacrificial flame. Each one bore the same chilling message:

189

MIDNIGHT RODEO – ONE NIGHT ONLY

TONIGHT AT SUNDOWN

ADMISSION PAID IN FULL

People spilled onto the streets to watch the descent, dazed, their eyes hypnotized like moths fixated on a deadly flame. One woman clutched a flyer to her chest, weeping uncontrollably. Another grinned maniacally, pressing hers to her blouse while murmuring frantic prayers. Children stooped to collect the eerie pages with trembling fingers as if the paper might bite.

And then, the walking began.

Slow and unsteady, they emerged.

From trailer parks, from isolated farmhouses, from the seedy bar on Copper Street—they arrived. Some stumbled barefoot, their pajamas soaked with cold sweat, their faces ghostly and distant. Others, clad in their finest Sunday garments, wore cracked lipsticks and off-kilter ties, their eyes empty, as if emptied by despair. Some wept openly, tears carving sorrowful paths along dusted cheeks. Others displayed eerie smiles—too wide, too knowing, as if privy to unspeakable secrets.

They uttered no words—not to one another, not a single syllable to anyone.

They simply walked.

They moved inexorably toward the pulsing, infernal glow of red and gold lights, which now throbbed in the distance like a festering, half-healed wound. The rodeo grounds had been transformed into a beacon—a macabre summoning. The lights blinked in rhythm, like the slow, dreadful beating of a monstrous heart.

June watched from Mason's porch, her heart sinking into a pit of foreboding as she stared at the procession of figures gliding through the streets like apparitions from a nightmare. Mason stood beside her, shotgun gripped tight, his face a mask of grim determination. Eli peered from behind a window, his coin clenched in a trembling hand, whispering his name like a desperate curse.

Nettie said nothing. Words had no meaning now.

The show was about to begin.

And the town—every last fractured, frightened soul—was taking its seat for the unholy performance.

———

The dying sun splattered its final rays over Still Creek like blood from a vicious wound. The sky burned through gold and violent crimson before plunging into an abyss of black—and as the last fragment of daylight vanished behind the hills, the gates violently yawned open. No calloused hand manipulated them. No mortal bolt was turned.

The twin archways guarding the rodeo grounds, hewn from twisted wood and corroded iron, groaned open of their own accord, as if summoned by the exhalation of an ancient, malevolent force stirring in the bowels of the earth. A rancid wind burst forth from within, choked with the acrid tang of burnt sugar, scorched leather, and sodden soil—a stench reminiscent of a graveyard masquerading as a saccharine carnival.

The crowd converged with grim inevitability. Like moths magnetically drawn to an infernal flame, the townspeople shuffled toward the spectacle—alone, in clusters of families, pairs of uneasy souls—all shrouded in heavy silence or murmuring disbelievingly under their breath. Some arrived still cloaked in the day's fatigue, while others had donned lavish attire as though attending a somber ritual. Many wore faces stripped of emotion. And yet, a few... curled their lips into enigmatic smiles.

The first among them crossed the threshold—and that's when the clowns materialized. They slithered from the shadowed edges like ink bleeding across a white page. Some ascended ephemeral ticket booths that hadn't existed just the day before. Others loitered beneath fragmented archways, leaning casually against rusted posts, fingers trembling with predatory anticipation.

Their garb was that of a twisted rodeo—a patchwork of worn vests and grimy chaps, cracked boots and masks sewn from battered leather, each one more grotesque than its predecessor. One clown's face was obscured by smeared, runny paint that dripped like melting wax, his grin unnaturally stretched beneath hollow-eyed sockets. Another bore a nose drawn in what looked like congealed blood, while a third displayed a sheriff's badge, its metal having long fused with his flesh.

Whispers of forbidden names slithered among the gathering. Names spoken in hushed tones that resonated only with those they targeted. They inched near certain entrants, bending in to hiss directly into their ears:

"Alma Riggins... we remember."

"Past due, Thomas."

"You kept the child, didn't you, Mr. Greaves?"

Most who heard these names recoiled sharply; some halted dead in their tracks. One man crumpled to his knees, overcome with uncontrollable weeping.

Other clowns remained silent—merely fixed their unblinking gaze on the passersby. Their eyes burned with a searing, molten gold, like coins plucked from the heart of a funeral pyre.

A woman struggling with her walker ambled past one of these unyielding clowns. He responded with a twisted grin, revealing teeth that resembled splintered, whitewashed wood. He removed his hat and bowed in a grotesque parody of respect. The woman nodded numbly and shuffled onward, lost in a trance.

Then, without warning, came the bell.

No lofty tower. No snarling rope. No rational explanation.

But from the corners of existence, it tolled.

DONG.

It struck like a brutal blow to the ribs. The sound carried palpable weight, warping the very air, making teeth clench and fillings vibrate. From miles away, dogs howled in anguished response.

DONG.

Each toll descended slower than the last, deeper and more oppressive—a signal dropping through the earth's layers, summoning something unspeakable. Calling forth all things touched by dread.

And with its relentless rhythm, the Ferris wheel jerked to life.

Not with the languid creaks of a once-idle attraction.

No—it whirled.

Faster and faster, its cabins blur into streaks, while red and gold lights flickered in savage unison with the bell. The vast wheel groaned like a behemoth roused from a tortured sleep, its spokes bending unnaturally, spurting sparks from every joint. The grinding of metal on rust screeched through the air.

DONG.

By the third toll, the Ferris wheel decelerated, syncing its unnerving pace with the bell's morbid cadence. Each cabin now held an eerie silhouette. Some wore archaic hats; others donned faces painted in macabre designs.

Yet none possessed eyes.

They remained motionless.

Yet they did not need to.

Still Creek's children, inexplicably drawn by a primal instinct that eclipsed fear, scampered to the fence, giggling in innocent delight. Their parents advanced with hesitant dread, clutching worn Bibles or frayed talismans as they stepped beyond the threshold.

And then—from behind one of the tattered tents—a low, mournful chorus began to intone a broken lullaby in a tongue that defied understanding.

"Round and round the wheel it turns,

The light will burn, the truth returns..."

June stood on the crest of a hill, her breath a mist in the cold evening air, eyes wide with apprehension.

Beside her, Mason angled the barrel of his shotgun ever so slightly—not to fire, but to grasp a fleeting sense of control.

Behind them, Eli's gaze remained riveted on the open gates, his hand clenching a hissing coin so tightly that crimson stained his fingertips.

DONG.

The gates loomed open in ominous welcome.

The people poured in.

And with that, the Midnight Rodeo ignited its nightmare.

———

The Big Top loomed like a monstrous beast in the oppressive darkness—a living mass of canvas that throbbed with every howl of the wind. Its red-and-gold stripes shuddered and rippled under the erratic gleam of the flickering lights, as if sinewy muscles writhed beneath stretched, fevered skin. Overhead, the pennants hung in eerie stillness, as if the very air inside had been overtaken by an otherworldly force.

From the outside, the tent looked deserted—a yawning gash, a cavernous mouth eagerly awaiting its first gulp of terror. But inside, the atmosphere was a seething cauldron of more than mere anticipation. It vibrated with raw, crackling energy, heavy and stifling, palpably alive.

Within the tent's depths, pulsating shadows shifted with an almost malevolent rhythm. Lanterns swung wildly on impossibly long ropes, casting distorted, quivering circles of light on the sawdust-strewn floor. Wooden bleachers, ancient and creaking under invisible burdens, formed a ring around the center, their timeworn planks groaning with each unseen weight. And in some of those seats, filled with shapes that were not townsfolk at all, hung eerie, translucent specters.

These ghostly figures shimmered in the erratic glow, their faces hidden in a perpetual blur of half-formed memories. Some clapped in ominous silence, while others merely stared, their presence a dark promise of what was coming next—they were waiting.

June, Mason, Nettie, and Eli crept in through a concealed flap, stepping into the perverse arena with hearts pounding like war drums and breaths held in fearful suspense. Eli's coin, still murmuring its own secret, lay silent in his pocket, untouched out of dread. Nettie moved with a lethal, uncompromising grace, her black rodeo queen regalia transforming her into a widow at war—her jaw set like carved stone, her eyes ignited with fierce, unyielding flame.

"There," June hissed, tightening her grip on Mason's arm.

Frank.

There he stood at the ring's edge—a silent marionette with limbs dangling at his sides, as though waiting for unseen strings to writhe and command him. His mask, a grim and cracked leather visage with brass-rimmed eyes and a mouth viciously stitched shut, glistened in the hazy gloom.

He did not blink.

He did not budge.

Then, in a heartbeat, the spotlight burst to life.

It flared violently from above—a searing flash that slashed through the darkness like a sharpened blade, transforming the ambient gloom into a surreal battlefield of light and shadow. Dust erupted, dancing like desperate fireflies in the blaze, and at the very center of that blinding brilliance stood Rook.

Rook was a figure of divine menace, draped in a velvet coat of the deepest crimson, interwoven with silver thread that glinted like captured starlight. A cruel, ornate silver half-mask obscured one side of his face, leaving one eye and cheekbone hauntingly exposed. His wide-brimmed hat lurked low, just enough to reveal the triumphant, scornful sneer that curled over his lips.

With a preacher's fervor, he raised his arms aloft, his voice erupting like an inferno, booming and shattering the silence with sound crashing into spaces that should have been shrouded in quiet.

"Welcome, Still Creek. Welcome... to the First Act."

A sparse, disquieted crowd stirred like a writhing mass of leaves caught in a violent storm.

"Tonight, we invoke the old ways. Before gods reigned. Before kings commanded. There was only blood—a torrent of fire. And the searing sting of truth."

His arms fell, and the lanterns above convulsed in erratic flickers, as if recoiling from the impending horror.

"Let the first blood... be spilled."

The ground convulsed in response.

Sawdust erupted violently from beneath, spiraling upward in a column that glowed with a sinister red luminescence—as though ignited by an infernal flame from within. It pulsed in time with a dark, relentless heartbeat.

And then, from the far recesses of the tent, a scream—a raw, piercing cry—ripped through the air.

It was not some distant echo, nor a surreal phantom noise. It was real and harrowing—a terrified clamor from someone in town.

A woman.

She was hauled into the ring by two grim clowns with blank, unsettling masks and bone-carved rope in their cold hands. Her high heels dug furrows into the floor as she twisted and writhed, her yellow cardigan smeared with dirt and tatters, her eyes wide in wild panic and disbelief.

"No! Please—please, I didn't do anything!" she screamed, her voice breaking as she struggled fiercely against their grip.

"You were chosen," murmured one of the clowns, his voice a dissonant rasp that belonged to something not quite human.

Rook lifted his gloved hand and snapped his fingers with chilling precision.

A hidden gate creaked open beneath the ring, revealing that something dark and ominous was stirring, rising from the depths.

In the shadows, June's grip tightened on Mason's hand as she dared not look away.

The show had begun.

———

The sky descended into a suffocating darkness, yet the horizon glowed unnaturally, as if the sun defiantly clung to Still Creek. On the outskirts of town, Sheriff Mott's tires shrieked against the fractured asphalt as his cruiser tore down the decrepit state highway. His face was ghostly and slick with panic-sweat, eyes wide and frenzied behind the wheel. He ignored the speedometer, consumed by the need to escape.

"Gotta get out," he muttered through clenched teeth, voice taut with desperation. "Gotta warn somebody... somebody else..."

The radio crackled with sinister static and eerie laughter. Every station returned the same unnerving symphony—scratching vinyl, distorted calliope music, or silence as dense as a starless abyss.

Mott's knuckles blanched as he tightened his grip on the wheel. The road stretched into infinity, flanked by twisted oaks and decaying wire fences. Exit signs blurred by—Deadman's Hollow, Bristled Creek, Lone Mesa—yet something was dreadfully wrong.

He passed the same gnarled pine tree once more.

And again.

And again.

The highway veered sharply. He slammed the brakes. His cruiser skidded to a halt, dust erupting like a shroud covering a hideous secret.

The road ahead was barricaded.

A towering figure on horseback dominated the intersection—the very intersection he had left miles behind. The rider stood motionless, cloaked in ash-colored leather, a wide-brimmed hat casting a shadow over his features. Yet Mott could discern the grin.

It was grotesque. Unnatural. It stretched impossibly beyond the confines of a human face.

The rider lifted a gloved hand, tipping his hat with deliberate mockery.

Mott's revolver quivered in his lap.

He was paralyzed.

The horse advanced, hooves eerily silent on the pavement. The rider's grin widened into a ghastly smile.

Behind him, a soft sound reverberated across the road.

A second horse.

Then a third.

The Pale Riders were closing in.

Sheriff Mott's scream tore through the night.

But it was swallowed by the fog that rolled over the asphalt like the lid of a coffin sealing his fate.

Chapter 9: The Price of Admission

The woman's final scream didn't simply vanish—it lingered in a raw, agonizing tension, stretching across the air like taut, exposed sinew before breaking into silence. Her blood pooled in the sawdust below, and as her last ragged breath shuddered from her broken chest, she began to rise. There were no wires, no pulleys.

Her body ascended as if hauled by invisible threads, her limbs dangling like a mutilated marionette caught between defiance and despair. She spiraled slowly, arms flung askew, her hair drifting in the lantern's light like underwater weeds caught in a current of uncertainty. Blood continued to drip, curling into the flickering glow like whispered, unsettled curses.

The crowd—both living and otherwise—erupted in a torrent of conflicting emotion. Some stood and applauded with almost manic fervor, while others moaned in an ecstatic, uneasy rapture, their bodies swaying as if in the grip of a bittersweet trance. And many, especially those wearing their own faces, watched with tears silently trailing down conflicted cheeks, clapping as if compelled by forces beyond their control.

Even the half-formed specters in the upper rows, flickering like a poor signal in a broken world, leaned forward in reverent, doubtful anticipation. Every gaze was fixed on her.

June's hand clutched Mason's, her nails digging in as if trying to anchor herself amidst the chaos. "That's not gravity," she whispered, her voice trembling with both awe and anxiety. "That's not anything natural."

Mason's eyes slid downward to where his holstered pistol should have been—gone. The rifle had vanished, so had the knife tucked into his boot, and the spare mags once nestled in his jacket. He looked up at June, whose belt—a belt that once secured the Sig—was now empty, and even her boot dagger was missing. The vest Nettie had given her earlier, stuffed with tools, lay hollow.

"What the hell?" Mason murmured, disbelief lacing each word. "They're… gone."

June's lips parted as if to protest, her voice wavering, "I checked. I had it before we came in—"

"They took them." His tone was low, a conflicted mix of anger and disbelief. "This place stripped us clean."

June's eyes swept the tent—the unnatural lights, the ecstatic, almost tormented crowd, and the levitating corpse that defied all natural order. "Then how the hell do we fight back?" she asked, her voice a quiet battle cry amid the mounting uncertainty.

Above them, the lights swelled brighter, and that was when the other acts began. From the upper beams, ropes snapped taut—strands wrought from horsehair and bone, intertwined with barbed wire and glistening sinew. They stretched across the tent like a web spun by something both ancient and cruel, a snare designed for the damned.

From below, new contestants were pressed forward. The school librarian, the butcher's boy, a teenage girl in a faded prom dress with a wilted, mold-darkened corsage—they were shoved into the spotlight by clowns clad in rusted leather vests and distorted rodeo gear, eyes hidden beneath cracked goggles, smiles smeared with greasepaint that barely masked their conflicted intent. The high-wire formed before them—no safety nets, no balancing poles—just a narrow path laden with risk and regret.

A voice, as if stitched together from the murmurs of those lost to Still Creek, hissed down from above, "Balance your guilt. Walk your shame."

The girl went first. With every uncertain step, she trembled, the conflict in her heart palpable. Halfway across, a clown dropped inverted from a bungee-like rope, leaning in as if to whisper secrets meant only for her. Her scream burst forth—a sound of terror mixed with defiance—and then she fell. There was no jarring impact; just a sharp, dissonant jerk as she vanished into the consuming blackness below, her scream echoing like an unanswered lament. The crowd's roar was a unsettling blend of approval and mourning.

Next came the librarian. Books tumbled from his coat pockets as he walked, igniting mid-air like paper soaked in accelerant, each falling volume a testament to forgotten knowledge. He made it further than the girl until suddenly, the line beneath his feet twisted into a mad, upward spiral, coiling like a snake ready to strike. He slipped, vanished, and was swallowed by the dust as if devoured by the earth itself. And still, the Big Top shook with applause that rang hollow with conflict.

Mason gritted his teeth, a bitter irony in his tone. "This is a slaughterhouse dressed up in sequins."

"And we're unarmed," June replied, her voice hard with both disbelief and a fierce vulnerability. "Helpless."

"No," Mason countered, turning toward her with clenched determination despite the sinking despair in his eyes. "Not helpless, just… declawed, for the moment." Their eyes lifted as they searched the chaotic sky.

Above, the woman continued her ascent, her movements now guided by a twisted, almost mournful rhythm. Her body seemed to dance a tragic waltz, limbs jerking in time to a slow, off-key melody from a violin forged of bone, played by a clown with too many fraught, trembling fingers. From the ring's edge, a shadow stirred.

Frank.

He stood alone now, his cracked leather mask peeling away as if by its own accord, revealing a face as pale as regret, eyes black and brimming with unshed tears. His mouth was sewn shut by a living thread that pulsed ominously, tightening with each ragged, conflicted breath. He turned toward June, their eyes meeting in a moment rife with unspoken sorrow and strife. And in that collision of despair and determination, he slumped. Yet beneath the collapse, he was still fighting—a silent war waging within him.

The spotlight snapped on, cutting through the gloom like a scalpel through raw, conflicted flesh. Rook entered the ring not with a walk but a glide, his crimson velvet coat trailing behind him like a wound that refused to close. The silver half-mask he wore gleamed with a malevolent luster, one exposed eye staring out—hungry, amused, and burdened by its own inner conflict. The tent seemed to breathe around him, the crowd falling into a deathly, ambivalent silence.

Rook raised his arms and the lights dimmed to a choking ember. His voice, warm yet saturated with venom, slithered around every ear. "They've all been drawn to Still Creek. To this Midnight Rodeo. Not for the sake of games or mere spectacle." He turned slowly, his eyes piercing through the tumult of the crowd. "But to answer for their past. To face what must be faced."

A final wire snapped into place above as a disheveled man—drunk, shirtless, screaming the name of a long-dead child—was flung into the air. He landed on the wire, slipped, and dissolved into a curtain of swirling smoke, a fitting symbol of lost hope.

Rook's smile split his mask as he continued, "Each attraction, each act, every performance—it is not theater." His voice fell to a conspiratorial whisper that carried despite the oppressive silence. "It is revelation."

He gestured toward the flapping tarps at the far end of the tent where the pulsing red and gold lights of the midway beckoned with a savage allure—both inviting and repelling in their seductive promise. "Beyond the veil of lights lies a midway of truths."

There was a heavy pause—a beat pregnant with defiance and dread. Then his final decree: "Choose your path. Choose your price."

And then, with a final whispering sigh, the lights died. The woman's corpse tumbled downward, bones snapping like brittle twigs as she collapsed into a perfect heap of blood and silence, with dust spiraling upward from her remains. A bell tolled—no tower or visible mechanism in sight—its sound cavernous and final, marking an end steeped in conflicted sorrow.

Far in the distance, beneath the eerie red glow of a Ferris wheel spinning defiant against gravity, the carnival began to hum—a haunting, ambivalent overture to a night that promised neither salvation nor certainty.

———

The tattered canvas of the Big Top trembled violently behind them as June, Mason, Nettie, and Eli sneaked through a narrow gap in the maddened crowd. The murmurs of the spectral audience clung to them like skeletal hands trailing icy fingers down their spines. Outside, the air was oppressive and warm—a suffocating blend of burnt, sugary popcorn and the bitter tang of decaying greasepaint. The carnival roared to life, hungry and vengeful, its insatiable desire palpable in every shadow.

They trailed behind a broken procession of townsfolk, their eyes glazed with a vacant stupor, their movements sluggish and marionette-like beneath the cruel night. Clowns drifted among them like malevolent shepherds, their gestures grotesque, beckoning silently toward twisted "events" with exaggerated bows and hollow, staring eyes. Each attraction flickered with sickly, unnatural hues— rancid spinning wheels, grotesque prize booths that sneered, stalls oozing toxic neon decay beneath torn, striped awnings.

Nettie halted before a decomposing funhouse entrance, its warped wooden façade grotesquely carved with grinning, sinister faces and emaciated, skeletal horses. A crooked sign loomed overhead, its failing bulbs sputtering weak, haunted light:

MIDWAY OF MIRRORS

See Yourself As You Really Are.

"This is it," Nettie whispered, voice steeled with grim determination. "This place will strip you to your very soul."

"Fantastic," Eli scoffed bitterly, his gaze fixed on the warped doors. "Because every moment up until now was just the opening act."

They slipped into the maw of the funhouse.

Inside, a chilling void replaced the outside warmth— not merely a drop in temperature, but an absence of all comfort and hope. Gas lanterns in tarnished iron sconces flared with erratic violet flames, casting long, twitching shadows that seemed to slither with deliberate malice. The air reeked of rusted metal, damp stone, and a sickly sweet trace of embalmed perfume.

And then the maze began.

Mirrors towered in every direction—warped, cracked, and smothered in layers of grime. Yet each one offered a perfect, unnervingly true reflection of those who passed before them, unaltered and immediate.

And then... the fragmentation commenced.

June turned to speak to Mason—and he was gone. Not evaporated, but severed—trapped on the far side of the glass. The corridor she had known changed with a cruel twist, curving into unfamiliar, nightmarish angles. The walls pulsed with every ragged gasp she took.

She stumbled backward—and froze.

In the mirror before her, she saw her mother: Youthful, radiant, draped in the scarlet sequined rodeo gown of a long-forgotten photograph. Her face glowed with a nostalgic warmth, her lips upturned in a gentle, loving smile.

"Mom?" June whispered, reaching out with trembling hope.

The image blinked, distorting.

That tender smile twisted into a malevolent sneer. Crimson began to seep from her mother's scalp, staining her flowing hair like fresh wounds. Her majestic dress decayed into a tattered remnant of rotted lace, and her eyes hollowed into vast, accusing voids.

"You abandoned me," the reflection spat, her voice a venomous hiss dripping with betrayal. "You always do."

June screamed, stumbling as the mirror's surface clung to her terror—the glass following her like a magnet drawn to despair. Her locket—the fragile relic cradling her mother's image—blazed with a burning heat against her chest.

Elsewhere in the twisting maze, Mason wandered among flickering reflections. His own face stared back—etched with lines of hardened anger and a bitterness that was older than he remembered.

Then, in the mirror before him: the boy.

Small. Smirking. Clad in a hoodie and jeans. Simply standing there, silent but ominous.

"Rosie says hi," the boy chirped with an unsettling smirk.

Mason edged forward, his chest constricting with dread. "What—how—?"

The boy's smile contorted, teeth sharpening into predatory daggers, lips stretching grotesquely until they split into a rictus of horror.

"You only save the dogs, right?"

The mirror erupted in a fractal explosion, spiderweb cracks splintering outward from the center and distorting the boy's face into a nightmare. Mason lunged forward, his fists clenching in desperate fury—only to find nothing but an echoing laugh reverberating like fiery detonations in a cursed crypt.

Eli's corridor was a claustrophobic tunnel that pressed in with sinister intent. His breath fogged the glass as reflections multiplied—but they no longer mirrored him. They exchanged whispers, some recoiling in terror, one bleeding darkly from its mouth.

Then, one voice cut through—the voice of Rook reverberating with grim familiarity.

"You've been wandering in circles since your first sin."

Eli shrank back, voice trembling. "No. Shut up. I didn't—"

"The drunken girl in the storm. The money you hoarded. The door you never opened."

Reflections swarmed him—dozens of Elis encircling him, each emblazoned with damning sins scrawled in crimson: COWARD. THIEF. TRAITOR.

"You've already lost to me, Eli," the mirror rasped like grinding stone. "You were condemned the moment you ran."

A shard of glass broke free and hovered, a jagged sliver suspended in the air, inches above his quivering heart.

He screamed and bolted into the labyrinth.

Nettie stood motionless before her mirror. It was void—completely empty. No reflection, no flicker of judgment, just the relentless presence of her own being.

"You don't scare me," she murmured, voice unwavering. "I already died once."

In that instant, the mirror shattered, folding in on itself in a silent, devastating implosion.

The others reconvened near the ragged end of the funhouse—breathless, skin pale, trembling with raw terror. The walls convulsed with ominous shakes, dust cascading from above like the ashes of lost hopes. The entire structure groaned, its ancient bones straining against an unspeakable force breaking free beneath it.

Just as they neared the exit, a ghastly hand erupted from the mirror beside June—her own reflection. It lunged, yanking the locket from her throat with a snap that echoed like brittle thread under immense strain.

She screamed, reaching desperately for the talisman, but the reflection only grinned—the same abhorrent, twisted smile her mother had borne—and then dissolved into the dark abyss beyond the glass.

The mirror split wide open with a violent rupture.

And then shattered into oblivion.

The exit burst before them like a gaping wound in reality.

They staggered out into the stifling, oppressive night air—hearts hammering, lungs scorched by fear and adrenaline.

The carnival had grown louder, wilder, and far more monstrous.

They were no longer the same souls who had entered, forever scarred by what lurked within.

And somewhere, echoing from the shattered remnants, the mirrors laughed—a mocking promise of the horror yet to come.

———

The sound of screams—harsh, untamed, and achingly human—ripped through the carnival air like a chainsaw tearing through raw flesh.

June barely had time to react before Nettie jerked her head toward the source. "That isn't a spectacle," she growled. "That's a sacrifice."

They ran.

Darting between warped funhouse shadows and the jagged backbones of decrepit booths, the group burst into a clearing lit by a dozen towering carnival floodlights, each flickering erratically as if powered by a dying heart. The ground underfoot was a slick, obsidian mire—sawdust entwined with something darker and viscous.

At the center of the chaos loomed a mechanical bull, a grotesque fusion of warped rusted chrome and patched, molten leather that hissed like boiling tar. Its eyes burned red, and its mouth was locked in a permanent, horrific grimace of agony.

Strapped onto its metallic back, bound with ropes woven from horsehair and barbed wire, was Tommy Hutch—a local teen once known only for dodging math lessons and racing ATVs along creek beds. Now he clung to the bull in a state of delirium, his head jerking violently as the beast bucked with a terrifying, predatory precision.

Then his face began to warp.

First, his skin drained to a ghostly pallor. It tautened and stretched, his cheeks ballooned grotesquely, and his lips split into a nightmarish grin. His eyes sunk into cavernous voids as his nose swelled into a bulbous, reddened eruption. A piercing, deranged laugh tore from his throat—it wasn't Tommy anymore.

217

It was a clown. And his face was disintegrating before their eyes.

Encircling the arena, a maddened crowd—locals and unspeakable entities alike, with stitched-shut mouths or features missing entirely—began chanting in a single, unsettling tone, swaying in a trance of possession.

"Ride or die. Ride or die. Ride or die."

Without a moment's hesitation, June vaulted the fence.

"Mason!" she screamed, her voice raw with urgency. "Control box! Over there!"

Mason's eyes locked on an ancient control panel, crudely nailed to a splintered plywood post. It was a relic, rusted and barely clinging to life, with wires sparking like furious, venomous serpents.

Lost in instinct, Mason drew the pistol he no longer had, feeling the phantom weight of an empty holster. Cursing under his breath, he hesitated only a heartbeat before Nettie, right behind him, slipped a small revolver from beneath her coat.

"I didn't bring it for you," she said evenly, her tone void of pity as she passed it over. "I brought it for the bull."

Mason nodded grimly, took aim, and fired.

The bullet found its target with unerring precision—piercing the heart of the control panel. Sparks erupted in a violent, screaming burst of blue and white. The bull shrieked—not with the cold clatter of metal, not with the hiss of hydraulics—but with the agonized cry of a dying beast.

Its joints locked; the savage spinning halted.

Tommy was hurled from his mount like a discarded ragdoll, crashing into the dirt with bone-crushing impact. His face flickered incomprehensibly between boy and monstrous clown before desperate flesh reasserted itself—barely.

June vaulted the fence, her strength unwavering, as she dragged him away. Her fingers dug into the scorched earth for traction while the searing heat from the bull's disintegrating body blistered her back. The monstrous frame crumpled in on itself, collapsing as if it had been a fragile shell all along, with smoke spiraling upward like incense at a funeral.

Its burning eyes dimmed to nothingness.

Then, silence.

A suffocating stillness that felt hard-won but left a dirge of emptiness in its wake.

Kneeling beside Tommy, June watched as his eyelids fluttered weakly open. "He said I had to stay on for eight seconds," he croaked, voice trembling. "But... I think... I think the seconds lied."

Suddenly, a voice shattered the silence.

Not Rook.

Not the huddled clowns.

Something ancient, something vast, whispered from every corner.

"He cheated."

"The price... is doubled."

All the lights blinked out simultaneously—one after another—until the arena was swallowed by an eerie shadowlight, a darkness that illuminated every dreadful secret.

June rose, terror and disbelief mingling in her wide eyes. "What does that mean?"

Mason's voice, barely a whisper carried on raw breaths, answered, "It means this wasn't the final ride."

High in the newly appeared stands—bleachers that had risen like gothic pews against a stormy sky—a lone figure emerged.

Frank.

Or what remained of Frank.

His silhouette was draped in Rook's coat—luxurious, velvet-red with silver stitching glinting like cold menace. His arms hung uselessly at his side, and his head was lopsidedly tilted, as if he were a marionette abandoned by its puppeteer.

The last tendrils of smoke wound towards him like ghostly fingers.

He did nothing.

No nod, no wave—only an unyielding, silent vigil.

June's voice, quivering with hollow dread, broke the silence. "He's not... is he...?"

Mason's grip on the revolver clenched tighter until the metal bit into his skin.

"I don't know," he rasped, "but he's wearing the ringmaster's coat now."

———

The path snarled again, its sound morphing— screams dissolving into an eerie, twisted carnival anthem. This was not the nostalgic jingling of carefree days; it was a demented melody, as if an ancient record were groaning through a filthy Victrola. It groaned, stuttered, sometimes reversing course in jagged bursts of sharp brass that seemed to jeer at the listener.

From the depths of the mechanical bull pen emerged June, Mason, Nettie, and Eli, stepping into a Midway that reeked of forgotten transgressions and raw, bleeding secrets. This was no ordinary fairground of simple pleasures—it was a decayed shrine constructed of history and confession, forged from lies and carnal betrayals.

Stretching out in relentless, impossible rows beneath sputtering, rusted bulbs and sinister crimson banners were carnival games: ring tosses, balloon dart booths, high strikers—all manned by grotesque clowns in tatters, their burnt makeup and vacant eyes slicing through the dim light like shards of broken glass. But it wasn't the games that chilled the blood—it was the exorbitant, soul-crushing stakes they demanded.

A trembling figure approached the ring toss. June's heart lurched as she recognized him: Harlan McKeen, the propane peddler who once sneered that she'd never escape Still Creek's suffocating grip. Now, stripped of his scorn, he was a quivering specter. With hands that shook uncontrollably, he hurled a ring onto the neck of a battered milk bottle—and as it slammed home, the game bell shrieked.

A clown's grin split his face as he reached behind a grimy counter, unveiling a prize swathed in a faded blue hospital blanket. It was a baby doll, wrapped like a secret tragedy. Harlan let out a nervous chuckle ready for dismissal—until the doll began to cry. A raw, wet, strangled sob erupted, desperate and muffled. His face crumbled into despair as his knees buckled. "I gave her up," he murmured, clutching the doll to his chest like a cursed ember. "I gave her up, I gave her up—I thought I'd forgotten—how does it know?" Dropping like a marionette onto the dirt, he rocked violently while the clown's silent, malevolent laughter glinted under the gloom.

At the balloon dart booth, a small boy—Danny Rhoades, no more than ten—fumbled with trembling hands as he tossed darts. Missing the final balloon by mere inches, his fate was sealed. A sinister clown stepped forward, a painted hand falling like a cold benediction upon Danny's head, tousling his hair. Then, as if devoured by darkness, Danny's shadow peeled away—slithering into the booth like smoky tendrils sucked by a void. With wide, disbelieving eyes, he blinked once and turned in slow, agonized confusion. "Mama?" he called, his voice warping into a distant, tinny lament. "Mama, it's cold." And just like that, he vanished—no flash, no echo, only an emptiness that screamed loss.

June's lungs seized with panic. Every booth, every cursed prize, was a confession bathed in torment. She moved toward a nightmarish game where Mrs. Radley—the ravenous, tear-streaked widow from Elm Street—hurriedly hurled softballs at a pyramid stacked with jars. Her fingers were raw, oozing blood as if they bled out her silent agony.

"What is she trying to win?" whispered Mason, his voice trembling with dread.

June's gaze fell on the prize wall. It wasn't a collection of playful trinkets but a macabre gallery of living faces, entombed behind grim, thick glass panels. Their expressions twisted in torment— eyeballs rolling in silent horror, mouths contorting in endless sobbing. One face stirred, turning toward her with a desperate urgency. It was her mother, her lips distorting into a plea: "June… help me…"

June staggered forward, a mix of terror and desperation flooding her veins. "No. No no no—" she cried out, her hand reaching, fingertips grazing the glass. It rippled like a surge of static-laced water beneath her touch.

A warm breath whispered against her ear—a voice, smooth as broken silk and cutting like razors, cooed, "All you have to do is play."

Spinning, June found Rook next to her— unannounced, ominously calm. His mask was gone, revealing a face in constant, maddening flux—a blur of her father, her lover, her child, herself—all intertwining in a grotesque dance of bleeding identities and eerie smiles.

"Win, and maybe you walk away with what you want," he murmured, leaning in so close his lips nearly brushed her temple. "But win or lose... the house always keeps something."

Enraged, June spat, "Go to hell."

Rook's smile widened into something feral as he replied, "Sweetheart, you're in it." At that moment, the flickering lights surged, and for a breathless instant, every prize, every tortured face, screamed— not with noise, but with raw, overwhelming sensation: grief, rage, betrayal—a cacophony of guilt and regret shattering through glass.

Mason yanked her back just in time as Nettie stepped forward, her voice steeled with defiance, "No more games."

"Then you'd better hurry," Rook called out from a twenty-foot distance, seated nonchalantly atop the high striker booth. "Because the Queen's Procession is almost here. And she loves her finale." In a blink, he evaporated into darkness.

With a final glance at the prize wall, June's eyes fell on the vacant space where her mother's face had been. Where once there was a pleading visage now stood a mirror of her own—her eyes blinking restlessly in the vacant, accusatory glass.

———

The midway's cursed carnival music still roared behind them as June, Mason, Nettie, and Eli surged over the rise overlooking the arena of despair. Below, the scene twisted into a waking nightmare—a vision warped by relentless madness. Infernal crimson floodlights sliced the pen with savage halos of red and gold while choking smoke clung low over churned, desecrated earth. The stench—of burnt rope, bitter rust, and rotting meat—coiled into their nostrils like a poisonous incantation.

Then a horn bellowed—a low, thunderous, maddening note—as ancient gates shrieked open. Grotesque clowns spilled out, dragging five terrified townsfolk toward the center like sacrificial livestock. One man staggered and sobbed in despair. A woman's scream split the air. And at the end of the line, bloodied and with one swollen, lifeless eye, stood Sheriff Mott.

June's breath seized in her throat.

But Mason surged forward, muscles taut with unbridled fury, descending the embankment without hesitation. "Mason—!" June cried, but he was already flipping open the revolver Nettie had given him, his eyes afire with raw rage. "I won't just stand here," he spat. "Not this time—never again."

He reached the bottom just as the first monster emerged from the holding pens. Not horses. Not machines. These were nightmarish abominations—twisted constructs bound by sinew and scarred iron. Smoke hissed from their ruined joints while metal hooves hammered against blood-dark mud. One beast yawned open its maw and let out a scream like a man burning in hell.

The sordid throng—a mix of living, spectral, and unholy things—roared in frenzied anticipation from the rising bleachers.

Mason sprinted toward the arena gate. A deranged clown hissed, stepping in his way with a baton fashioned from ancient vertebrae. Mason raised his revolver and fired—a bullet singing through the clown's chest. The foul creature staggered, its laughter devolving to a gurgling mockery before dissolving into a cloud of ash.

He vaulted the gate.

Inside, Hank Carver—the gentle florist—was thrust onto a monstrous bronco against his will. The creature convulsed into life, bucking with a violent, inhuman rhythm. "Get off!" Mason screamed, racing after him. "Jump—jump, damn it!" Hank's eyes met his in terror, only to be flung like a rag doll into a cold, unyielding steel post. His spine snapped with a sickening crack, his neck shattered—and in that moment he was dead.

Mason skidded to a halt as the very ground beneath him began to pulse, glowing a vivid red as if an artery were rupturing deep within the earth. A ghostly whisper slithered into his ear: "You don't get to save them. Not this time."

Dead, spectral hands erupted from the soaked soil, clamping around his ankles with the cold, inexorable strength of iron. Mason roared, firing his revolver once, twice—but the shots echoed uselessly as the ghostly grip dragged him down. In his agonized struggle he saw another soul—a trembling diner woman—trying desperately to flee, only to be caught. Two frantic steps, then a bronco skewered her in the back, sending a spray of blood arcing under the harsh lights. She was dragged, shrieking in raw horror, spinning in ragged circles until she vanished beneath a cart overflowing with grim bones.

June reached the barrier, screaming Mason's name, but he waved her away fiercely. "Don't come in here! Stay out!" He wrestled with the phantom grip, tearing one leg free just as another hideous bronco was unleashed. Two more fragile souls—quivering, sobbing with terror—were forced to mount these living nightmares, clinging to the grotesque offer of motion rather than the promise of abandonment.

And then the ride began.

The arena transformed into an orgy of chaos. What had been simple sand now curdled into thick, slow-moving blood; the air shimmered oppressive heat, radiating agony, as vile laughter—inhuman and misplaced—echoed around them.

In a desperate bid, Mason crawled toward one of the riders—a terrified teen he barely knew. Almost within reach, the bronco bucked, hurling the child through the air. His body crashed into the dirt, limbs twisting in a dismembered tableau. As Mason reached out, the teen's eyes—hollow, stitched shut in grim finality—met his. In that horrifying moment, the teen dissolved into dissipating steam... gone.

Then the final bronco appeared: a beast as dark as obsidian and as silent as death itself. It trotted slowly toward Sheriff Mott, who now sobbed openly, on his knees in desperate regret. "I kept this town safe," he choked, voice trembling with guilt. "I enforced the rules..." The beast bowed its head as if to scorn him. "I was the law..."

With trembling desperation, Mott reached out to Mason. "Mason, please—I don't want to die!" Mason lunged forward again, but the ghostly hands pulled him down hard, slamming him flat on the ground.

He roared with unrestrained fury, teeth gritted in defiance. "Let me save him! Damn it, LET ME—" he bellowed, as Mott clambered shakily onto the bronco.

Then the ride transformed. It did not buck or twist—
it metamorphosed. The bronco's hide peeled away
like wet, rotting paper to reveal a nightmarish fusion
of burning gears, searing fire, and brittle bone. It
spun Mott in frenzied circles until he was thrown
horizontal, arms flailing in terror. Then, with a final,
merciless flip, it split him apart.

Mott was hurled into the air like worthless refuse, his
body striking the ground with a bone-crushing snap
that silenced the bloodthirsty crowd. He lay still.

Breaking free from his spectral bonds, Mason
charged toward Mott just as a stark spotlight fell on
the grisly scene. Rook emerged—a spectral arbiter in
a shadowed coat, boots drumming like a death
march—as he walked through the blood-soaked dust
like a judge presiding over a macabre execution. He
knelt beside the shattered sheriff, leaned in close,
and in a voice cold and final whispered, "Your
judgment is complete." With a single, decisive snap
of his fingers, Mott vanished. Only his hat remained,
spinning slowly in place like a token of lost authority.

Mason crumpled to his knees beside the forsaken
hat, blood and dust merging over him as all hope
faltered. From the outer stands, the maddened
crowd roared in sick, furious triumph. Rook swept his
gaze over them, eyes piercing the encroaching
shadows. "Let the procession begin."

——

Smoke billowed like ragged prayer flags across the blood-drenched arena as the crowd tore itself away—not with relief, but with the heavy, shuffling reverence of souls escaping a sermon that had nearly crushed them. June staggered through churned, seething mud toward the ring's edge; every step was a battle, as if the earth itself was clawing at her boots, desperate to imprison her. Her lungs blazed with burning pain and her hands trembled uncontrollably, and only when salt and blood mingled on her tongue did she realize that tears had silently fallen.

Mason loomed near the jagged fence, his tattered shirt stained with ash and sweat, his shoulders heaving as if carrying the weight of the world. His gaze was fixed on Mott's hat, still spinning sluggishly in the swirling dust, and he had remained mute since Rook's jarring crack.

From the darkened fringes, Nettie emerged like a revenant, her black coat drenched and clinging to her lithe form. Her face was unnervingly calm—an eerie stillness that masked a storm of brutality, confined behind invisible glass.

June's eyes darted wildly as terror hammered at her chest. "Where's Eli?" she gasped, her voice cracking under the strain.

Silence answered her.

Spinning around, she scoured the murky edges of the arena—through stalls, bleachers, and creeping shadows. "Eli! Eli, where are you?!" she shouted into the oppressive dark.

Mason turned, his jaw clenching with unspoken fury.

At the broken fence post where Eli had last stood, something small and silver glinted in the dust.

June sprinted to it, collapsing to her knees.

Eli's coin lay there.

But it was shattered.

Divided into two flawless halves, one edge still pulsing softly like the last gasp of a dying heart in her trembling palm.

Nettie stepped up to her side, her voice eerily devoid of shock or sorrow:

"He's been claimed. Left the stage, one way or another."

June's stare burned with accusation. "You knew this would happen."

Nettie met her gaze, eyes as hard and unyielding as iron. "Next is the Queen's Procession. That's when it truly begins."

Behind them, a sound began to surge—at first faint, then growing louder, metallic and heavy.

Hooves.

A rhythm, deliberate and relentless.

Not one horse.

Many.

From somewhere far beyond the twisted edges of the rodeo, past the half-lit midway, from fields where no trail had ever been etched— they were coming.

And looming in the distance, like a dark omen incarnate, the Ferris wheel began to churn once more.

This time, it spun with wild, frantic speed.

Each rotation flared into a violent burst of red and gold—a maddening beacon that seared the horizon with its unhinged glare.

June slowly stood, a grim determination replacing her despair.

Mason shifted beside her in silence.

The four of them—now three—stood on the edge of something that had long since abandoned the pretense of mere entertainment.

June's eyes fixed on the advancing dust, where ominous shapes began to emerge.

And with a voice scarcely louder than the howling wind, she whispered,

"We're not just caught up in this rodeo anymore... we're part of the act."

Chapter 10: The Queen's Procession

The final echo of Sheriff Mott's disappearance still clung to the air like scorched gun smoke—bitter, charred, absolute. And then, something far more terrifying took its place.

Silence.

Not a peaceful void, but a suffocating absence of possibility. No laughter. No breath. No movement.

It was a silence that whispered you weren't meant to exist under its oppressive weight.

June stood rooted at the edge of the arena, her eyes riveted on the slowly halting spinning hat that once crowned the sheriff. It had finally come to a stop.

Then, without warning, the dust on the arena floor began to rise.

At first, stray motes lifted aimlessly. Then they swirled into frantic eddies. There was no wind—yet the dust churned and contorted in midair, swirling like phantom smoke with no source.

And then it transformed.

Before their eyes, the airborne dust darkened and softened into delicate, lifeless petals—thin as whispers, weightless, and utterly dead. Dozens at first, then hundreds, descending like a mourning shroud draped over Still Creek.

Some crumbled instantly upon contact; others clung to trembling shoulders and parched lips, leaving behind a bitter taste of coal and iron.

And then—there were the bells.

Not pealing effortlessly through the heavens.

But emerging from below.

The ground trembled subtly—as if some monstrous entity was exhaling deep within the core of the rodeo grounds. The bell tones were low, muffled rumbles that vibrated up from the earth, shaking bone and marrow more than any noise could shatter eardrums.

DONG. DONG. DONG.

The sound did not merely command attention—it seized it.

All around them, the townspeople began to reappear—some crawling from beneath the bleachers, others shuffling out from the midway like sleepwalkers awoken from a haunted dream. Their faces were stony, eyes vacant and glassy, reflecting nothing but the crimson glare from the arena lights and the haunting spin of a distant Ferris wheel.

They moved with a mechanical inevitability, as if manipulated by unseen puppeteers.

They did not speak. They did not even glance at one another.

Instead, they drifted into prescribed lines and circles encircling the arena's heart, each person silently accepting their morbid destiny, guided only by the dark force pulsating beneath their trembling feet.

"Mason," June whispered, her voice a ragged thread of terror. "What's happening now?"

He remained silent for a heartbeat too long. His grip on the revolver tightened—a futile gesture in a situation where their weapons meant nothing. He scanned the mass and stepped toward a teenage boy dressed in a crisp white shirt and scuffed church shoes, his limbs slack, his face void of expression.

"Hey, kid," Mason called out cautiously, stepping closer. "You don't have to do this. We can leave— come with us."

The boy didn't falter in his pace.

Mason reached out and grabbed his arm—a firm, commanding hold with no trace of aggression.

The boy stopped dead in his tracks.

Then, slowly, he turned to face him.

His eyes were impossibly wide, the pupils swallowed entirely by unyielding blackness. When he spoke, his voice was not merely his own. It resonated with an ancient, knowing quality—a voice that belonged to something far older.

"She calls for us."

The words were soft yet seismic, echoing within the depths of their souls.

"You'll hear her too."

Then the boy pivoted and resumed his march, merging into the ever-tightening spiral encircling the arena's heart.

Mason staggered back, swallowing hard as dread clawed at him. "We've lost them," he muttered. "We've lost the entire damn town."

A slick, wet sensation slid down June's cheek.

She brushed it away.

It wasn't tears.

It was ink.

Dark, petal-shaped ink—which dripped from the heavens, the earth, from deep within her.

And still, beneath their pounding hearts, the bells relentlessly tolled.

DONG. DONG. DONG.

———

The circle was finally sealed. The townsfolk stood frozen around the central ring, their silhouettes thrown into sharp relief against the burning red glare of the Ferris wheel and the cascade of black petals— like plague-ridden snowflakes—drifting around them. June's grip on Mason's arm tightened until her knuckles blanched, her breath catching like a snare. The bells had fallen silent, leaving a vacuum of dread.

Yet something monstrous was approaching.

The very ground groaned—not a tremor, but a deep, agonized moan, as though the very earth were crying out in torment. Then, with a violent, unforeseen rupture, the soil at the far end of the arena split apart. It tore open with a sickening sound of wet leather ripping, yielding a jagged chasm that belched scorching smoke and searing heat. The crowd remained immobile—no whispers, no screams. They waited, hearts pounding in terrified unison.

From that bleeding wound in the arena emerged the Float. It did not roll; it ascended, as if pulled upward by unseen, gnarled hands rising from beneath the soil—a land that had longed for its morbid return. It was a creation birthed from nightmares, an abomination of rusted rodeo wagons fused with shattered wood and bleached-bone relics, forming a horrifying base. Jagged spikes of barbed wire erupted from every seam like the thorns of a vengeful,

239

dormant deity. Its wheels, like serrated gears, spun without ever kissing the ground.

It was alive. And it screamed softly—a sound that was equal parts lamentation and malignant glee.

Drawing the float behind it were four skeletal steeds, their flesh in tatters trailing in bloody shreds, ribs flung open like the secrets of broken altars. Their hollow eyes ignited with coals of furious fire. On their withered backs rode the Hollow-Eyed Riders—tall, unyielding figures clad in decayed parade garb streaked with corroded rust and dried blood. Their faces were vanished, replaced only by curling, jagged antlers wrapped in crimson ribbons that dripped like oozing, living wounds.

June's stomach twisted into knots. "Oh my God," she uttered in a trembling whisper.

At the pinnacle of this dreadful spectacle stood Her.

The Queen.

Tall. Immutable. Cloaked in a gown of moth-devoured silk the sullied hue of spoiled gold, threaded with shimmering, shifting runes that defied understanding. Her train trailed behind her like the slow unraveling of eternity.

And her face—

Her face was eerily familiar—it was her mother's, yet grotesquely altered.

Too unnaturally smooth. Too unnervingly serene. Immaculate, as if molded by a memory devoid of real warmth. Her skin radiated with an otherworldly light, her hair was woven with interlaced teeth and bloodstained ribbons, and her eyes...

They were raging tempests, a thousand furious storms none of them human.

She raised her head, lips parting to release a voice that belonged to no single soul. It was not hers alone, but a discordant symphony of women—a layered cacophony of weeping, laughing, and screaming that clawed at the very marrow of June's bones.

"The Midnight Rodeo has turned."

The crowd offered no reply—they needed not. They belonged to her.

"The ring no longer harbors your sins..."

With a single, bony hand—adorned with rings forged of obsidian, rust, and cruel human teeth—she elevated her threat.

The arena's dirt pulsed and shimmered with a dreadful red glow.

"It harvests them."

In a collective, fevered moan, the crowd swayed in a rapture of ecstasy. Several townsfolk crumpled to their knees, arms raised in either maddened praise or surrendered defeat. One man convulsed, foam erupting around his lips as the Queen's words carved into his mind.

The float began its slow, deliberate circle around the ring—drawn inexorably by the skeletal horses, each step exuding a haze of smoke that bled with every agonizing stride.

Mason's teeth clenched in defiance. "That's not your mom."

June's silence was an admission. She could not speak—because a part of her had believed, had dared to cling to hope—until she met those eyes.

Those hollow, empty eyes.

The Queen's head swiveled slowly, and her gaze latched onto June—not with recognition, but with a possessive declaration.

The float halted.

The bell tolled again—this time a titan's knell that shook the bleachers, splintered the ancient supports, and forced June and Mason to brace themselves against the slick, dust-coated fence.

And the Queen—this twisted version of June's mother—smiled with a cruel, unsettling grace, her lips parting in a smile that betrayed never having offered a single goodnight kiss.

———

The float settled into the arena like a malignant tumor, pulsing with a sinister, infectious rhythm as its bone-engineered core vibrated with a gruesome cadence. Overhead, the Ferris wheel writhed in reverse, jerking violently with every turn as though it were trying to unspool time itself.

Then a new force stirred.

From the shadows beneath the bleachers and the pitch-black gaps between the lanterns, clowns emerged—not frolicsome harlequins, but grim figures resembling cult priests or ruthless executioners in tattered, broken boots. Their faces, once smiles now smeared into grotesque masks of bone and melting latex, betrayed raw, unvarnished truths. Clutched in their grasp were black satchels and corroded urns—implements designed for collecting memories.

They advanced through the crowd in a precise, eerie silence.

Following in their ominous wake came the pale riders, antlered phantoms aglow under their dark cloaks, trailing tendrils of smoke and the acrid stench of scorched hair. With each step, the people withdrew as if a sinister force had swept over them.

The silent mandate was unmistakable.

Tributes.

Not of flesh—no, that would be tragically simple.

These were offerings of memory.

June watched, her stomach churning with dread as the town surrendered not only possessions but the very essence of its soul.

A woman stepped forward—a resolute figure, Marla Jessup, the seamstress. With trembling hands, she extended her wedding ring. The instant it met the outstretched palm of a waiting clown, it dissolved into a shimmering golden haze and ascended, absorbed into one of the glass jars dangling from the Queen's float like spectral dream-catchers.

Marla smiled weakly before turning to the man beside her—her husband—and her smile faded into a scowl.

"Can I help you, sir?"

Her words fell like a curse. For him, her name had become a relic of the past.

An old, hunchbacked man, his body shaking as if in perpetual agony, pressed a small music box into her hands. The clown nodded, winding it sharply once, unleashing a haunting melody that slithered into the air.

Instantly, the man's face contorted.

He spun toward his wife, fear and horror flooding his features as he cried, "Who are you? Where's Mary? I... I can't recall your song..."

She could only weep, clinging to him in desperation.

But he barely acknowledged her embrace.

Then a child approached—barefoot and eerily devoid of tears, as if she had long since emptied her reservoir of sorrow. Clutched in her tiny hands was a carefully folded crayon drawing of her family, set beneath a forlorn blue sky.

She surrendered it without hesitation.

As the paper was devoured by the jar, she opened her mouth to speak—only for the sound to vanish into a void.

Her eyes widened in terror. She scanned the chaos around her, panic etched into every line of her face.

She had forgotten how to speak.

June's breath hitched, caught in her throat.

Mason then shattered.

With a furious cry, he lunged toward one of the jars—its violet glow swirling with curling wisps of a woman's cherished memory. He recognized her instantly: Becca Langley, the beloved teacher.

In a blind surge of rage, he smashed the jar with the cold, heavy butt of his revolver.

The blast of shattering glass was accompanied by a scream—not from the jar, but from the Queen herself.

Behind Mason, Becca gasped, clutching at her chest.

"I remember—my baby—my baby! You stole him! You stole—"

Before her words could fully form, a clown, emerging silently from the shadows, plunged a needle of bone into his side.

Mason collapsed, teeth clenched in searing agony, his eyes wide with unspoken torment.

June rushed to him, scraping through the dirt to shield his crumpled form.

Blood blossomed across his shirt, a macabre bloom.

With warped resolve, he looked up, gritted teeth managing a desperate whisper: "Don't… let them erase you, June…"

She supported him, staggering backwards as clowns encircled them—nailed in silent vigil. They struck not, only watched with predatory patience.

Then Nettie stepped forward.

Unyielding, unbowed, she moved as if entirely forsaken by fear and grief.

The clowns hesitated as she advanced, uncertain how to confront such a force of defiance.

She stared up at the Queen, who loomed aloft amidst the madness, arms raised like a malevolent conductor orchestrating oblivion.

Nettie's voice, raw and ragged yet resoundingly clear, tore through the dissonance:

"You already took what I cherished. You took her. You stole my sister. You'll claim nothing more unless you earn it, witch."

The Queen tilted her head in slow, deliberate calculation.

And then, she smiled.

Not with warmth, but with a ravenous hunger.

For a breathless, suspended moment, the glow of the jars dimmed.

Then it flared back—brighter, fiercer than ever.

More souls stepped forward into the sacrifice.

The cost was rising, inexorably, as the jar filled to the brim with names destined to be forgotten.

——

The air turned oppressive, each breath a struggle—like dragging smoke through splintered, shattered glass. The cascade of black petals had ceased, and the arena itself seemed to pause in trembling anticipation. At its very center, enshrouded by a blood-tinged miasma, the Queen lifted her arm, her skeletal fingers cradling June's stolen locket. It pulsed with a fierce, violent heat, casting jittery, twitching shadows across the arena—as if it were trying desperately to mimic the furious beat of her own heart.

"You were born under this cursed ring," the Queen intoned, her voice erupting in every register, from shrill to guttural, human to something monstrously other. "You bear my blood, my anguish, my undoing."

The ground itself convulsed beneath them.

All around, the arena began its relentless transformation. Bleachers elongated into nightmarish spires, twisting upward like jagged vertebrae clawing at a perverse heaven. The audience—mask-faced, soulless—clapped in a slow, discordant rhythm that chilled the marrow.

Behind them, the Ferris wheel screamed into a reverse frenzy, spinning with impossible velocity while erratic lights flared and bolts leapt like wild sparks. With every brutal turn, the skyline of Still

Creek writhed and contorted, its buildings bending and buckling like trees in a voracious inferno.

Beneath June's boots, the familiar earth cracked open to reveal ancient glyphs buried just below—blood-red symbols etched in bone ash, pulsing with a serpentine, ominous rhythm. The ring was no longer a mere stage—it had become a womb of torment, a crucible of fate, a searing throne of damnation.

June advanced, her mind ablaze with static and her heartbeat echoing the frantic pulse of the locket. It wasn't mere walking; it was as though the Queen's voice, like a sinister lullaby, compelled her forward. She passed Mason, whose trembling fingers reached out in a desperate plea, silenced by overwhelming dread. Nettie's lips moved in mute agony.

Then the world dimmed—before the vision struck her like a bang, a raw, violent reality crashing sideways into her skull. She stood in the arena once more, not in the present but many agonizing years ago. The terrain was arid, the air heavy with the stench of hay and gasoline. There were no clowns, no aberrations—only her mother, solitary in the center of the ring, sweat beading on her brow, eyes blazing with unyielding defiance.

In her hands was a crown forged from twisted antler, cruel wire, and ancient gold rodeo coins—each coin etched with a perpetual, blood-curdling scream. Clutched in one hand was a match, futilely attempted to ignite the crown's destiny, yet the wind maddeningly refused to give life to the flame. And then the crown stirred—it slithered up her arms, coiling around her wrists, dragging her mercilessly to the earth. In desperate terror, she screamed June's name, and the arena swallowed her whole.

June jolted back to the present, gasping for breath. Now, the Queen stood at the edge of the float, the locket hanging inert in her grasp, while her other arm extended, palm open. Resting there was the crown, identical to the one in her vision: twisted antler, venomous black wire, and gold coins suspended in eternal, agonized scream.

The Queen descended with a predatory grace, each step etching a withered, charred boot print into the dirt. Reaching June, her voice was a silken promise of doom. "Wear it... or watch the town decay into rot."

June stared at the crown—it hummed with a vicious, insatiable power. All around her, the world leaned in with malignant intent; the riders, the demented clowns, the masked, soulless crowd, and even the very ring itself. One step forward... and everything would shatter beyond return.

———

The crown convulsed violently in the Queen's grasp—a living, breathing hunger pulsing in its core. June's eyes locked onto it, transfixed. The gold coins glinted fiercely, each one flashing with twisted reflections of friends, strangers, and even a tormented echo of herself, all contorted in raw agony. The wire coiled tighter, hissing dark promises too sinister to name.

The Queen tilted her head, her stolen face blazing with the fever of triumph. "All you have to do is wear it, child. Embrace what you were always meant to become." In her other hand, the locket pulsed like a desperate, final heartbeat.

June's fingers curled around the crown until its vicious thorns tore into her skin. With a determined heave, she raised it high. In an instant, the arena itself leaned in with malevolent anticipation. The clowns froze mid sway, the pale riders reined in their monstrous steeds, and the faceless, masked crowd watched with a breathless, dreadful expectancy.

Then, with one slow, resolute step... June stomped the crown into oblivion. The impact rang out like a cannon blast. Brittle antlers shattered, gold coins burst apart into a cascade of glimmering shards, and the barbed wire screamed, recoiling like a wounded serpent.

The arena erupted in a primal cacophony—not merely from the people, but from the very ground itself. The earth bellowed like an enraged beast, its cry tearing through the bleachers that shuddered and cracked like brittle, ancient bones under a scorched, blackened sun. The Ferris wheel howled, spinning out of control as its bolts shrieked against twisted metal.

The Queen staggered back as the force of the destruction ripped through her. Her beautiful, stolen face—the very visage of June's own mother—glitched and contorted. In one horrifying moment, kindness melted into a cruel, mocking reflection of June, and then morphed into something older, scaled, and skeletal, with teeth like shards of broken mirrors.

June staggered, her heart pounding like war drums and her hands bleeding from the remnants of the crown's cruel barbs. From deep within the crowd, a spectral figure flickered into view—Eli, or what was left of him. His form was fractured, like a stuttering VHS tape; half his face was missing, exposing a ghostly jawbone and a void of darkness, yet one searing, intact eye remained fixed on June.

He whispered through the maelstrom, "This isn't her true form. She's using you to anchor herself." The warning sent a spike of ice through June's veins.

Behind her, Mason burst forward, seizing her wrist and yanking her away just as an unseen force cracked the very ground where she'd stood. "Come on!" he roared, dragging her toward the arena's edge where Nettie loomed—hunched over like a battle-scarred lioness. Nettie ripped off her glove, revealing a palm branded with an ancient glyph glowing an infernal orange, its lines twisting like barbed wire. With brutal force, she slammed her palm into June's shoulder, the burning heat searing through her shirt.

June's cry was swallowed by a surge—a barrier forming, cutting the Queen's oppressive pull as if a part of it had shattered. She staggered upright, breaths coming in ragged bursts, eyes aflame with defiant fury.

Above the wreckage of the shattered crown, the Queen—whatever monstrous guise she truly wore—stood, screaming a soundless torment as her glitching face fought to reclaim control. June stepped forward, her gaze locked onto the cursed entity, and in a voice razor-sharp and low, declared, "If I bear your blood, I'll use it to drain you dry."

The Queen's scream erupted—not as a sound, but within the very minds of those present. Far above them, the Ferris wheel convulsed in a disturbed dance—its lights flickering, its metal warping grotesquely—until, with a deafening, shattering crack, it exploded, scattering a thousand tons of twisted iron into the void.

From the splintered hub poured forth not a creature, not a person, but a sound—a primordial scream that began as a low rumble, barely perceptible, then grew louder, swelling into a horrid, all-consuming wail that tore at the edges of reality itself. It was the cry of something ancient—too old to be born, yet ravenous, restless, and ready to ride into the consuming darkness.

Chapter 11: Broken Arena

The arena erupted in a cataclysmic burst behind them, showering ash and molten iron as Mason, June, and Nettie tore through a jagged rip in the fence, hacking up choking clouds of black dust with every desperate breath. Each step seared the scorched remains—the shattered bones of the rodeo's illusion splintering under their boots like brittle glass.

The Ferris wheel screamed its final death cry, its final shuddering turn collapsing into chaos like a drunkard crashing into a gutter. Flaming spokes plummeted from the sky in agonizing, apocalyptic arcs.

June barely dove clear as a massive shard of debris fell, her heart hammering wildly against her ribs.

"Go, go, go!" Mason roared, yanking her wrist and hauling her upright with raw urgency.

They raced across the barren dirt field, lungs burning, the charred carcass of the rodeo smoldering behind them—and an unknown terror looming ahead. The black petals had vanished, replaced by deep, burnt footprints gouged into the earth like the mad scribblings of a deranged cartographer. They spanned in every possible direction—into the suffocating woods, toward the flickering phantom lights of Still Creek—twisting into maddening patterns that blurred June's vision when she stared too long.

Every scorch-marked print smoldered at its edges, as if its maker was still caught in a relentless, unfinished inferno.

Nettie skidded to a halt at the tree line, her breaths ragged. "This isn't just about the rodeo anymore," she rasped, fear and fury mingling in her voice. "It's devouring the whole damn town."

Still Creek stretched out before them—distorted, fractured like a painting ruined by a violent storm. Streets jittered like faulty film reels; buildings leaned and contorted into impossible angles when not looked at directly, while streetlights sputtered overhead like dying stars. From a cracked side street came the warped, nightmarish jingle of a carousel, its notes scraping against their nerves like shattered glass.

The midway—with its twisted booths and blood-spattered rides—bled into the town's edges, infusing its streets, yards, and even the very bones of Still Creek with sinister intent.

Mason dropped to his knees, hands clutching his chest as he desperately fought for breath. "We're running out of time."

"What the hell are we supposed to do?" June gasped. "This whole place is—"

"—infected," Nettie interjected grimly. "It's like a festering wound that just won't close."

They exchanged haunted glances—bloodstained, battered, and exhausted—yet still breathing. Still fighting.

Mason pushed himself up, his face set in hardened determination. He slammed a fresh round into the battered revolver with a force that echoed through the chaos. "We find something real. Something that can wound Rook. Hurt her. Something alien to this nightmare."

June's nod was fierce, fists clenching as the blood from her crushing blow to the crown still pulsed and the Queen's shriek burned in her ears.

Nettie stepped back, her expression tightening into grim resolve. "I can't follow you right now," she stated firmly, voice low and unwavering. "There's something I buried. Or maybe it was buried for me."

Mason began, "Nettie—" but she cut him off, eyes cold with unmistakable finality.

"I have to remember. If we don't unearth the full, brutal truth, we're merely rearranging deck chairs on the Titanic." With that, she pulled a small, rusted charm from her pocket, pressed a tender kiss to it, and tucked it deep into her coat. "Meet me at the courthouse. If I'm not there by sunrise... finish it without me."

257

Before anyone could protest, Nettie spun on her heel and sprinted toward the dying edge of town, her form vanishing into the shifting mists and snarling shadows.

Mason cursed under his breath. "Damn stubborn women."

June managed a tight, resolute smile through her terror. "You're the one who's always chasing after us."

He chuckled bitterly and scanned the desolate road ahead, where the ghost of Still Creek loomed ominously. He suddenly pulled her into his embrace, eyes locking with hers, their lips meeting passionately. "Come on," he muttered with a glint of mischief, eyes burning with relentless determination. "If we're gonna die, let's at least make it unforgettable."

Together, they plunged forward—chasing the scorched footprints that burned a trail into an uncertain future, each step fueling a hope that was fading faster than they could grasp it.

———

The house was a scar on the landscape, worse and more foreboding than memory could recall. Mason and June stood in the dying light, eyes locked on the collapsed porch and the roof that, with its peeling, skewed lines, betrayed decades of decay. Old Man

Thompson's home—once an odd, benign relic—now lurked like a carcass waiting for the grave.

"He's gone," June hissed, her voice a trembling wisp in the gloom. "Just… gone."

Mason's jaw set into a harsh line. Mysteries unsettled him; he thrived on concrete clues—suspects, evidence, the cold precision of a crime scene. This was something darker, something far beyond the realm of simple disappearance.

"Maybe he ran," he ventured, his tone flat and empty of conviction. "He must have known what was coming. Did he say anything else?"

June's head shook, her eyes haunted. "No, but you're right—he knew. The old man wasn't caught off guard by this chaos."

The air reeked of ancient wood mixed with a tang of fresh decay—the scent of rusted iron bleeding into damp, sodden earth. They forced the creaking front door open; its protesting whine echoed like a dying cry.

Inside, the house was a mausoleum—emptied of life rather than abandoned. The furniture lingered, yet every surface and every room had been scrubbed squeaky clean of any human presence. Family portraits had vanished from the mantle, and the curtains hung as if mourning their lost purpose. Even the dust seemed disturbed, as if it carried the memory of unseen, sinister movements.

The house listened.

"We were here just days ago—what the hell happened..." Mason murmured, disbelief ringing in his voice as he took in the lifeless scene.

June advanced warily through the living room, her fingertips skimming over the brittle remnants of an armchair. "We need clues," she whispered urgently. "Any sign of why he vanished."

Mason's hand hovered near the cool steel of the revolver tucked against his hip as they split up, combing through drawers and checking closets. That's when June's eyes caught something peculiar.

Across the far wall stood a pristine glass case, miraculously immaculate even when everything else lay stripped bare. Inside, a single plaque gleamed under a suffocating film of dust:

"For when the Devil rides."

The case was empty.

June's skin prickled as if every hair had been electrified.

"Think that's a clue?" Mason muttered as he joined her side.

"It's more like a damn warning," she replied, voice tight with unease.

Their search led them to the fireplace, its structure half-collapsed into itself. Mason kneed aside a loose brick, sending a cloud of ashen dust swirling into the stagnant air. In that dust, June's flashlight caught a barely perceptible seam in the stone—a detail so out of place it screamed of hidden purpose.

"Hold on," June commanded softly. She knelt and, with a determined yank, pried a loose slab free, exposing a concealed iron ring. Their eyes met in a silent exchange of grim resolve.

"No guts, no glory," Mason growled, and together they tugged. The hatch protested with a shriek that reverberated through the lifeless corridors of the house.

Below lay a narrow, choking cellar, a cavern of shadows and damp that reeked of long-forgotten graves. They descended inch by agonizing inch.

At the bottom, in the wavering beam of their flashlight, something impossible took shape: a rifle, suspended in stark contradiction to both modern ordnance and antique relic, its presence otherworldly. Its stock, hewn from wood that shimmered with an oily black sheen, was etched with silver glyphs spiraling into veins of pulsating black opal. It exuded an icy aura that seemed to carve into the marrow.

Scattered beneath it, strewn across the dirt floor, lay yellowed sketches, battered maps, and feverish journal entries rambling about the Midnight Rodeo, the Ring, and the enigmatic first Rook. June crouched, her voice trembling as she read aloud:

"The Devil rides when the ring is broken. The first Rook fell by Griefwine—sorrow distilled. Only a willing sacrifice carries the shot."

Mason's brow knit in confusion and dread. "Griefwine? What in the hell is that?"

June flipped the brittle page and her heart seized in terror. Rendered in shaky, desperate lines was an arena—a spectral coliseum—adorned with glyphs and a bullet immersed, almost alive, in a vial of dark, viscous liquid. Scrawled in massive, irregular letters were the words:

"Break the ring. Bleed the anchor."

Her blood turned to ice.

Lifting the rifle, June felt an unnerving sensation: it didn't shun her touch, it embraced her, as if it had been fated to wait for this moment.

"This isn't just about Old Man Thompson vanishing," she said, her voice a mix of awe and horror, staring down at the dark gun cradled in her trembling hands.

"He knew what was coming. He left us the only thing that could stop it."

Mason stepped to her side, his jaw clenched tight enough to break. "If grief's the price... we've got plenty to pay."

Above them, the sound of a distorted reality thickened—a twisted cacophony of metal tearing apart and children's laughter morphing into savage howls. Time was running out.

And now, in their trembling grasp, lay a weapon that promised devastation. But the cost—oh, the cost was yet to be measured.

———

The house seemed even smaller now, a tight, collapsing reminder of its former self. It sagged in on itself, tired and battered by a storm that felt more like a curse than a downpour. Nettie Carson stood before the crumbling porch, her elongated shadow wavering under a bloodred twilight. Each shallow breath felt like a battle against a world whose skin was closing in.

She hadn't been here in what might have been months, or perhaps years—time had become a fickle, untrustworthy companion. With hesitant resolve, she touched the door; it creaked open without protest, as if the lock had long since ceased to fight. Inside, a heavy silence greeted her. The house remembered every sorrow—even if she struggled to do so herself.

Every step on the creaking floor mirrored the turmoil inside her. Her boots dragged over memories left in the dust, while her hand grazed a banister thick with the weight of forgotten days. Peeling wallpaper, like old, scabbed wounds, revealed remnants of a night filled with fire, raised voices, and the unbearable loss of something cherished. The echoes of that night seeped from the walls, blurring past and present until they mingled like rising water.

In the flickers of her memory, she saw a younger version of herself—lips pressed into a tight line, fists clenched in anger—locked in a silent battle with a shadow crowned by the wild arrogance of a rodeo king. In another flash, June's mother—her own sister—stood resilient and unwavering, a blazing beacon amid the nightmarish chaos. The walls seemed to pulse, and the kitchen swirled around her, the house singing a language of memories that were as painful as they were familiar.

Stumbling into her old bedroom, Nettie was swarmed by scents of cedar and bygone days. The dresser slumped against the wall with a drunken tilt, and a cracked mirror fractured her reflection into a hundred broken selves. There she stood, shivering from more than the cold—a shiver born of deep, inner conflict.

A half-remembered nursery rhyme wound its way back from the depths of her mind, a haunting refrain:

"When the Devil rides and the wheel turns black,

Find the place he can't crawl back.

Behind the pane, where memories sleep,

Lies the blood, the tear, the secret you keep."

With eyes closed, Nettie surrendered to the house's dark guidance, grappling with the remnants of a past she both yearned to escape and desperately clung to. Pushing aside the dresser with trembling strength, she felt dust and grief swirling around her. Her hand, searching along a cracked wall, discovered a seam—a small, familiar panel. With a press, the old hinges groaned, and a hidden compartment creaked open.

Inside lay a bundle of tattered journals, all tied together with a faded black ribbon; a small, rusted tin held yellowed scraps of parchment, soaked with time and something far darker. At the very bottom, wrapped in weathered oilcloth, rested a single sheet of brittle paper, scrawled in a dark, ruddy ink that whispered of forbidden truths. The name at its center struck her like cold water: Ezekiel Rookman.

Nettie's breath came in a staggered hitch. That name pulsed with a dangerous promise, as if speaking it would awaken what she had long tried to bury.

Below the name, in frantic, broken handwriting, the ritual was laid out:

Break the Ring.

Bleed the Anchor.

Sever the Queen's hold through willing sacrifice.

Bind the unbound with sorrow given freely.

Her vision wavered as conflicting emotions roiled within her. The very walls of the house quivered, and for an agonizing moment, she saw everything—the true, brutal memory unfolding. The night of her escape from the rodeo flashed before her eyes. It wasn't a matter of sheer luck or raw strength. It was her sister—June's mother—a woman who had selflessly taken Nettie's place. She had stepped right into the heart of the Queen's circle, into that merciless ring of sacrifice, trading her own future for Nettie's fleeting chance to run free.

Nettie recalled screaming, fighting, begging even, while her sister only offered a wry smile and whispered, "You're the strong one. You'll remember for both of us." And then... silence, a void where love and loss tangled in unresolved regrets. Rook had swept away the truth, burying the unbearable memory under layers of dust and time. Until now, when the floodgates of buried agony burst open.

Falling to her knees, Nettie clutched the journals tightly, sobbing into the settling dust. In that raw moment of clarity, she saw that June wasn't merely a survivor or an unlucky soul—she had been molded by destiny, born within that cursed lineage, too close to the ever-hungry ring. And now, unless the cycle was broken—unless the chains of ritual were shattered—June would be consumed, claimed entirely by the Queen, transformed into a fresh anchor of sorrow, a new blood price paid in full.

With determination mingled with inner torment, Nettie wiped away her tears roughly and gritted her teeth. No more running, no more choosing to forget. She tucked the journals and the ritual safely into her coat, cast one last conflicted glance around her haunted house, and stepped out into the bruised evening. Outside, the wind carried a fractured carousel tune, echoing the conflict of her soul.

She had a war to fight, and a debt of memory and sacrifice to finally repay.

————

Ash tumbled like cursed snow over the midway, a relentless, choking pall that smothered every jagged booth and creaking ride. It clung to the fractured carnival—adhesive to the splintered booths, to the sagging rides, to the skeletal ferris wheel that groaned as if in agony against a bleeding, bloodstained sky. The deranged carousel convulsed in mechanical suffering, its once-proud horses now snarling in silent torment as their forms melted into the scarred, broken earth.

Through this hellish wasteland staggered Eli Boone. Or what remained of him. Each step convulsed his body in tortured shudders. Red and white face paint oozed from his pores like rancid war paint, seeping down his cheeks as if it were the blood of battles he never chose to fight. His hands had betrayed him—transformed into monstrous appendages with spidery, twisted fingers that writhed like something out of a nightmare.

Inside his skull, a swarm of maddened whispers buzzed with feral intensity—a hive of deranged voices bent on obliterating his sanity.

"Smile, smile, boy."

"Juggle your sins, dance for the Queen."

"Forget your skin, forget your soul."

He fought back with every ounce of his being, clenching his teeth until blood seeped from the fractures in his gums, each drop a testament to his desperate battle for control over his crumbling mind.

Around him, a legion of other clowns swayed and lurched—soulless marionettes trapped in an eternal, grotesque pantomime. They clattered invisible cymbals with hollow applause, weeping bitter black tears as they marched in a fevered trance under the Queen's silent, tyrannical command. Most of them were empty husks, vanished identities in a sea of decay.

But then... one clown stood apart.

Emerging from the chaos, Eli stumbled toward the shattered ring-toss booth, where a lone clown leaned nonchalantly against a battered post—defiant. Not advancing in blind obedience. Not drooling in submission. Not cowering. This clown sported a tattered red coat and a bowler hat half-devoured by flames. His mouth was stitched into a gruesome, bloody grin, yet his eyes burned with a wild, unapologetic fire. With a slow, deliberate wink, he locked eyes with Eli.

For one heart-stopping moment, the maddening whispers faltered. The clown tipped an invisible hat, then spoke in a voice that shattered the madness—a voice as clear, as cutting, as thoroughly human as it was fierce. "They think they own you, boy. But coins always turn. And I kept the other side."

Eli's stomach contorted in searing agony as his already fractured mind reeled. The coin—the damnable, burning curse the clown had given him at the very start—was more than a trap, more than just a brand. It was a key. If he could cling to it, if he could salvage even the last remnants of who he once was, maybe he could defy his fate.

Gritting his teeth, Eli staggered to his feet, gasping in ragged breaths. His half-painted hands trembled violently, curling into punishing fists. With trembling resolve, he clutched the shattered fragment of the cursed coin—the shard that had fallen after the stampede—and tucked it close to his heart beneath his jacket.

The mysterious clown bestowed upon him a solemn nod before melting into the ash-laden void. And in that charged, burning moment, Eli understood something vital: not all clowns bowed slavishly to the Queen. Some only feigned subservience until they could strike at the very core of tyranny. A quiet rebellion simmered in the nightmare, a brutal war waged in the shadows.

Even as he stood broken and half-transformed, Eli Boone realized he still had a vital role to play. With a twisted, defiant, bloodstained grin, he spat out, "You want a clown, Queen? You're about to get the wrong damn one."

———

The courthouse towered before them like a shattered, malevolent fang set against a sky that hemorrhaged despair. Its clock tower stood broken, time forever arrested at 11:59 with hands twisted back in an agonizing mockery. Cracks festered across its walls like festering wounds, while tattered flags whipped violently in an unseen, savage wind. The building groaned under the weight of an ancient, cruel force—something far older and harsher than any law it had ever upheld.

Inside, Still Creek rotted with a malignant decay that seeped from its very soul.

And there, three solitary warriors stood in its dying shadow.

June stormed forward, boots slamming against the fractured pavement as if daring the past to challenge her. The rifle—a relic of Thompson's legacy, interlaced with grief and cold vengeance—was slung across her back, its stock relentless against the worn fabric of her jacket. Her hands trembled, not with fear, but with the searing certainty of what must be done.

Mason followed, limping from the brutal scars of the night's earlier battles, his jaw so clenched that the harsh grind of his teeth resounded like a death knell amid the ruins. His revolver dangled low, a grim symbol of his half-prayer, half-promise to defy the darkness.

Nettie brought up the rear, cradling the ritual journal to her heart as though shielding a wounded, vital secret. Her coat was torn along the sleeves, crusted with dried blood, yet her eyes—icy and unyielding— burned with steely determination.

They were the last flame amid the engulfing night—

And perhaps, the only hope left to ignite salvation.

Beyond the courthouse square, reality twisted into a feral nightmare.

The sky bled like a slit throat, while shadowed, twisted midways sprawled down the streets, devouring streetlights and paving alike. Buildings writhed in grotesque forms under a maddening gaze, and street signs scrawled eerie messages in languages not meant for human tongues.

On the horizon, as if spawned from the fury of a tempest, the Pale Riders emerged.

Silhouetted against a bruised, burning sunset, these monstrous figures rode forth—beasts with hooves that thundered like war drums, cloaked in tattered shrouds, their riders masked in cracked porcelain with antlers curling like the limbs of some dark, ancient deity.

There were many now—

Dozens swaying in a macabre dance, perhaps even hundreds, their forms pulsating as they waited, breaths held in dread anticipation.

It was as if the entire world held its final, gasping breath, bracing for the death rattle that would soon follow.

In the suffocating gloom behind them, Eli lurked in the shadows. Bent unnaturally between the innocence of his former self and the monstrous destiny the Queen had tried to force upon him, his skin flickered in streaks of deathly white and blood-red, even as his eyes blazed defiantly with a stubborn human fire. The shattered half of the ancient coin drummed against his chest like a forbidden heartbeat.

He was not yet lost.

And Still Creek was not beyond salvation.

June's gaze pierced the encroaching darkness as the weight of the rifle—a conduit of ancient, sorrowful power—grew unbearable in her grip. With every step, its gravity bore down on her, laden with the crushing cost of responsibility.

Still, she did not waver.

Turning to Mason and Nettie, with the looming silhouettes of the Pale Riders engraving scars upon the crumbling earth, she spoke in a voice low and unyielding:

"Still Creek isn't just dying," June declared, her eyes locked on the rifle with steely conviction. "It's being devoured—eaten alive by the very decay that surrounds us. And we might be the last ones left to tear it free."

The night swallowed her words, devouring them with an insatiable hunger.

And in the distance, the Queen began her relentless march.

Chapter 12: Breaking the Rodeo

The earth trembled violently.

Not with mere footsteps or the simple growl of thunder.

It convulsed with something ancient, monstrously heavy, ravenous.

Mason, June, and Nettie stood locked together at the crumbling courthouse steps, where their elongated shadows fractured across the shattered square.

From the east, the Pale Riders materialized.

First a few, their hooves battering the asphalt in a nauseating, relentless cadence. Then dozens. Then an onslaught—the riders robed in ashen cloth and patched leather, their masks twisted into grotesque porcelain grins, antlers gouging deep scars through blood-soaked air.

Streetlights overhead shuddered and died one by one as the Riders thundered past, their beasts exhaling clouds of smoke laced with metal shards.

Still Creek convulsed in terror.

The long-silent courthouse bell began pealing a death knell, each toll resonating without mortal hands.

June's grip on the rifle tightened until her knuckles blanched to bone-white. The weapon vibrated in her grasp—not from fear, but a fervent recognition.

It knew what was coming.

Beside her, Nettie frantically scoured the ritual journal, pages scrawled in rust-red ink blurring beneath her trembling fingers.

"The blood..." Nettie gasped, her breath hitching as the words leaped from the page. "It's reacting."

June's eyes slid downward—and there it was.

Blood—her own, still sticky from crushing the Queen's crown—had secretly seeped onto the ancient, yellowed pages.

The glyphs drank it in ravenous hunger.

Dormant lines ignited into fierce, blazing red, bursting forth like veins pulsing under a blacklight.

Mason spat a curse under his breath. "She's the catalyst," he muttered. "It's June. It's always been June."

The Pale Riders decelerated.

Their steeds exhaled curling black vapor. Heads turned unnaturally, each masked face honing in on June with predatory precision.

The weight of their stare bore down like a vice, squeezing the air from her lungs.

The nearest rider dismounted with a sickening lurch, his limbs bending in impossible, spidery angles, bones clicking in protest. In one calloused, gloved hand he dangled something sinister:

A noose.

Woven from human hair and tangled barbed wire.

He hurled it at June's feet without a word.

An offering.

An invitation.

The courthouse square plunged into a darkness as if a second night had fallen.

The Queen was coming—June could sense her ominous presence—storming in from behind her malevolent horde like a tempest with razor-sharp fangs.

Yet something stirred fiercely within June as well.

Not terror.

Not despair.

But incandescent resolve.

Nettie thrust the journal into her arms. "You don't have to," she choked out, her eyes wild with raw grief and burning fury. "You're not merely their pawn, Junebug. You're ours."

June met her gaze—unyielding and ironclad.

"I'm the one who has to end it."

Stepping forward, her boots clashed against broken stone. She abandoned the shattered town, the fractured past, and the listless promises.

She strode into the circle of Riders, into the snaring noose they had cast.

The rifle slung across her back throbbed with a rising, furious energy.

Above them, roiling clouds churned sickly yellow, as lightning seared jagged scars across the sky.

Deep within her, the Midnight Ring pulsed awake— an ancient force older than her mother, beyond Rook, transcending memory itself.

The lead Pale Rider surged forward to block her path, brandishing a rusted axe the size of a coffin lid.

Without even a flicker of hesitation, June raised her rifle in one smooth, cataclysmic motion.

BOOM.

The shot blasted through the rider like a seismic cannonball. The glyph-inscribed bullet shredded not only flesh but the very essence of his soul, disintegrating it into a tempest of ash and wailing agony.

The remaining Riders recoiled in a reckless huddle.

For the first time, they faltered.

For the first time, dread clawed at them.

June leveled the smoking barrel at them, her voice slicing through the rising tempest with unyielding defiance.

"I'm not here to die for you."

She cocked the rifle once more.

"I'm here to end you."

From behind the ruined courthouse, something vast and glittering stirred—

The Queen.

Half-hidden by the shadows, her silhouette draped in a gossamer of gold-threaded terror, a dreadful halo of screaming visages swirling around her like shattered moons.

And with her, came the final, unrelenting reckoning.

——

The square trembled under the relentless, bone-rattling pounding of hooves. Mason's hand lashed out for his revolver as June's grip on the rifle stiffened, her fingers trembling with the premonition of carnage. From the bleeding, dismembered line of the Pale Riders, a deformed bronco burst forth—a monstrous hybrid of beast and decaying metal—snorting searing steam and dragging jagged, broken chains like the toll of a death knell.

Atop this infernal creature sat a rider, a grotesque parody of man, his face half-hidden by a shattered porcelain mask splashed in sickly, ominous hues—a mirror of the Rook's malevolent glare, crudely mended with threads of filthy red. And in that grim moment, June recognized him immediately.

The bitter taste of bile flooded her mouth.

"Frank."

Not the Frank she had once kissed beneath flickering neon lights, not the Frank who had raced through Still Creek on a stolen bike, whiskey clinging to his devilish grin. This Frank was something twisted—a corrupted knight forged in unrelenting rage, seething regret, and the rot of his own decay. His bronco howled its wrath as it charged, unstoppable, straight for them.

Mason yanked June behind him, gun raised like a final barricade. "He's not coming to talk," he snarled through gritted teeth.

The bronco bucked with savage fury, hurling Frank into the air until he crashed hard against the shattered pavement, his body crumpling into a crouch as if surrendering to the inevitable. His fractured, masked visage lifted toward June, hollow eyes burning like branding irons incinerating all hope.

With a deliberate, chilling motion, Frank drew a rusted blade from his belt—not with hesitation, not with any vestige of recognition, but with pure, vicious intent.

Before Frank could close the distance to June, Mason surged forward. The two collided like living battering rams—fists, blades, and raw, bone-shattering fury intermeshed in an explosion of brutal combat.

Frank fought with the cunning brutality of a cornered beast—aiming savage, ruthless blows at Mason's throat, his knees, his gun hand. A jagged cut blossomed along Mason's ribs while another gash tore across his forearm; every strike was a promise of agony.

Mason staggered under the barrage, ducking, blocking, and countering desperately.

"You son of a bitch!" Mason roared between furious strikes, but Frank only grinned—a splintered shard of madness tearing across his face beneath the ruined mask. A savage punch to the gut sent Mason reeling, and Frank pounced, smashing Mason's revolver from his grasp and kicking it across the pavement like a discarded toy. Lifting his jagged blade as though it were a scythe of death, he moved in for the kill.

June screamed. "FRANK!"

That single, desperate cry allowed a moment's pause—a heartbeat in which the knife's deadly thrust wavered. It was all the opening June needed. The Griefwine rifle recoiled harshly against her shoulder and then exploded in a thunderous BOOM, the glyph-etched bullet slamming against Frank's chest. The impact just grazed him, yet it unleashed a cascade: the shattered Rook mask burst apart in a cloud of splintered porcelain and ashen dust.

Frank staggered, his breath coming in desperate, gasping bursts.

In that fleeting heartbeat, June saw him—the man beneath the monster, the Frank who once had swept her away from the drudgery of small-town life, only to plunge her into deeper damnation.

Frank's eyes, wild and brimming with raw, desperate humanity, locked onto hers as blood bubbled around his cracked lips.

Staggering a single step closer, he rasped, "Tell her... tell her I tried... I tried to save her..." His voice was a raw, broken whisper, and then his knees buckled as he crumpled face-first into the dirt, lifeless.

The bronco let out one last, keening shriek—a horrifying lament of metallic death—and collapsed into a smoking, steaming wreck behind him. Mason, panting with the weight of fury and loss, retrieved his fallen revolver and stood in grim silence over Frank's broken body.

There was no mourning here, only the cold necessity of survival.

June stood immobilized, the smoking rifle sagging uselessly in her arms, as her past—what little she had left—bled out in dunes of regret and blood. Overhead, the looming, relentless silhouette of the Queen's army swelled ominously, and the Ring pulsed violently beneath her skin, demanding her blood.

The final, apocalyptic battle had only just begun.

———

Ash rained down like inky black snow over the twisted, forsaken midway, each flake smothering the world beneath a velvet shroud of decay and death. Eli Boone stumbled through this apocalyptic blizzard, a creature in limbo—no longer wholly human, yet not fully transformed into the monstrous abomination he was becoming. His torso spasmed with erratic, inhuman convulsions; limbs contorted into grotesque, elongated claws. The clown makeup that once adorned him now seeped like malignant

283

ooze from every pore, an unmistakable sign of the malediction that ravaged his very soul.

Inside the confines of his skull, a chorus of deranged voices exploded, shrieking in cruel unison. "Smile, Eli. Dance, Eli. Die, Eli." Their spectral claws raked ferociously at the remnants of his consciousness, unearthing memories he had battled fiercely to preserve. The cursed face paint constricted over his features like a sentient mask, both binding and suffocating him with every passing second. Overwhelmed, he crumpled to his knees, a spattering of blood and ash mixing on his skin, a grim testament to his internal war.

Around him, the midway groaned under the weight of its ruin—rusted rides convulsed in futile rotations, and the remnants of long-dead neon lights winked mockingly in their flickering dance. In the distance, the forlorn sound of a courthouse bell tolled a discordant, fragmented knell—a prelude to the end of the world itself.

Eli was teetering on the brink of oblivion. Yet then—a glimmer caught his eye amid the swirling vortex of smoke and ash. There, barely perceptible against the dying light, lay a fragment of chrome glinting like a forlorn memory, its surface marked by a shard of deep, electric blue paint. With eyes narrowed through the veil of blood and dust, he dragged himself forward, each agonizing step a desperate bid for salvation.

His fingers clawed through relentless mounds of ash intermingled with brittle bone shards and splintered wood. And there, emerging from the decimation, was his motorcycle—half-entombed by the debris, half-doomed to the consuming flames of despair. Yet it persisted, a tangible relic amidst the ruins, a defiant symbol of hope.

In that moment, Eli's heart shattered open like a wounded animal, spilling torrents of raw, visceral emotion. He pressed his bloodstained hands against the pitted, scuffed metal of his bike, and a single, ragged sob burst forth—a cry that resonated more with the wildness of a beast than the vulnerability of a man.

A flood of memories crashed upon him with relentless force: his father's steady presence behind him as a teenager, guiding his tentative hands onto the throttle while a gruff laugh rang in his ears— "Give it hell, son. Don't let the road scare you." He recalled summer nights filled with dizzying speed down dirt roads, the stars blazing fiercely overhead like watchful guardians, and the comforting presence of a warm beer tucked into his jacket. The image of Rachel appeared, her arms a haven wrapped tightly around his waist, as they raced down endless backroads toward nothing but the promise of freedom, away from a life destined to imprison him. These recollections were fragments of the life he once dared to believe in, the life he clutched desperately as his future.

But even as these memories surged, the deranged clown voices intensified, their guttural screams growing ever more desperate and furious. The ceaseless grip of the paint slithered tighter across his skin, an oppressive force determined to pull him back into that abysmal nightmare. With a defiant roar that transcended the boundaries of human sound—a sound torn from the depths of despair—Eli gouged at his face with his own bloodied, twitching fingers. He tore the cursed pigment away in ragged strips, each rip a searing agony that scalded as though fire rained upon his flesh, peeling his skin raw and making him feel as if he were tearing pieces of his soul away.

Yet, driven by sheer will, he pressed on through the torment. Tears mingled with the ash on his cheeks as his labored breaths punctuated the silence of the dying world.

"I'm still Eli Boone!" he bellowed, his voice a tortured crescendo against the choking sky.

"I ain't your jester, you rotted bitch!"

With that declaration, another strip of paint fell away, a crimson rivulet trickling down his neck as something inside him finally snapped free. The demonic whispers stuttered, their unholy cadence faltering as the spectral masks shattered.

Eli emerged from the ashes of his own despair. With a guttural snarl of rage, he hoisted the battered motorcycle upright. Cascading waterfalls of ash cascaded off its frame—each drop a testament to battles past. Though the ignition switch lay half-melted, the tires deflated and scarred beyond recognition, and the chrome marred by deep gouges, the machine growled beneath his touch like a wounded beast primed for a final, furious war.

He swung his leg over the seat with determined resolve, gritted his teeth into a snarl, and forcefully kicked the starter. The engine erupted into a relentless, guttural roar, shaking the very foundations of the midway with its violent clamor. Every malformed clown, still shambling in the engulfing dust, turned to face him; their hollow, wild eyes widened and their stitched, sinister mouths quivered in astonishment.

Eli revved the throttle once, then twice, unleashing a torrent of noxious smoke that howled from the pipes like a demon set free. A broken, bloodstained grin spread across his face as he steered the motorcycle toward the decaying courthouse square.

"Time to burn your whole damn circus down," he declared, his voice laden with fury and defiance.

In a cataclysm of tortured metal and a dazzling shower of sparks, the motorcycle surged forward, carving a violent path through the bleeding midway. Ash and fragmented nightmares were scattered in its wake as Eli Boone raced toward the courthouse, toward the battle that awaited him, toward the sole future still worth fighting for.

———

The courthouse square bled darkness and ruin into a bruised, screaming sky. Jagged pillars of smoke and debris tore across the heavens as the ritual glyphs under June's boots pulsed like a beating heart—sigils splattered in her own blood, carved by ancient transgressions and fiercer bargains. Nettie knelt in the rubble, her voice a ragged incantation from a crumbling journal, hands quivering with terror and desperate hope. Mason towered above them both, every muscle taut as he gripped his shotgun with a white-knuckled fury, eyes scouring the turbulent, swirling shadows.

At the edges of the square, the Pale Riders circled in slow, predatory arcs, wolves on the prowl waiting for the signal to frenziedly tear their prey to shreds. They were nearly upon them. Nearly prepared. Nearly—

Without warning, the very ground convulsed and split apart. A piercing sound, like innumerable needles lacerating soaked cloth, sliced through the charged air. From the collapsed husk of the courthouse emerged the Queen, stripped of pretense—no shimmering glamor, no deceptive beauty, only unyielding, brutal truth. She was a monstrous mosaic of the dead—her body crudely stitched together with gold thread and crimson, a patchwork horror of weeping visages and withered, gnarled limbs. Her eyes were fathomless voids, empty craters of relentless despair, and her crown of twisted wire and bone pulsed with names carved deep into its sinister roots—Still Creek names. June's family names.

Her shattered mouth echoed with a macabre choir, cackling in derision: "Did you really think you could bind me, little one?"

Mason, driven by raw instinct and fury, stepped in front of June, throwing his body into harm's way. "Stay behind me," he roared, voice like thunder, "No matter what happens!"

June barely began to protest when Mason's wrath cut her off. "You're the one who matters, June! The rest of us are nothing—we're expendable! For once, do as I ask!" His words seared through her soul; she knew he was right, the truth in those words churned her stomach. Still, she kept her ground, clenching her rifle tightly against her chest, defiance blazing in her eyes.

The Queen advanced, drifting closer with arms outstretched like a predator beckoning a stubborn, stray child.

"You're not here to battle me, child," she cooed, voice as silky and deadly as poison. "You're here to complete me."

The glyphs beneath June ignited, chains of bloodlit energy snapping around her ankles and wrists, shackling her with an agonizing precision. Every desperate struggle seared her flesh like liquid fire.

In a surge of raw desperation, Mason fired. A deafening explosion shattered the square—a furious roar that tore through the cacophony—but the buckshot met only empty, enchanted air, devoured by the Queen's mocking laughter. With a languid gesture, she dismissed Mason's futile attack, sending his shotgun cascading across the broken ground. Cursing, he lunged toward June, battling the malevolent chains that scorched his skin with cursed light as he fought to free her. "Let her go!" he bellowed, raw anger boiling over.

The Queen leaned in, her tone as sharp as a honed blade: "She can't go anywhere. She belongs to me."

At that, Nettie scrambled forward, voice cracking as she hurled desperate words from the ritual. The Queen's many faces contorted into mocking smiles as she regarded Nettie with a chilling tenderness.

"Your sister thought she was saving you," she snarled, tone dripping decay, "But she wasn't rescuing anyone. She was bargaining with fate."

The air thickened, alive with static, as the Queen unleashed her grim revelation: "The ritual was never meant to free this wretched town. It was devised to seal the bloodline forever. And you, child... are not merely the anchor."

June's blood ran cold as she froze in place. Nettie's face crumbled, horror unfurling in every line, while Mason's fists clenched until his knuckles bled, crimson droplets mingling with scorched earth.

"No," June gasped, voice trembling in disbelief. "What does that mean?"

The Queen's grin grotesquely widened, the stitched scars on her face writhing in a fevered glee. "You carry his cursed blood. You were bred for this—to be the final, sealing bond of the Rodeo."

Nettie staggered, collapsing to her knees with trembling hands roughing the dust, whispering brokenly, "My sister... She didn't save June. She condemned her."

Below, the glyphs beneath June's feet burned with blinding, violent intensity.

The Queen raised a gnarled hand, golden threads dripping and trailing like venom, poised to interlace June into the abomination of the Rodeo.

Without a second thought, Mason lunged—throwing himself between June and the vile Queen, arms wide in defiance, a man facing his own demise head-on. "You'll have to kill me first," he snarled, venom dripping from every word.

The Queen tilted her head in a baleful curiosity, and for one agonizing moment, the square held its breath—the Riders, the wreckage, even the shattered clocks paused in morbid silence.

Then, with a hiss that cut through the tension, the golden threads surged like malevolent serpents. With sheer determination, June gritted her teeth and hurled the Griefwine rifle toward Mason's feet.

"Use it!" she screamed, her voice cracking with raw anguish.

Mason snatched up the weapon at the precise moment a lethal thread sliced towards his throat. The rifle bucked in his hands, unleashing a burst of sorrow and unbridled rage that exploded into the Queen's malevolent midsection.

She shrieked—not from pain, but in furious, otherworldly rage—as the venomous threads recoiled, hissing like infernal snakes ignited in flame. In that fleeting, brutal moment, June tasted freedom.

They all tasted it.

But the Queen was far from vanquished—not yet.

Above them, the courthouse clock bellowed midnight as the sky fractured wide open. The true final act of this grim, relentless saga was just beginning, and in its merciless heart stood June—the living embodiment of the Queen's blood, bone, and damned destiny.

———

The Queen reeled back, black ichor sizzling from the gaping wound Mason's shot had ripped through her flesh. Golden tendrils snapped wildly around her, lashing the air like enraged, venomous serpents. She clawed at her shattered ribcage with savage talons, her stitched-together body convulsing as the damned souls trapped within her skin howled in unholy torment. Yet, bleeding profusely, she rose. Even broken, her smile burned with a defiant, frenzied madness.

As the last glyphs beneath June's boots ignited in infernal red, the Queen hoisted her tattered crown high and whispered in a voice woven from countless stolen tongues, "June Rookman."

The name crashed over them like a hammer striking the soul. Mason stood frozen, paralyzed in silence, while Nettie gasped and staggered backward, her bloodied hand shattering against her mouth. Even the Pale Riders wavered in their endless circling, their skeletal steeds pawing the cracked earth with uncertain fury.

The Queen's laughter erupted, guttural and relentless. "You are his heir, his daughter, the debt long overdue," she sneered, her words coiling around June like iron chains. "You carry the seed of the first betrayal. You are the heart of the Ring—its pulse, its prison, its key. You can never outrun what you are."

June's legs buckled, and she crashed to her knees, the Griefwine rifle slipping from her slack fingers and clattering uselessly onto the blood-slick ground. The glyphs at her feet pulsed faster, feeding hungrily on her despair, while inside her skull, her mother's voice screamed out in a relentless, maddening echo.

The Queen drifted closer, golden threads unraveling from her wounded form like demonic vines reaching out with sinister intent. Instinctively, Mason stepped in, his hands raised in sacrificial defiance, ready to lay down his life for her. Nettie, sobbing brokenly, crawled across the ashen stones in a desperate bid to reach June.

"No," June whispered, the sound crumbling beneath the weight of every shattering blow, "No, no, no..." Yet a brutal truth gnawed at her from the inside: her father was not some faceless ghost—he was the monstrous architect of the Rodeo.

With a grotesque flourish, the Queen extended her arms in a demented welcome, every stitched seam on her abominable body straining to contain her, "Come home, daughter. Come be what you were always meant to be."

And then—the roar.

A sound fiercer than the pounding hooves of the Pale Riders, louder than the Queen's maniacal laughter, more earth-shattering than a town's death.

Eli Boone burst onto the scene.

His motorcycle erupted into the square like a bolt of furious lightning—tires screaming, engine belching fire and smoke—smashing through the hulking figures as if scattering delicate, brittle dolls. He barreled straight toward June, weaving unflinchingly through collapsing glyphs and shrieking shadows until he skidded to a smoking halt beside her, his boots churning up clouds of searing black dust.

Without hesitation, Eli lunged, seizing the front of June's jacket and yanking her onto the motorcycle's back seat. Her world spun wildly as his defiant, bloodstained eyes locked with hers. "You're more than just his blood, June!" he roared over the chaos. "You belong to us, to Still Creek—you are YOU!"

Those words sliced through the bedlam, shattering the Queen's twisted spells faster than any bullet. In that moment, something inside June snapped open—a defiant liberation, unbound by blood, unchained from her name.

It was her choice.

She leapt from the bike, landing squarely on her feet. With trembling determination, she retrieved the Griefwine rifle from the ashen ground. The weapon hummed in her grasp, its heat burning like a living heartbeat against her skin. Rising slowly, with purpose burning in her eyes, she faced the enraged Queen. The golden threads lashed out in fury, but June did not flinch. She stood before her not as a daughter, not as a doomed sacrifice, but as herself.

"I'm not your daughter," June declared, her voice honed to steely defiance. "And I'm not your sacrifice." Lifting the rifle high, she watched as the sigils around her feet erupted into a blinding white inferno.

The Queen's scream fractured the sky, and with unyielding resolve, June pulled the trigger. The first shot shattered the very fabric of the world.

Chapter 13: The Shattered Rodeo

Still Creek didn't merely cease to breathe—it suffocated in a torment of its own decay. It hovered in a state of raw, agonizing limbo—caught between a death rattle that clawed at its very soul and a silence so fierce it drowned out any spark of life.

The sky itself had mutated into the ghastly hue of ancient bone, a choking, unholy gray that swallowed every stray beam of light. Dawn had bled into dusk without a single ray of sun, trapping the town in a suffocating, false twilight that burned like acid on the eyes.

A low, malignant wind stalked the ruined streets, a restless predator slithering through shattered doorways and drooping window frames, whipping ash into twisted, serpentine specters. The air reeked of burnt flesh, corroded iron, and an eldritch stench—something primordial and malevolent that had no place in the realm of men. Buildings hunched together like dying warriors, their frames collapsing under unseen weight.

Streetlamps convulsed in spasms of repulsive yellow light before snuffing out like dying hearts. Even the pavement pulsed with an ancient, ravenous hunger, vibrating beneath the sorrowful tread of broken boots.

Still Creek wasn't simply dying—it was decaying into oblivion, its identity rotting away piece by agonizing piece. At the far edge of Main Street, the Pale Riders loomed, motionless upon their emaciated steeds. Not even a trembling hoof disturbed their morbid stillness. Behind their shattered, antlered masks they surveyed the devastation like merciless judges—grim arbiters awaiting the final, inevitable condemnation. The black bones of their horses hissed against the frosty air, swirling mist rising from every exposed joint like the breath of specters. Their shadows elongated unnaturally, clawing across the fractured asphalt as if yearning to reclaim what once was.

They waited. Always waiting.

The few survivors—pitiful remnants of a once-living town—huddled along the sidewalks like abandoned dolls. Eyes were wide, empty voids of despair; slack mouths were frozen in mute agony; faces were smeared with soot and blood like grotesque masks of mourning. They stood shoulder to shoulder with deranged rodeo clowns and eldritch nightmares—as if the horror had seeped so deeply into Still Creek that human and monster had melded into one indistinguishable terror. Some trembling souls clutched rosaries, Bibles, and wedding bands as if in desperate prayer, while others only grasped at their own empty limbs, hollow with despair. The clowns grinned without mirth, their painted smiles cracking to weep a black, viscous ichor, their dead, starved eyes harboring only an insatiable hunger. It was impossible to separate the living from the damned.

June Weaver stalked through this pandemonium like a revenant, half-interred in the quagmire of decay. Her boots shattered broken glass and singed bone beneath each step. The Griefwine rifle, a pulsing beast at her shoulder, drummed a relentless heartbeat against her spine, a grim metronome counting down doom. Mason King trailed unsteadily beside her, his left arm looping around her neck as if tethered to a collapsing world. His breaths came in harsh, ragged gasps, leaving a trail of scarlet breadcrumbs along cracked, blood-soaked pavement. His revolver dangled loosely in his other hand, yet his eyes burned with the ferocity of one prepared to perish in combat.

Nettie Carson trudged just behind, her grip trembling on a battered ritual journal until her knuckles blanched like cast bones. Her lips moved in silent incantations, a litany of fragmented prayers disintegrating on her tongue.

And then there was Eli Boone—a beast incarnate—roaring down the ruined street on his sputtering motorcycle, which vomited foul black smoke. Blood clung to him like a second skin, his matted hair a testimony to neglect, his face—a canvas half-devoured by the cursed clown skin—set in a grimace of raw, defiant fury. With a single, guttural rev the motorcycle growled, a living monster challenging the oppressive void.

Together, they trudged down Main Street—their spirits the last feeble sparks in a town already starved of itself. The buildings on either side blurred in June's view, their forms contorting like grotesque wax figures melting under an infernal heat, only to snap back moments later before crumbling entirely under the pressure of a disintegrating time. Reality itself seemed to unravel, bleeding its very essence into the void.

The wind surged anew, transforming into razor-sharp squalls that lashed at them, carrying with it disembodied whispers—names, voices from the past that clawed at June's sanity. Friends. Neighbors. Echoes of voices long silenced, now pleading in despair from shattered doorways and gaping windows. "Stop," they urged. "Run." In a rasp that brooked no defiance, they murmured: "You can't win. You can't undo this legacy of ruin."

Still Creek was no longer besieged by mere malevolence—it had become a living, breathing Circle of Despair. Every crumbling brick, every scattered bone, every desperate heartbeat was part of the endless ring.

At the end of the street, beneath a sky devoid of mercy, a shape began to form—a figure emerging from the swirling chaos. A man in a dark, tattered coat and a wide-brimmed hat, he advanced with a lethargic inevitability. His boots struck the debris in a measured, final cadence that resonated against the shattered ruins. As the figure drew nearer, even the deranged clowns ceased their twitching madness. The Riders tilted their heads in eerie unison. The survivors trembled, rooted to the spot.

June recognized him before a single word fell from his lips, before he even unhurriedly raised his hand. Rook.

The taste of blood surged in her throat with bitter foreknowledge. Mason stiffened against her side, barely clinging to life, his pallor deepening into a grisly, deathly hue. Nettie's fingers spasmed over the journal, white-knuckled in terror. Eli's motorcycle growled a low, furious snarl, poised to burst forward. Still Creek itself clutched its breath in dread.

The end had arrived.

And it wore a familiar, merciless smile.

——

The shattered remains of Still Creek's Main Street lay in a deathly silence under a bruised, bleeding twilight, every fractured window and sagging awning trembling under the weight of the impending storm. They first caught sight of him as a dark, ominous shadow—a long coat whipping violently in the dry, maddening wind, his boots pounding the cracked pavement with a slow, relentless beat. Rook.

He advanced with a swagger forged by bitter memories rather than arrogance—each measured step a tribute to the once-familiar cracks of the street he'd once roamed alongside Nettie Carson, back when life was a precious coin just waiting to be risked. His hat, cocked low, plunged his face into deep, deadly shadows, yet his grin fractured the darkness like a sharpened shard of glass. Confident. Menacing. Unstoppable.

He didn't hurry. He didn't have to.

The small, battle-worn assembly—June, Mason, Eli, and Nettie—stood in the heart of Main Street, hearts slamming against their chests as though the very earth were holding its breath. When Rook finally spoke, his voice was a silken menace, smoothed by years but honed to a cruel edge.

"Well now… look at you," he drawled, his tone laced with scorn as he tipped his hat slowly. Golden eyes burned with a mocking fire. "Still standing. Still defying fate. Nettie, my dear, you always had a knack for stirring sentiment."

Nettie said nothing. Her eyes were hardened flints, her jaw clenched so fiercely it threatened to shatter.

Rook clicked his tongue like a master chiding a recalcitrant beast.

"Decades," he murmured, stepping closer with predatory grace. "Decades I gave you. Time to let go. Time to live. You could've been a queen, Netta. Ruling by my side. But you chose… the ashes."

He halted a few paces away, hat still clutched in his hand, his tousled hair whirling in the taunting wind. His smile melted away, replaced by something icier, older—even though beneath that frost lay a raw, wounded hurt.

"But here we are again, sugar," he whispered, his voice seeping with both regret and menace. "You and me. Just like that fateful night under the harvest moon… when you shattered your promise."

Nettie's hands balled into fists, her nails digging into her skin as if to anchor her resolve.

"I kept my promise," she spat, voice laced with heartbreak. "I paid a price you'll never understand."

A low, harrowing laugh escaped Rook—a sound twisted with regret and cruelty.

"Oh, I understand, darlin'. You traded me for her." His gaze slashed sideways, landing unflinchingly on June.

June stiffened as if a toxic weight had settled upon her shoulders, ancient and venomous.

"You really think it'll end differently this time?" Rook continued, words dripping like poisoned honey.

"Think you can outsmart the rodeo again?" His tone fell to a dangerously intimate murmur. "Blood answers to blood, Netta. You can't rescue her. Not from me. Not from what she owes."

He extended a gloved hand towards Nettie—a gesture that was both invitation and irrevocable decree.

"Once more, sweetheart. Come back to me. Reclaim the family you abandoned when you struck that deal so many years ago. Stand by my side—and I'll spare her." A pause stretched as his voice softened to a ruinous echo of tenderness that betrayed what might have been.

"I'll make her shine like the star you dreamed. I can give her that."

The air crackled with a suffocating intensity, every fiber of tension palpable. June's breath hitched, her heart pounding in terror. Nettie wavered, caught in a battle of memories and anguish—the long, sultry summer nights, whispered promises, and the searing cost of betrayal surfacing in a painful torrent.

But when she finally spoke, tears streaking across her grimy cheeks, her voice was resolute despite the sorrow.

"No."

One word—a heartrending death knell for the past they had both tried to bury.

Tears scorched her eyes, yet she never faltered.

"I'd rather watch this town burn than crawl at your feet again."

Rook's outstretched hand slowly clenched into a fist. For a fleeting moment, sorrow flickered in his eyes before it was extinguished by the hunger of the beast within him. The false warmth in his smile drained away, revealing only the predator beneath.

"Well then," he said softly, tipping his hat back onto his head, "I guess y'all made your choice."

Above them, the dying sun tore open the clouds, unleashing a seething darkness that bled across the sky like ink on death's canvas. The creatures of the rodeo leered and lusted in anticipation. The ground trembled, and the wind howled a mournful dirge as the pale rider's steeds neighed—a disquieting prelude as the final act began.

——

The wind fell eerily still, as if the very air braced itself for the conflict about to erupt. Ash hung suspended like frozen breath—each speck a silent witness to the brewing storm. Under the dying gray light of the bone sky, the figure before them morphed in a sudden, jarring shift. The confident swagger slowed to a halt, and the cruel grin that had once promised malice now faltered. Before their eyes, Rook's form wavered, flickering as if on a disrupted transmission, until the vicious young ringmaster they knew dissolved into the worn, battered shell of Old Man Thompson.

He stood amid the ruins of his old flannel shirt, boots caked in layers of dust from years of neglect, his hat trembling in weathered hands. Yet his eyes remained unchanged—those sharp, gold-flecked eyes that burned fiercely behind time-worn wrinkles.

Nettie staggered back, her mouth parting in a strangled gasp. "Thompson?" June whispered, stunned. Mason's hand jerked toward his gun in a reflexive motion, though hesitation held him captive for a heartbeat.

Old Man Thompson offered a tired smile—neither cruel nor mocking, but filled with a deep, aching sorrow.

"Always was me," he said, voice cracking like dry branches. "I kept a piece of myself hidden here. Buried so deep even I started to believe I was just another ghost rotting with the town."

Nettie's fists trembled as she glared at him. "You lied to me."

"No," Thompson said softly. "Not at first. I loved you, Netta. I loved this place. I loved what we could've built." Every crease on his face deepened with regret as he continued, "But the rodeo don't love," he murmured. "The rodeo don't forgive. It eats, and it twists, and it binds. I fought it for a time. Fought real hard. Hid myself away. But you can't outrun the blood forever." His gaze locked onto Nettie's with a raw, unshielded intensity.

"I never wanted it to come to this. I swear it. I shielded you as long as I could." Turning slowly, he faced June, Mason, Eli, and Nettie, his back bowed as though burdened by the weight of inevitable retribution.

"A price has to be paid," he said simply. "That's the law the Rodeo's built on. Always was. Always will be. And whether I do it or someone else does it, what's owed always comes around."

The ground trembled beneath them while the sky deepened into a hue of ruin.

"I'll give you a choice," Thompson rasped. He dropped his hat onto the cracked pavement and squared his shoulders, drawing a worn Colt from its holster. "One of you faces me. One draw. Winner decides what happens next."

His face twisted in pained acceptance. "I don't want it to be you, Netta," he said, so quietly it broke something in her chest. "But the Rodeo... it demands the challenge. If no one steps forward, it'll take what it's owed anyway. Not in blood. And not just yours. Your souls."

Silence seized the square as if defusing the charged air itself. Mason stepped forward first—no hesitation in his resolve.

"I'll do it," he said, voice low, firm, as he gripped his revolver.

"Mason—" June started, but he simply shook his head. "I ain't watching someone else bleed for me."

Thompson—no, Rook—nodded once in respectful acknowledgment. "I always liked you, kid," Thompson bowed slightly, momentarily transforming back into the younger Rook—a silent salute to an old code older than either of them could fully fathom.

They took their positions—ten paces apart, boots scuffing over the cracked, scorched earth like echoes of past battles. In that lingering stretch before the coming storm, every moment throbbed with the promise of bloodshed.

Rook and Mason locked eye's, the Ringmaster holding a gold coin. "When the coin hits the ground, we draw. Understood?"

Mason simply nodded.

A simple flick and the silver coin flipped end over end through the air then plummeted toward the street, the shiny perfect edge hitting the cracked asphalt.

Then—gunsmoke shattered the stillness of the sky. Mason's shot split the air, his hand trembling under the sting of blood loss. Rook's bullet found its mark— low and brutal—striking Mason in the side. With a guttural cry, Mason crumpled onto one knee, blood seeping into the dust beneath him, yet miraculously, he clung to life. It had not been a killing shot; Rook had intentionally spared him.

June screamed and surged forward, but Nettie caught her arm. Nettie's face was as white as the ash that surrounded them, her voice hoarse as she pleaded, "I'll go," she choked out, stepping forward with arms spread wide. "If that's the price, I'll pay it. Let the girl go. Let them all go."

Rook's weathered face, momentarily haunted by the ghost of his past, flickered with raw grief as he lowered his weapon. For a long, painful heartbeat, it seemed he might relent and accept Nettie's sacrifice. But then June broke free of Nettie's grasp.

Advancing steadily, her boots crunching on the unforgiving, cracked earth, she positioned herself between Nettie and Rook—standing as the barrier between what had been and what might be. With a voice as clear as a bell ringing through the dying world, she declared, "No." Her gaze, steely and unyielding, locked onto Rook. She had Mason's pistol in her hand, the Griefwine rifle lying next to her fallen lover.

"I challenge you."

Around them, the swirling ash roiled in chaotic fury, and even the sky seemed to hold its breath in anticipation. Rook's form wavered once more, shifting back into the younger man—the Ringmaster—with his hat casting deep, ominous shadows across his face. Yet when his eyes met June's, something unmistakably human trembled behind that golden glow.

"You sure about that, Junebug?" he said, the familiar nickname echoing like claws across her soul.

June stepped forward, chin raised high. "One draw," she said. "Just you and me."

Behind her, Mason gasped as he struggled to rise; Nettie wept silently, overwhelmed by despair. High above, Eli, astride his rumbling bike, revved the engine once—a grim promise that if June fell, he would ride headlong into hell after her.

Rook smiled—a slow, sad, monstrous smile that carried the weight of countless regrets. "Well," he said, tipping his hat in a weary salute, "ain't you just your mama's spitting image."

As the dust churned violently and the guns glinted ominously in the fading light, the wreckage of Still Creek bore witness once again to a relentless turn of fate—a wheel set ever onward toward fresh, inevitable bloodshed.

———

The world narrowed to a point—
Ash churning in a tight spiral around June and Rook, two figures standing alone at the broken heart of Still Creek.

Rook's coat flapped in the dead wind, his gold-flecked eyes never leaving hers. He spun a battered silver coin in his fingers, its surface glinting with unnatural light.

"You know the rules, Junebug," he murmured, voice like velvet over razors. "We flip... and draw on the fall."

He tossed the coin skyward with a lazy flick of his wrist.

It spun higher, catching the last flickering light of the ruined sky—
Tumbling end over end like the fate of the world itself.

But this time—
June didn't wait.

Her body moved on pure instinct, the iron pistol heavy and burning in her hand.

She squeezed the trigger just as Mason, blood leaking from his side, raised the ancient Griefwine rifle from where June had tossed it beside him as she rushed to his side earlier.

Their shots cracked out as one—
Boom.
Boom.

Mason's bullet struck first—clipping the spinning coin in midair with a spray of burning metal shards.

It shattered into a thousand glittering fragments, vaporizing in the space between life and death.

And in the same instant—

June's bullet slammed straight into Rook's chest.

The impact hit him like a god's hammer.

Rook's body arched backward, a violent convulsion that sent his hat spinning into the sky. Black ichor erupted from the wound in a geyser, spraying across the cracked pavement in writhing, serpentine rivers.

The street shook.
The sky ripped open.

Rook's form slammed into the ground with the force of a falling star, his scream—no longer human— shattering the windows of every hollow house lining Main Street.

The Pale Riders reeled back in shock.

For a frozen heartbeat, Still Creek held its breath—

And then all hell broke loose.

The Pale Riders roared like an unstoppable flood.
Scythes appeared in their bony hands, curved and
gleaming like crescent moons torn from the night.

They surged through the streets—
Slashing down every twisted clown, every malformed
monster birthed from the Midnight Rodeo's cursed
depths.

The rodeo clowns shrieked and flailed, but there was
no escape.
One by one, they fell—
Painted faces splitting like rotten fruit beneath the
Pale Riders' blades.

All but one.

Near the smoldering wreckage of the Tilt a Whirl, a
single clown remained standing—
Its painted smile sagging, its form shimmering.

Before their eyes, the clown convulsed, bones
cracking audibly—
And morphed.

Into a man.

Eli's breath caught in his throat.

"Dad..." he whispered, voice shattering against the
sunlight.

There, blinking in stunned confusion, stood Eli
Boone's father—whole and alive, but forever altered,

the faintest trace of the clown's sorrow still flickering behind his tired eyes.

And then—

Silence.

Still Creek emptied like a dying breath.

All the other townsfolk—their faces twisted in grief, terror, or longing—simply... vanished.
Gone as if they had never been there at all.
Erased from the dream.
From the nightmare.

The skies above burned away the last shreds of storm, leaving behind a startling, perfect blue—
Clear. Blinding. Indifferent.

Sunlight spilled over the wreckage like molten gold, illuminating the battered survivors standing alone amidst the ruins.

Just Nettie.
June.
Eli.
Eli's father.
And Mason—
Mason, blood pooling at his feet, propped against a shattered bench, his revolver slipping from his grasp, yet a stubborn fire still raging in his battered chest.

They were all that remained.

Still Creek was silent.

Too silent.

No birds. No breeze.
Only the distant ticking of the broken clock tower, counting down to something none of them dared name.

June lowered the Griefwine rifle slowly, her arms trembling under the enormity of what they had done.

Nettie stood at her side, silent tears tracking down her dirt-smeared cheeks, staring at the black-stained pavement where Rook—where Thompson—had finally fallen.

And Eli...
Eli staggered forward, torn between wonder and fear, toward the father he thought he had lost forever.

The nightmare was over.
Or so it seemed.

But in the heavy, unnatural quiet, June felt the truth settle deep in her bones.

The Rodeo might be shattered.
Rook might be dead.

But some things—
Some debts—
Don't ever really disappear.

———

The survivors stood in shocked, wordless awe amid the shattered remnants of Still Creek, where twisted debris sprawled beneath a sky ablaze with searing light and barren emptiness. The town, in every sense, had become a haunted relic—a ghost town draped in dust and despair. The silence was absolute except for the occasional groan of settling ruins and the languid flutter of ash swirling in the unforgiving shafts of sunlight.

Then came a sound—a faint, persistent whistle. It was soon joined by a low, almost nonchalant melody that drifted down Main Street like a cool, unexpected breeze through the charred skeletons of dead trees. There was something peculiarly light, ancient, and almost cheerful about the tune.

At that moment, June's head whipped upward, her heart pounding like a frantic drum against her ribs. Mason, sitting stiffly on the ground, felt a grim, crusted film of dried blood harden upon his torn shirt. Nettie's eyes narrowed as fierce emotions of fear and hope battled deep within her. Meanwhile, Eli, struggling to support his staggering father, turned toward the mysterious sound with a look of utter bewilderment.

Drawn irresistibly together like moths to a flickering flame, they moved as one towards the source of the strange, impossible tune. Rounding the corner that led to Nettie's battered home, they suddenly saw him.

There he was—Old Man Thompson.

He was rocking slowly in a creaking chair positioned on Nettie's sun-beaten front porch, his gnarled hands steady as he whittled away with a faded knife whose blade gleamed in brief flashes. Wood shavings danced across the weathered boards near his worn boots, and the same battered hat sat perched atop his head. His timeless, tired smile curved his lips as if nothing out of the ordinary had occurred—as if the world's end were merely another dusty Tuesday afternoon.

Meeting their confused and wary eyes, Thompson offered a lazy nod and drawled, "Well, well, I knew I was dealing with the right folk," as he continued carving an elegant, slender figure from a scrap of cedar.

June's mouth opened in mute surprise before sealing shut; she fumbled for a pistol that was no longer there. Mason, his instincts flaring, had prepared to lunge at Thompson—only to realize with a jolt that his own injuries had seemingly vanished. Thompson chuckled softly, a sound imbued with a strange, knowing affection as he set aside the newly whittled figure and leaned forward on his knees.

"You did good," he said in a gentle cadence, "better than most. You fought hard. You clung to each other when it mattered most. That—more than you know—is what counts."

The quiet was broken by Nettie's trembling voice. "Rook... what in the hell is this? What's happening?" Her question trembled in the heavy air, as Thompson's eyes flickered with a golden gleam beneath the faded brim of his hat.

"You're dead," he stated simply, as if speaking an undeniable fact of nature. The words struck them like a sudden, deafening thunderclap—yet no thunder followed, only the profound silence and the frantic beating of their hearts, their eyes darting into one another as if to confirm the terrible truth.

"You've been dead for a long time now," Thompson continued softly, his voice imbued with the gentle sorrow of someone imparting shattering news to a child. "Still Creek isn't real. It never was. This is Purgatory—a sorting ground where souls discover what remains of themselves... or mourn what they have lost. It's where you get sorted."

Eli shook his head incredulously, murmuring, "No... no, I remember—" but Thompson only smiled sadly.

"You remember fragments," he said quietly. "Let me help fill in the rest."

With a graceful motion belying his age, Thompson rose from his creaking chair and stepped down onto the scorched, cracked earth. His words fell heavy and deliberate like stones onto the abandoned street.

"Eli... you and your daddy were on your way to that motorcycle show, weren't you? A little road trip, just the two of you." At this, Eli's breath caught in his throat as a sudden memory crashed upon him: the piercing glare of headlights, tires shrieking against the pavement, the bone-crushing impact of metal and glass, and the harrowing scream of his father echoing in his ears.

"A semi crossed the line," Thompson murmured, his voice gentle as a whispered confession. "It took you both out before you even had a chance to see it coming."

Eli's father squeezed his shoulder, a silent exchange of pain and reluctant understanding passing between them. "It's true, son. I remember now," he admitted, as his eyes filled with the weight of recalled tragedy.

Thompson then shifted his attention to Mason. "And you, Deputy... shot down in the line of duty. Protecting a waitress named Rosie and a busboy at that roadside diner. The busboy you believed all this time was a thief." Mason staggered as vivid, brutal memories rushed back—blood hissing upon cracked tiles, a convict's gun flashing in the dim light, his own desperate act of shielding two innocent souls—and then, nothing. There was never a K-9 named Rosie or a shoplifter. His mind had somehow tricked him.

June took a trembling step back as Thompson's golden gaze found her once more. "And you, Junebug," he said, his voice heavy with sorrow, "you didn't go out in a blaze of glory. No grand heroic exit. Just Frank—too drunk, too enraged to know what he was doing."

The memory of Frank's wild, crazed eyes, the crushing weight of betrayal, the split-second flash of a gun, and the numbing cold that followed overwhelmed her.

"And afterward," Thompson murmured softly, "he turned that same pistol on himself."

"Are you my father," June asked in trepidation.

Thompson's sad smile seemed to fall even more so. "No dear," he said with regret, "I am not. Though I tried my best from afar."

June clutched her mouth in a pained gesture as a tortured sob clawed its way up from deep within, threatening to shatter her resolve. "I'm so sorry, my dear," Thompson intoned, his tone a tender mix of regret and compassion.

Finally, he turned his somber eyes to Nettie. "But you, Netta..." His voice faltered under the weight of his grief. "You were never just June's aunt. You were her mother. You gave your life for her, holding her tiny hand until you slipped away, unable to watch her grow."

Nettie gasped, staggering backward as fresh tears cascaded down her face in unbidden rivulets. Locking eyes with June—who stared in wonderment and sorrow—the two found solace as Nettie swept her up into a fierce, tearful embrace.

"Oh my God, oh my God, my baby...it's truly you," Nettie whispered amidst her sobs, the sound of their reunion filling the silence with bittersweet, heartfelt joy.

Only then did Thompson speak once more. "And here... in Purgatory..." His voice softened even further, imbued with a gentle warmth. "I found you all—lost, broken, and unsure of who you were. I couldn't bear to let them take you, so I wiped your memories. I hid you away. I loved you, in the only way I knew how."

Before their tearful eyes, the figure before them began to transform—not reverting back into Rook, but evolving into something older, yet infinitely greater. The weathered features smoothed into something serene, the hunched posture straightened into dignified calm.

His battered garments slipped away, replaced by a simple dark coat that floated around him without the slightest hint of wind, while a halo of golden light crowned his figure—radiant, not menacing, but ancient and inevitable.

Thompson smiled down at them—a smile filled with kindness, timeless sorrow, and boundless understanding. "I'm not just Thompson," he declared, his voice deepening into a resonance that spanned the ages. "I'm Death."

Mason began, "But Death is…" only to be gently cut off by Thompson's wry wink.

"…not the one you should fear," he added with a familiar, comforting drawl. "I merely guard the crossings and ensure the games remain fair."

"But why?" June asked, perplexed by all the revelations.

"Souls are a tricky thing," Thompson began, "they have to be weighed and measured. Nothing does more to reveal a soul's true nature than conflict under duress."

The entire world seemed to spin around them as June gripped Mason's arm, seeking stability amidst the cosmic upheaval. In a low, broken whisper, Eli asked, "What now? What happens now?"

With a grin reminiscent of a doting grandfather who has just shared a secret joke, Thompson—now Death—pointed down the ruined street. There, waiting under the endless, scorching sun, stood five majestic horses.

Their manes shimmered like spun gold, and the intricate symbols embossed on their gleaming saddles spoke of mysteries older than language itself.

"Ride off," Thompson said simply. "Ride into eternity, toward new beginnings, and into whatever dreams you're brave enough to chase. It's your choice. It always has been."

The survivors stood, silent and spellbound, as fragile hope began to blossom at the edges of their weary hearts. Then Thompson turned once more to Nettie. Before their eyes, he changed again—not into the grim visage of Death or the monstrous Rook, but reverting to the young man he once was: the real Ezekiel Rookman. Handsome and strong, his eyes shimmered with mischief, sorrow, and a love that defied time.

Stepping forward, he extended his hand toward her. "Come with me, Netta," he said, his voice trembling with earnest emotion. "Let's finish what we started properly this time. I don't want to face this alone—especially not without you."

Overwhelmed, Nettie blinked back tears as she gazed at the man she had loved, lost, despised, and mourned all at once. A long, shuddering breath escaped her, and then she smiled—a radiant, heartfelt, and heartbreaking smile that spoke of long-awaited redemption. "About damn time," she whispered tenderly as she placed her hand in his.

Together, they turned toward the waiting horses, toward the golden horizon bathed in celestial light, and onward into the unknown future.

Toward freedom.

Toward forever.

Epilogue: Where the Road Ends

The sun poured molten gold over the vast, undulating plains, its liquid light smoothing over the scars of past sorrows. Behind them, the town of Still Creek—its ghostly, deserted streets, its crumbling, timeworn buildings, and its shattered, faded memories—dissolved into a whisper of smoke, vanishing with every steady, rhythmic hoofbeat.

June rode in an almost sacred silence, her warm leather reins held loosely in her gentle grasp. Her horse, a magnificent creature with a coat as brilliant as burnished copper, moved with the fluid grace of a companion who had journeyed through endless lifetimes alongside her, each step a testament to their eternal bond.

Beside her, Mason maintained an imposing presence. Despite the rugged scars that marked his body, he exuded strength and quiet resilience. His hat, pulled low to shield his eyes from the relentless glare of the sun, shifted slightly when he noticed June's glance. In that tender moment, their fingertips met across the narrow gap between them—a silent, unhesitating affirmation of their shared journey.

Ahead, Eli and his father charged forward with unbridled delight, their laughter pure and unburdened, mingling with the bright expanse of the sky. Their spirited horses stirred up twisting clouds of dust as they galloped toward an unseen horizon, momentarily convincing everyone that the world could be reduced to nothing more than fresh starts and endless, open roads.

Farther back, moving at a measured, timeless pace, were Nettie and Rook. They were no longer the haunted remnants of Still Creek but had transformed into the youthful dreamers of yesteryear—reborn and reinvigorated. Nettie leaned in close to whisper something secret into Rook's ear, and the result was a hearty laugh that burst forth like the resonant tolling of a long-forgotten bell echoing across the vast plain. They refused to glance back, for nothing in their past bore the weight of a future worth their attachment.

As the golden haze swallowed the town entirely, June felt a tremendous weight lift from her shoulders—the release of a burden she had unknowingly carried from the moment of her birth. Turning with a slow, deliberate twist in her saddle, she cast a lingering look over her shoulder at the spectral remains of Still Creek. All that existed now was a delicate shimmer, a ghost town at peace with its settled debts, whispering a quiet farewell on the wind.

With a tender smile fighting back tears that burned in her eyes, June shifted her gaze forward, tightening her grip on Mason's hand as she murmured into the quiet—perhaps a tribute to her mama, perhaps an affirmation to herself: "We're free. We're finally free."

In that moment, she urged her horse into a spirited run, and one by one, the others followed suit. Their laughter and exultant cries blended with the rising wind as they sped together into the vast, unbroken light that stretched beyond the known world—an expanse where no rodeos, no lurking monsters, and no lingering regrets could ever touch them again.

Only freedom.

Only forever.

——

Far from where Still Creek once whispered its quiet secrets—beyond the horizon where June, Mason, Nettie, Eli, and the others rode off into a shimmering eternal sunset—somewhere in the oppressive emptiness of nowhere... a small town lay in restless slumber.

Nothing about it screamed of life: a scattering of rusted mailboxes, porch swings that sagged like tired ghosts, and cracked asphalt roads twisting aimlessly toward oblivion. A gas station with a shattered Coke machine, a diner clinging to peeling layers of paint, and a lone bar where the jukebox blared the wrong tune in a mocking loop.

This was a place that most souls barreled through without a backward glance.

Only one sentinel defied its insignificance—a lone, flickering yellow streetlight at the town's sole intersection.

Blink.

Blink.

Blink.

Its lonely, relentless pulse stood as a grim reminder, steady and unyielding, waiting.

Yet on this night—when the moon retreated behind a choking shroud of mist—something deep and irrevocable shifted. A low, primal rumble tore through the silent fields.

Dust swirled in unwelcome spirals, unnaturally sluggish and ominous. And then, as if conjured from the very essence of the dark itself, a rodeo materialized at the outskirts of town.

Tattered tents erupted like violent bruises under a sickly starlight. A decrepit Ferris wheel groaned to life, its slow, creaking arc twisting the very air into a poisonous miasma. Raggedly stitched banners— crafted from remnants of what should have remained broken—flapped defiantly despite the dead, motionless night.

At the twisted heart of this macabre carnival, a solitary figure in a crimson velvet coat slouched against a battered ticket booth. His wide-brimmed hat shadowed his face, yet when he smiled, a flash of gold ignited beneath the brim—an omen in that bleak landscape.

He spun a weathered silver coin into the night air; it caught the lurid wink of the yellow streetlight as it tumbled in a dizzying dance—blink, spin, blink, spin—before nesting perfectly in his calloused palm.

The figure pivoted to face the dormant town, his voice a languid velvet drawl that slithered through the stale air, echoing far beyond reason: "Come one, come all... Midnight's fixin' to ride again."

In the distance, the Ferris wheel howled like a dying beast, while the carousel trembled, its spectral horses frozen mid-stride before jolting into tortured motion with the groan of anguished gears.

Beyond the chaotic fairgrounds, that solitary yellow streetlight maintained its steady, accusing blink—as though it alone bore witness to the unfolding nightmare.

Deep beneath the cracked, desolate earth, something ancient and ravenous stirred... and grinned with terrible delight. For in this cursed town, where debts are forever unpaid, games twist into eternal torment, and rides never truly end—once the

Midnight Rodeo finds a new haunt, its relentless wheel inevitably comes back around.

About the Author

I had dreamed of being a writer ever since I was a little boy growing up in Northeast Texas. My imagination has always been wild and carefree. My first typewriter was a little plastic blue toy typewriter when I was 10 years old. I wore that thing out writing stories and screenplays, even though I didn't know the first thing how to do so. When I was in high school, I told myself and my friends that I would write a novel one day, and then life happened. It took me a long time to complete my first novel, Hale County. In the meantime I was writing non-stop on many other stories, but never really completed them. A few months ago something in me clicked one night and I have been writing non-stop ever since. This book you are reading is one of those projects I started and finally finished. I hope you enjoy this work.

There are many more stories to tell.

www.ingramcontent.com/pod-product-compliance
Lightning Source LLC
Chambersburg PA
CBHW070724280626
47159CB00023B/2587